Library of
Davidson College

RECENT FICTION FROM CHINA 1987-1988

Selected Stories and Novellas

Edited and Translated
by
Long Xu

Chinese Studies
Volume 1

The Edwin Mellen Press
Lewiston/Queenston/Lampeter

Library of Congress Cataloging-in-Publication Data

This work has been registered with the Library of Congress

This is volume 1 in the continuing series
Chinese Studies
Volume 1 ISBN 0-7734-9664-5
ChS Series ISBN 0-88946-076-0

A CIP catalog record for this book
is available from the British Library.

Copyright © 1991 The Edwin Mellen Press

All rights reserved. For information contact

The Edwin Mellen Press The Edwin Mellen Press
Box 450 Box 67
Lewiston, New York Queenston, Ontario
USA 14092 CANADA L0S 1L0

The Edwin Mellen Press, Ltd.
Lampeter, Dyfed, Wales
UNITED KINGDOM SA48 7DY

Printed in the United States of America

TO MY PARENTS

CONTENTS

EXCITING
Wang Meng   1

FIREBOAT
Wei Shixiang   7

RECOMMENDATION
Xing Hongliang   45

OLD ACQUAINTANCE
Han Shaogong   55

CLASSMATES
Shen Rong   65

FRUSTRATIONS OF THE YOUTH AH DE
Cen Zhijing   81

KITCHEN SMOKE AGAIN, KITCHEN SMOKE AGAIN
Ma Bende   99

FLUID PERSONALITY
Li Xingtian   117

WHEN I THINK OF YOU AT NIGHT, THERE IS NOTHING I CAN DO
Chao Naiqian   159

ABORTION
Li Songjing   169

SMART LADY
Liu Yufeng   213

PREFACE

Readers interested in China may still be baffled by the recent drastic changes leading up to the crackdown in Tiananmen Square on June 4, 1989. Perhaps the stories selected in this book, all published shortly before the bloody event, can provide a glimpse of the catalysts -- deeply rooted in the history of the People's Republic -- which seemed to point to the great possibility, if not inevitability, of such a disastrous showdown.

The later day collapse of the communist regimes in eastern Europe and *Peristroika* in the Soviet Union created an unprecedented fear among the hardliners who clung to Mao Zedong's dogma of tight ideological control, while the intellectuals and entrepreneurs, the two most radical groups advocating further reform, were experiencing increasing frustration due to the economic difficulties and political crises. Corruption, nepotism, and inflation were alienating the regime further from its people; and it was widely believed among the educated members of society that the time had come for them to take a more active role in shaping the future of their country. The general view among them was that the on-going economic reform and open policy could not attain the desired results without fundamental changes in the political system. And the brewing of this popular belief was well represented by the writers of these selected stories.

Since the founding of the People's Republic in 1949, never had writers been allowed more freedom to reflect on the decades of social evil as of June, 1989. As the reforms went on, they encountered serious problems that no one seemed to know how to handle; then frustration surfaced in a myriad of forms. Disillusionment, anger, bitterness (to name but a few), so long embedded in the past, came back to haunt the present, but with new perspectives. To understand the past in a new era, writers were struggling to define what the past recommended, how it was affecting the road forward, and trying to offer predictions about the future. They did a convincing job in exploring the roots of their frustration because they were constantly aware that the past could not be undone -- and its aftermath still remained overwhelming in the present -- yet their search for a plausible way out had to continue. Nevertheless, in these stories, they have shown (in their unique artistic way) what they rightly prefer.

Indeed, these stories continue the early trend toward a much more genuine and serious expression of the social realities in literary circles, which began shortly after the end of the Cultural Revolution in 1976. Mao Zedong and his colleagues, including the "Gang of Four," had been promoting a "new literature" during their thirty-year reign which transpired to be little more than propaganda. With only a handful of exceptions, the "realities" painted in literary works before 1976 were simply what they chose to see, and the romanticism they instilled in them were lies and untruth. Once the "Scar Literature" (stories exposing the wide-spread social injustice and sufferings during the Cultural Revolution) caught the attention of the reading public in 1979, writers and poets -- both of the old and new generation -- began to vent their pent-up emotions against the misrule of the communist regime. And the trend, in view of the Tiananmen massacre and the subsequent suppression, will probably go on for some time in the future. However, toward the middle of the 1980s, the scope of the writers' exploration of the past and present quickly expanded to include an examination of the traditional values, which some believed had helped hinder the social progress of contemporary society. While attacking, for example, bureaucracy, submissiveness and passivity, they had an eye on their origin. They seemed to realize that in order to effect positive changes, they had to go beyond the thirty some years of communist rule to challenge the make-up of the Chiness people. To modernize the country, the minds of its people had to be modernized first.

Naturally, they searched the farthest and remotest corners of the land, and the deepest recesses of the mind. Controversy and hot debate mounted as the probe became more penetrating -- and as the subject matter widened, the tone grew increasingly sarcastic. Feeling threatened, the hardliners in the ruling circle repeatedly tried to suppress it, labeling it as a form of "spiritual pollution," but the killing on June 4, 1989 would only temporarily succeed in repressing the voice of the writers.

The primary purpose of this book is to provide scholars and students of contemporary Chinese literature, as well as sinologists in other fields, with some stories which may shed light on the almost "inherent" political turmoils

Preface

in China today. At the same time, it is hoped that these contemporary Chinese stories, through their soul-stirring and insightful representation of the changing era in this popular art form, will arouse further interest among the reading public.

"Exciting" ("Lai Jin," from *Beijing Literature*, January, 1987), by the noted writer Wang Meng, is more than experimental in utilizing stream of consciousness to underscore the overwhelming confusion and frustration of the new era. "Fireboat' ("Huochuan," from *Controversial Literary Works*, February, 1987) and "When I Think of You at Night, There is Nothing I Can Do" ("Dao Heiye Wo Xiang Ni Mei Banfra," from *Beijing Art and Literature*, May 1988) are thought provoking in dealing with incest in their different social contexts. The motif had been virtually banned from the literary scene for over forty years. It is noteworthy that the authors tried to show that the sin is committed due to extreme social and economic circumstances rather than immorality of the individual directly involved.

Another form of frustration represented in the book is mainly caused by the gap between beneficiaries and victims of the communist rule, as well as in "Classmates" ("Tongchuang," from *Beijing Literature*, June, 1987). It is further drmatized in "Old Acquaintances" ("Guren," from *Zhong Shan*, May, 1987) as the highly emotionally charged scene appears valid only in its unique political setting.

"Abortion" ("Liuchan," from *Story Writers*, May, 1988) and "Smart Lady" ("Qiaoniang," from *Feitian*, July, 1988) are piercing examinations of human behavior distorted by social pressues new and old. Sarcastic, and even cynical in their way, the writers explore the lingering power of the social norms that confront and destroy what could otherwise have been fulfilling relationships.

The rest of the stories deal with various problems arising from the economic reform over nearly ten years. "Recommendation" (Jianxian," from *Shanghai Literature*, February, 1987) highlights a crisis in building up the leadership needed to carry it forward. "Frustration of the Youth Ah De" ("Qingnian Ah De zhi Fannao," from *Literary Works*, June, 1987) accentuates the futility of doing new business in old ways. The fate of Yang Hongshan, the chief protangonist in "Fluid Personality" ("Liudong de Renge," from *People's*

Literature, October, 1987) remains precarious, as the threat posed by the political conservatism is still very much alive. And it is obviously calling for a more stable and constructive political environment in which the entrepreneurs can fully realize their potentials. The reforms undoubtedly bring about some hope and excitement, but frustration as well. Some reap immediate benefit, though not without a price; others stand by and scrutinize the moral implications of the price. One question raised in "Kitchen Smoke Again, Kitchen Smoke Again" ("You Jian Chuiyan, You Jian Chuiyan," from *Shanghai Literature*, August, 1987) is how high a price each individual is willing to pay in adjusting to a new era of progress and uncertainty. The dilemma caused by the need to establish a new value system at the sacrifice of personal moral integrity, partially conditioned by years of propoaganda, has not yet ended.

Finally, I wish to express my deep gratitude to all the authors whose stories are included in this book. I am also indebted to Furman University for its generous support for this project. Dr. Tony Esolen, of the Department of English, Furman University, kindly read the whole manuscript, and offered many valuable suggestions, for which I am very much grateful.

Long Xu
Greenville, South Carolina

EXCITING

Wang Meng

You can call the protagonist of our story Xiang Ming, or Xiang Min, Xian Ming, Xien Ming, Xian Min, Shang Min, or Xiang Ming Xiang Ming Xiang Ning Xiang Nin, and so on, and so on. Three days ago, which is also five days ago one year ago two months later, he who is also she has a vertebra problem which is also a problem with spine, dental caries, dysentery, epilepsy, breast cancer which is also good health longevity nothing wrong. On the forty first of November which is eleventh twelfth of the fourteenth month a sudden spinning dizziness strikes, then takes pictures B ultra sound electroencephalogram cerebral angiography for final diagnosis. Then could not make an appointment with the doctor could not find connection so does not go see the doctor so there is nothing wrong so plays ball games swims drinks wine delivers speeches watches TV series and there is nothing wrong with vertebra or simply has no vertebra. Relatives friends enemies all say or say nothing you're so young you're so old you're so strong you're so weak how could you have anything wrong how could you avoid falling ill! It makes him her laugh cry eh eh eh keep mouth shut.

So takes a fast ride on highway in a luxury sedan. Gets a taxi after much trouble, two eyes staring at the meter, full of apprehension and suspicion, fearing might get ripped off. On an ox cart on newly harvested fields with roots and ditches still there untouched unleveled. Bottom is bouncing high and aching. On a horse better still on a camel passes desolate gobi, sacsaoul branches make you shudder several times. Perhaps there's no big difference from two feet walking on beach or desert. Plane takes off, a stewardess brings juice full of ice listens to dialogue and background music while watching movie and headset with abrupt enigmatic interludes. First class train carriage is also full of speculators, trading blue jeans, bras, live tortoises and black rice. Xiang Ming takes business trips, travels, conducts investigations elsewhere, buys, sells, pushes sales, rejoins his family, visits, goes on study tours, learns from others' advanced experiences, attends gatherings for writers, organizes commodity shows, receives awards, enjoys summer vacations in resort areas, rests for winter, establishes connections, inspects and emulates, competes, calls on old friends, meditates on the past, makes personal visits, escapes arrest, goes on casual tours or inspections. Lives in hotels guesthouses classrooms of elementary schools public air-raid shelters basements public bathrooms under bridges in detention centers prison cells. Then she he arrives finds misunderstands gets lost overlooks misses the places he she wants to go.

So many motorcades come to welcome present flowers fire popcorn salutes keep waving hands burst into thunderous applause. All say he was a reformer a path-breaking entrepreneur a white collar criminal a man who raises hell in people's interests a braggart a man supported by higher authorities a man on blacklist. So no one knows anybody else it could not find the one who is scheduled to meet it the one who is scheduled to meet it could not find it. Sparse applause, expressionless faces. So comrades-in-arms and their wives hold his hands tight, "You've not changed," "You're much older," "I recognize you right away," "I can hardly recognize you," then whisper ask if he wants to buy haw plum ginseng. Then toss luggage on shoulder with one jerk of hand. Then goes to report loss of it in luggage department.

He goes to his post at once declares three administrative principles at welcome meeting. She calls everywhere to find a place with good room board accommodation less expenses. It does not find the person feels hard to account for trip when goes back so calls emergency long distance several times. The first time she attends review committee meeting proposes resolutely all award decisions mustn't be interfered with by connections or balance considerations. Once registered he hands in manuscript in Chinese and English while collecting meal tickets. It has all organs checked in a hurry receives injections of every newly invented imported drug. He begs from one government agency to another asking for compensation of unreceived salaries punishment for slanderers. It searches for written audio video materials researches day and night listens to demonstrations works on evaluations. She visits all old acquaintances superiors pays respect in turn time and again. Upon arrival it tries all it could to get return bus boat horse dog tickets tries three rounds seven rounds.

Feels this a really lovely place. Slim attractive lakes, rock mountains full of inscriptions by famous figures, a feast for eyes. Feels lack of sound management proper maintenance enough protection. Population explosion dust pollution garbage everywhere. Feels it has really changed, high-rises paved streets woolen sweaters on display in all department stores, their styles colors defy all recollection imagination. In them look like foreign gentlemen ladies. There are more duck tongues goose comb fish bear's paws than fairies in heaven. Feels it's still poor shabby, replaces wood with concrete without a piece of marble. So-called private section in cafe is only fit to drink brown mixture toothache liquid. Young men's long hair unwashed for many days unlike hippies but convicts on the run. Ties hang loosely disclose soiled shirt collars. Not a piece of granite on buildings not a single fountain not a single bronze sculpture. Feels not at all backward not only is calligraphy popular but also classic symphonic music Qigong[1] artistic gymnastics lion dance figure swimming utterly routed and a girl's planning to start an international stock trading company of bombers. Not only is there realism but revolutionary modern Beijing Opera plus modernism impressionism stream of consciousness Fei Feiism. Fei Fei Fei is an acrobat in Tian Qiao.[2] Feng Feifei is a famous singer in Taiwan. And amid blasts of music one or several black horses stud bulls piglets male elephants are led onto stage. Feels better to build a few decent rest rooms first to avoid spitting and pissing wherever it's convenient, all the while squeeze push bump making calls like cursing riding bus with expired season tickets. Drink beer till vomit violently like cholera patients, thirty cents of deposit for using a dirty plastic cup.

So goes to see operas, movies, songs and dances, fashion shows on invitation. To enjoy, appreciate, understand, evaluate, judge, decide, determine, help, cultivate, modify and improve art. There are loud hubbubs and cool fade ins, libido of ancient Chinese sages and convulsion of brains of men in computer age, sincere appeals and cynical laughters plus false cries. There are real exploration and fake mysterious empty inspiration. Real tears and pretentious brows. There are critics who have swallowed seasoned delicacies of artists and writers as well as those who got spat upon, who are always worrisome, or rigorous, careless, timid and slippery, devoted. There are the newest challengers of cliches who breed trash but claim to have awakened to own values.

So says this art is full of newness, is old socks thrown away by foreigners, is earthen human figures buried with the dead before Qin and Han Dynasties,[3] is a new mixture of east and west aesthetic civilization like mixing Costa Rica coffee with Napoleon brandy or using Parthia aniseed for Xingjiang kebab,[4] is something similar to that of the 40's and 50's unable to break away from old conventions, is figures by ghosts beyond even my

---

[1] A system of deep breathing exercises.

[2] "Fei" means to fly. Tian Qiao is a popular market place in Beijing.

[3] Qin (221-207 B.C.) and Han (206 B.C.-220) are two ancient dynasties in Chinese History.

[4] A famous local delicacy of mutton cubes roasted on a skewer. Xingjiang is an autonomous region in northwest China.

understanding, is the best Gold Monkey Gold Fish Gold Fan award winning stuff voted by audience, is a piece of rock that blocks the path forward, is flowers and silks unprecedented in history, is a sewer that opens too wide to be stopped now, is a new cross-eyed perspective, is a small topic under urgent discussion. Anyway he she it and they all clap hands all suffer from diarrhea in the end.

Receptions and banquets follow discussion. Boiled noodles eggs in chicken broth ginseng with garlic eels in cowhide soup. All propose toasts for Xiang Ming with wine vinegar pepper mustard. Say so young but so experienced must be commended worshiped star of new generation breakthrough. With several men of this type the twentieth century is real twentieth century till models of twenty first century bring faint light or strong light bring cocaine bring hormone bring depth bring sense of contemporary time bring future bring tides of wildness. Other comments you may neglect. Say very dangerous if go on like this downfall halfway after getting lost crash into mountain into pieces with loud bang of radiance. Say anyway breakthrough finally ends in pissing in Confucius" buddha palm founding solidifying getting rid of burrs benefaction accomplished satisfactorily disappearing unharmed becoming outdated like that under skullcap or tail. Say whatever you say Chinese moon is not round except he himself is more perfect than the hollow in the sun. Say you'd better concentrate in your own professional work don't take business trips attend meetings. Say you got to know and see more which creative people path-breakers really do as passenger plane Concord of European Common Market. Say you haven't divorced by now is there something wrong with your concept. Say now human desires prevail unlike ancient sages better promote morals wipe out human desires. Handwriting of Kong Decheng[5], Secretary of Council of Inspection in Taiwan, hangs high in Confucius' home in Qufu. Even Liulichang[6] has already built a Confucius Restaurant. Also sells roast ducks shall die with everlasting regret without eating it.

Xiang Ming cannot but asks the following questions! Are yolks ultimately conducive to heart attack or health? Could time past come back again? Is old or new convention more likely to rot more easily quickly? Do more college diplomas mean progress in education people's cultural

---

[5] A direct descendent of Confucius.
[6] A street in Beijing, famous for selling cultural relics, books, calligraphies, paintings, etc.

EXCITING

accomplishment or contrary? Are things one says most often things one most likes to say most wants to say? Smoking taking rarest most expensive traditional medicine watching TV series, which brings early death? Does bringing others down by accusation mean oneself is smart? Some say he's going too fast some say he's going too slow could it be proved he's going at exactly right speed? Is it really so those who can speak English will help brothers-in-law go abroad after finding a foreign mate? Which is more vigorous and active private collective or government ownership? How many among those indulging in loud empty talk are not swindlers? Is quadrangle[7] or high-rises more modern? Why don't linguists who distinguish retirement with from without official rank and correction from rehabilitation get bonus? Who would win in a tug-of-war ancient men or contemporary? Is huge centipede gold dragon kite bigger than Boeing 747 jumbo? Is man doing job smarter than man talking gesticulating? In which season is one more likely to contract infection of upper respiratory tract, winter or summer? Is speech on memorial service or routine meeting more reliable? Is streamlining administrative structure or increasing staff members more effective? Which is more full of loftiness heroism, Gongfu[8] or Scar literature?[9] Who is more neurasthenic, theorist or artist? Which is more costly, business trip or personal travel? Does it return to original place to go one hundred steps forward then one hundred backward? Has man with enteritis committed crime of wasting food? Do hospitalization and being discharged have something to do with illness? Is it true that non-poet painter pianist must understand less poetry painting piano music that poet painter pianist couldn't understand? I love you I hate you which is more expressive of love? Foreign exchange money or RMB,[10] which is more representative of national cultural tradition? Which has more enterprising spirit, loneliness or enthusiasm? Water or wine, which is thicker? Art or money, which is more beautiful? Which one is more like myself, Xiang Ming or Xiang Min? Park or prison, which is better for the practice of Qigong? Does fake old diehard or imitation foreign devil partake more of quintessence of Chinese culture local special product? Is new low proof Yanghe liquor watered down? Doesn't man

---

[7] Houses of traditional architecture common in Beijing.

[8] Marshal arts.

[9] Literature about injustice and sufferings, appearing in the late 70's and early 80's.

[10] Foreign visitors are required to exchange their currencies with Foreign Exchange Money to use in China instead of RMB, the Pinyin abbreviation of Chinese currency.

awake have dreams? Could any foreign guest invite you to visit abroad? Do you run fast because there is a mad dog after you? Is it adaptation or creative writing to make novel into movie? Who earns more, those who work or those who don't? Is it true that all women are beautiful all scientists scientific? Must chopsticks in paper bags be cleaner than chopsticks put on table? Why can't one make wheezing sounds while drinking soup? Why do Chinese have to succumb to European table manners? How can one enjoy food without making squelches? Must water closet be more advanced than chamber pot?

He she it, while staggering running down questions, is driven out by electrical club led out politely invited respectfully onto rostrum operation room seat for distinguished guest mortuary makeup backstage. Granted Xilibergendang Award of International Geobiological Year 1982-328, chosen for world celebrity list black list voted best male female boiling feet[11].

Xiang Ming guesses things now are really exciting!

---

[11] A Chinese homophonic phrase for leading actor or actress.

FIREBOAT

Wei Shixiang

I. Ferry Crossing of Wide Slope

The river, a mile wide, stretches northward over vast shoals. Across it, only a few dark yellow ridges can be seen. Blown by the yellow wind after the Beginning of Spring,[1] the sky is yellow, the river is yellow, the big or small shoals are yellow, and so are the uneven banks. Even the setting sun looks dizzily yellow, as if it has been soaked in the yellow water of the river. It shines dimly on this old and gloomy land that extends to the end of the sky and water.

A handful of black sesame seems to be thrown on the endless slope of yellow soil beside the river; it is the small Village of Wide Slope.

Ah Hua, a lunatic woman, is lying in a dirt hole in the village street near the wall of Liu's Diner, which solicits business from ferry passengers. A group of pupils just out of class from the locally sponsored Ferry Elementary School surround her, clapping their hands and making fun of her:

> A black chick searching in the hay stack,
> What he gets is a stupid wife;
> She won't wash the wok as she's told,
> But jumps in it to wash her smelly feet;
> She won't clean the pot as she's told,
> But jumps in it to wash her bare ass.

Ah Hua's hair is as disheveled as a chicken coop. On one side of her plump, white face there hangs a piece of red paper. She is hopping up and down, clapping her hands, and laughing with a wide open mouth. The collar of her red damask padded clothes is open, disclosing her neck and half of her chest, which has turned blue with cold. She does not wear padded trousers; the crotch of her gray polyester pants is wet, and the legs of the pants are torn into threads. A wet red line drips with a bad smell down her calf.

San San is out of school, too. She has been sitting in at a locally

---

[1] Around February 5.

sponsored middle school about a mile away. She is coming down the yellow soil of the village street in her wine red padded clothes and blue trousers with a green school bag. Her body always carries with it a light sway like a tender willow branch in a breeze. She walks very fast, eager to reach her shed to cook for her father.

But she stops here. A few kids are picking up remnants of lotus roots or small turnips left behind by people who came for the early morning market, and are throwing them at Ah Hua. San San shouts in her crisp and loud voice, "Stop! Why are you bullying her?" She goes over to shield Ah Hua.

Ah Hua, smiling, reaches out her soiled hand, "You give me money, I'll take the train, find Xiao Jian, and marry Xiao Jian."

Bang--a piece of rotten napa cabbage hits San San below the ear. "Ha, ha!" the kids are in an uproar.

San San wheels around with her almond eyes wide open. "Don't you understand? She's a stranger here and is sick. Isn't she pathetic enough, being sold here from Yunnan?[2] If you throw anything at her again, I'll go tell your teacher!"

The kids disperse at once and run away.

San San peels the piece of red paper off Ah Hau's face, buttons up her collar, and dusts the dirt off her clothes. Suddenly her nose crumples and her eyes fix on the leg of Ah Hua's pants, "Oh, this is...."

A few country women come up, "My goodness, a girl over twenty doesn't even know to clean it when it comes...."

"O my, Hei Chou's got enough to worry about! A man nearly forty, he finds this woman thousands of miles away, and now what?"

"That's easy for you to say. If Ah Hua weren't mad and stupid, you think they'd let you take her for just five hundred yuan?"

Ah Hua drops flat to the ground again, murmuring, "You give me

---

[2] A province in the south, hundreds of miles away.

money, I want to take the train, to find Xiao Jian...."

San San rummages through her pockets, but she does not have any money with her. The women say to Ah Hua again:

"Stupid girl, you're still looking for Xiao Jian. If it hadn't been for that son of bitch, would your father beat you into a lunatic?"

"Well, well, how come they didn't send you to a doctor?"

"Doctor? How much would it cost? If her father had had the money, do you think he would have sold her?"

"Her mother would be so sad if she were still alive. Hei Chou said her mother died early, leaving behind a lot of kids...."

San San feels dizzy; she bites her lower lip for a long time and does not move. Her mother too has died young, on a grain boat in the Huai River in their home town. Her mother has just given birth to her and was lying under a ragged quilt in the cabin. Two factions were up in arms against each other,[3] and there were numerous people with torches trying to take over their boat. They were shouting that Luo Er, who dared to oppose the Party, socialism, and Chairman Mao's revolutionary line, had come back and was hiding in the marshes up the river. They were competing to get him first in order to hold a denunciation meeting ahead of anybody else. What could her father do? He tried desperately to move their boat to the middle of the river. Several torches were thrown onto the boat, and boom, it caught fire instantly....

She heard all this from her eldest sister Shui Xian, who was ten that year and knew and understood everything. Their father threw her two elder sisters into the river like mad and rushed into the cabin to pick up San San.... But in the end he could not save her mother, and all they got for her second sister, who was then three, was a drowned body....

San San squats down and seizes Ah Hua. "Come, come with me to our boat. I'll ask daddy to give you money. We have toilet paper, too."

---

[3] This kind of fighting for local supremacy was common all over the country in the late 1960's during the Cultural Revolution.

Ah Hua, the lunatic, jumps up, her eyes wide open in disbelief. "You give me money? So I can find and marry Xiao Jian?" Then she utters a cry, claps her hands, pirouettes twice like a whirlwind, and runs laughing and shouting toward the river.

II. Crescent Bend

The huge river turns into a waterfall through the narrow dog-toothed canyons. It gushes down the overhanging cliffs, rolls over, then forces its way and flees like a desperado for his life. It zigzags and rushes through countless mountain passes and gorges until finally it reaches the vast, flat plain.

As the sky and the land grow wide, so does the river. At last it is granted the freedom to flow, so it slows to a comfortable pace. And only now does it discover that it has been carrying so much heavy and useless yellow dirt. So it casually deposits it along its path, leaving behind goose-egg-shaped shoals after shoals above its surface. They turn into resting places for wild geese seeking after spring, slow the water down for fish afraid of wind and waves, and provide a living for men and women who hunt the geese and the fish.

Between the Wild Slope Ferry Crossing and the high stone dike a mile away, there is a shallow, crescent-shaped river bend. Twenty or thirty boats lie close to the bank, like a crab with its legs stretched out. These are small wooden boats, a dozen feet long and four feet wide, with flat bottoms. On the opposite bank stands a cluster of small rundown sheds propped up by sticks with walls made of mud and straw and roofs of plastic sheets, asphalt felt, or torn sail. Here is San San's home, which they carry along wherever they go. There are goose guns on the rackets and fishing nets hung to dry outside the sheds. Each shed has a stove and a bed for the woman and children. Most of the men pass the night on their boats.

None of these men, if over forty or fifty, is ordinary. They are either ex-prisoners, or have in the past few years been purged as "spies for the Nationalist Party," "run away landlords," or "reactionaries," .... They have left their homes and businesses and have been making a living wandering from place to place on the boat with their wife and kids, just for the sheer freedom of it, so that no one in the world can exercise any control on them.

One boat, which lies by a newly-formed, slim shoal like a water bird in the middle of the river, belongs to Da Yang Ma of the Jiangsu[4] Gang, who uses it as a casino.

Cripple Lao Ding of the Huai River Gang loses again. Da Yang Ma is playing as the banker and his long and thin face is crowded with smiles. He blinks his small eyes and strips away the five ten-yuan bills in front of Cripple Lao Ding.

Cripple Lao Ding's broad, dark and whiskered face looks withered; the shuttle-shaped scar on the right side is suffused with a whitish gray color. Only his eyes are as bright red as the charcoal fire of the stove in a corner at the back cabin. Fat geese are being cooked in the iron pot on the stove. These members of the Jiangsu Gang will gamble all night once they start! At midnight Lao Liu of the diner sneaks in like a ghost and shouts, "Well-baked and fried cakes." Then a boat paddles toward the bank. One yuan for a fried cake,[5] take it or leave it. Why not? Sometimes the whole basket of cakes is carried to the casino. Geese that have come to find fresh food in the wheat fields land on the shoals, and when the guns are fired, there will be wine, meat, and clothes! A goose sells for seven or eight yuan for its meat and down. Also there are the big Huang River carps with red tails; you can sell them anywhere for a good price. Eight or ten yuan is nothing! Cripple Lao Ding throws down his hand of soiled cards and takes from the side of his crippled leg his wine gourd, which can hold two pounds of wine. He will not give in to anybody, so he gurgles down some more wine, takes out several more bills and throws them onto the cabin floor. Once again his eyes catch fire like the incense sticks that catch the river breeze.

"Daddy, time to eat!" From afar comes San San's crisp, clear voice. She is annoyed.

Lao Ding pokes his disheveled head out of the canopy of the boat, snorting, "San San, you eat first, I'll be back in a moment." He discovers his own boat coming across a rapid current by a shoal. Throwing down her paddle for the bamboo punt-pole, San San plants herself firmly on the boat with her two feet apart, and stares at him. Her purses her little mouth like a

---

[4] A province in east China.
[5] A very high price here, as it usually costs about twenty cents.

silver carp. And there seems to be another woman sitting on the hatch cover.

"Has Shui Xian come back? You all go back and eat first." Shui Xian and Da Shun, his son-in-law, belong to another team of boats and are settling in the Pan Ma Bend some ten miles down the river. She comes to see him from time to time.

"I won't. I won't eat if you don't. If you don't come, I'll ask Uncle Luo Er to come for you." San San is coming closer, the black and white of her clear almond eyes can be seen clearly.

Da Yang Ma hastens to persuade with smiles, "Brother Lao Ding, go back please. Don't upset San San."

Cripple Lao Ding howls at San San, "Humph! Don't use your uncle to get me!" Still, he limps out of the cabin anyway.

San San's Uncle Luo Er is the chief of the Huai River Gang. There is no one on the scores of waterways who does not know him. A dark and powerful man, he is an excellent boatman and an expert goose hunter. He has killed boas as thick as a tree-trunk by the Erhai Lake in Yunnan Province, and vultures that stand half a man tall on the shoals in Inner Mongolia[6] as well. He has a lot of skills, and a quick temper, too. None of the fifty or so people in his gang, young or old, dares to talk back to him. But he has always been exceptionally lenient to Lao Ding, not only because he is his sworn brother but for many other reasons too. This time they happen to come across Da Yang Ma and his gang. If the gang stays on their own boats, Luo Er is polite to them and passes their boats with his eyes closed. But once when his younger son, Si Bei, gambled there, he snatched a tow board and gave him a sound beating. He did not say anything the first time Cripple Lao Ding went to the gambling boat. Today he only cast him a glance and says coldly, "Elder Brother, if you are bored, let me take you to see an opera in the county seat. It's not worthwhile throwing away your hard-earned money in the water!"

Lao Ding knows perfectly well that he should stop gambling, but he feels so bored and depressed. He returns to his boat with a sullen face, and finds that the one sitting on the hatch cover is not Shui Xian but a young woman with neatly combed hair and clean face, who is smiling at him in a weird way.

---

[6] An autonomous region in north China.

Isn't she Ah Hua, the lunatic who has been running wild everywhere on the shoals? His face falls instantly. The boat is still crossing that rapid current. He feels all at once that the waves under the boat are bumping each other like crazy; he reaches out to hold down the old guns that he has been using for more than ten years. The guns, which sit on a rack toward the back of the boat, are longer than the boat itself, each weighing more than a hundred pounds; their octagonal barrels, glowing dimly in the dark, are as thick as a tea cup. And their butts, hewn out of mature and sturdy Chinese scholartree, are gleaming with use. After his two daughters, the guns are as precious to him as his own life. While others move their guns onto the bank in off season, he does away with this precaution because it is hard for him to move around as a cripple. So he leaves the guns on the boat and keeps them company every night, as if they were his sons.

He sits at the head of the boat and takes out a cigarette. He is so bored that he wants to scream. Taking him completely off guard, Ah Hua stands up and jumps to him, smiling and shouting, "You give me money, to take the train...."

Cripple Lao Ding grows angry and hollers, "You stay put there and don't move!" According to the ancestral tradition, women are not allowed to touch the goose gun. Even daughters have to go around it on the boat. It is a worse violation of the taboo for women from other families to come on board. The year before, a young man went crazy and let a woman from another family touch his gun. When he was shooting the geese that night, the gun blew apart. The bottom of his boat suffered a hole two feet wide, and he was wounded too.

But Ah Hua, wriggling like a water snake, grasps him and will not let go. "You give me money, I want to find and marry Xiao Jian...."

Cripple Lao Ding is about to curse her when San San pouts like a spoiled child. "Daddy, give her a few cents, I've promised her."

"You!" Cripple Lao Ding roars. Nevertheless, he takes out some money and puts it in Ah Hua's hand, ordering, "Sit down! I'll throw you in the river if you move again!"

But Ah Hua claps her hands, waves the money, and shouts, "Ha, ha, oh.... I'll take the train to find Xiao Jian and marry him!" She jumps over the two guns while shouting.

Cripple Lao Ding explodes and dashes toward her in one giant leap. His face is all blue, and he seizes Ah Hua by the collar of her padded clothes. Then bang, bang, he boxes her ears twice, snarling, "You, you!" His whiskers trembling, he is too angry to finish his sentence.

San San, frightened, hastens to intervene. "Daddy, don't hit her. She lives on land and doesn't know the rule on a boat. Daddy, don't hit...."

Ah Hua, the lunatic, begins to cry out loud. She tries with all her strength to break free. And with a ripping sound her red damask padded clothes and the shirt inside split open, disclosing before Cripple Lao Ding's eye her shining white chest and two bulging breasts.

He is instantly stunned. He feels pins and needles in his scalp; the shuttle-shaped scar on his right face turns from blue to red to purple as if filled with blood. His two eyes fix lethally on Ah Hua's chest. He does not hear what San San says as she comes over to console Ah Hua; he only feels that his blood in the veins is as hot as fire, as if a host of single-horned ghosts were running wild and ramming upward, banging against the inside of his head and screwing up his thoughts. Oh, how many years, how many years has he not seen this....

His wife, Rong Rong, appears before him abruptly. Rong Rong's face and body were just as white, he just could never forget...

At that time his leg was not crippled, and his face was not scarred. When the fishermen's commune[7] was founded, he walked on a pair of twelve foot stilts, wore a brand new costume while playing in the Land Boat show,[8] and sang folk songs or operas with his clear voice... attracting Rong Rong all the way.

"Brother Ding, I've something to tell you." Rong Rong buried her head in his armpit.

---

[7] A more recent form of collective farming in China, which began in 1958 and was abolished in early 1980's.

[8] A traditional dance performed during festivals and celebrations.

"Go ahead." He tucked in the quilt for Rong Rong.

"Brother Ding, you... keep my nipple in your mouth."

"What for?"

"You fool, do as you're told. My granny said once a man held a woman's nipple in his mouth, he is her child. You're... my big child now, and you'll be...as close to me as my child."

Oh, my Rong Rong, my sweetheart, you died so early; you died such a miserable death!

There were two newly heaped graves. In one was buried his Rong Rong; in the other, his second daughter. His fishermen brothers did not let him come close while they were collecting the remains of Rong Rong. He heard later that there were only a couple of charred bones left. A few old men sighed, "O my, it was fire from heaven! The river god was angry, and he was punishing the sinners." Rong Rong had just given birth to San San, there had to be bloody disasters if she stayed on the boat! My god, how bitterly he has always regretted letting Rong Rong stay on board in the middle of such a mess. However, the movement to clarify the class ranks[9] was going on. At one time, they would find a "run away landlord," at another, a "spy for the Nationalist Party." He had served for five months as an odd-job man for an officer in the Nationalist army, so he himself was a castoff from the old society; and because he had set Luo Er free, he was considered a diehard follower of the reactionaries. He was so afraid that Rong Rong might die in his company while he was being paraded through the streets! But who had ever expected ....

San San has already tidied up Ah Hua's clothes and is now wiping away her tears and coaxing her. "I'll talk to daddy to let you play on our boat again, and give you more money. Daddy is a good and kind man. He just lost his temper for the moment." She turns back and says, "Daddy, is it true that you've lost a lot of money? If sister finds out about it later, she'll be worried sick about you!"

---

[9] Another political purge launched in 1969 and 1970 during the Cultural Revolution.

Cripple Lao Ding remains silent and still. Like the scar on his face, his two eyes are dull, blank, and wooden as those of a dead fish. Yet his hands, which look like a pair of old paddles, grip the two goose guns firmly.

The small boat moves to the bank. In front of the sheds, Si Bei is holding an imported cassette radio and doing disco with a group of young girls and boys. There is a great deal of laughter and shouting. Dust rises at their feet, and the radio is blasting, "You disappear after smiling faintly to me, where could I find you, where could I find your smile...."

Cripple Lao Ding clutches the wine gourd and puts it down again. A bitterness wells up his throat. He longs to sing and shout, repeating the familiar song he used to sing for Rong Rong:

Hei, the drum beats at nine and I listen near the door,
The young sister opens the door full of smiles,
Hei, she reaches out her hand and pull the sleeve of my blue garment,
And she calls me dear bother again and again.

But he does not sing it, and only waves to San San, telling her, "You go ashore first, and tell Ah Hua to eat too. Now I...really don't want to eat anything."

III. Moonless Night

A night without moonlight is the perfect time to gun down the geese. Luo Er has already given the word to get ready to sail to shoals far away. So every family has been to the market in the county seat, busy buying things for the monthly sacrifice for Duke Jing.[10]

Tonight is the month's first night without moonlight. The men of each family have already flushed out and brushed their guns with water and filled them up with gunpowder early. They have also stick a handful of goose feathers in the barrels. This, according to the rules, is not to be done by the women. What the women should do is to cook a square cut of pork ribs, put

---

[10] A river god they worship.

it in a clean plate, add four dishes of cakes and fruits, and dress a whole goose with its wings intact.

As it grows dark, the cabin canopies on each boat are all covered with white cloth. The wave absorbers, made of braided straw, are hung on the bows so that the guard goose cannot hear the noise when they approach the shoals. The men then wash their hands and faces, wrap a white towel on their heads, put on a white overcoat, and go on board all in white. Then they hold up a bowl of liquor and set fire to it, using the liquor fire to light up all the surrounding areas of the small boat in order to frighten away evil spirits. After that, they lay out wine at the head of the boats for sacrifice: the square cut of pork ribs is placed in the middle. Three chopsticks are stuck into it in the form of a triangle. Behind the pork is the dressed whole goose, with a wine pot and cups, and the four dishes of cakes and fruits on either side. Now everything is ready. The twenty-odd small boats line up with their bows heading toward the river. All are white; all are waiting for the order from Luo Er.

Their women and children are standing on the bank, forming a dense crowd; they lend impetus to the men on their departure. Shui Xian is also there. She has come from the Pan Ma Bend during the day on a truck that happened to pass here on the Yellow River dam. She does not bring her child with her, but has brought several bottles of wine, two cartons of cigarettes, and a pair of thick camel down padded trousers, which are rather popular at the time. Her father, now on the boat, has already put it on.

San San does not come, saying she has to do her homework. Though she has missed many classes, she really takes her study seriously. Shui Xian tells her to come out of the shed, but she tips her head, "Nope, haven't I seen this for a hundred times? If I ever get to be the chief, I'll do away with all this." Shui Xian is so frightened that she covers her mouth in a hurry, "My goodness! What a naughty girl! Wait for the retribution from the gods when they hear you."

The sky has grown so dark that the shadows of the shoals in the middle of the river can no longer be seen. Now Uncle Luo Er is standing on the head on his boat in the middle of the line. He waves his hand and roars, "Burn the paper!" Each boat responds by igniting bunches of yellow mount paper, which brightens up the whole dark Crescent Bend. After the wind blows the ashes into the river, each of them lights a bunch of incense sticks and insert them into the barrels of his guns. Luo Er leads them in kneeling down on the bow. He raises a cup of wine in both hands and prays, "We beg you, Duke Jing, to see that our guns fire well upon ignition, and that everything shall be fine...."

On every boat the men kneel down and kowtow three times to the river, then they spill their cups of wine into it and pray in unison, "Duke Jing, drink this cup, please...." After that they take their sharp fish knives and cut a piece of meat and throw it into the river. "Please have some meat, Duke Jing." Then they pick up a few cakes and fruits and toss them in the water, praying again, "Duke Jing, please grant us blessings and protection, so that every family will be safe... and have good luck...."

Uncle Luo Er waves his hand once more, "Go!" There rises the sound of the paddles, and the team of boats moves toward the gray and black shadows of the shoals far away.

Shui Xian is watching her father limping forward for the paddle, and she feels a sudden pain. Her heart aches and tears well up in her eyes.

Her father's leg was broken the year her mother died. Their boat had been burned, and two members of the family had died. When the two factions were fighting with each other, they left her father alone. So he left, carrying San San in his arms and dragged Shui Xian alongside. At first they tried to get milk everywhere, from women or goats, or corn gruel, or sweet potato soup.... Then they begged from village to village. Someone persuaded her father to give San San away, but he couldn't; a few others suggested that he find and marry some middle-aged woman, but he said nothing. He had heard Shui Xian, with tears in her eyes, sing the folk song,

> Young cabbages turning from green to yellow again,
> At age two or three they lost their mommy;
> Life isn't that bad with their daddy there,
> Only afraid that he will bring in a stepmother.

Since then her father would remain distracted for a long time; otherwise his eyes would become very red and he would clenched his teeth till they chugged. Her father changed. He stole grain and other things; he became a roving criminal.... Once he carried back a sack of coarse rice on his back, and was caught half way. His leg was broken right then and there; the whitish bone chips stuck out of the skin and the blood soaked the trouser leg.... From then on, no one has ever again mentioned finding a woman for him.

The river wind hisses over. Shui Xian wraps tight her green padded clothes and shivers with cold. The wind on the river must be even fiercer and colder! Father and others have to paddle their boats dozens of miles away and stay in water for the whole night. Every time they come back, a strong young man like Si Bei would be trembling with cold and his face would be turning blue. But father is over fifty, and he has that leg.... Oh! Since he joined Uncle Luo Er and made a living like this, more than ten years ago, how has her father endured it all!

Uncle Luo Er has been worrying about him and has said over and over, "Elder Brother, couldn't you listen to one word of mine and stop hunting geese? If you really don't want to sit idle, you could sharpen the fish hooks or mend the nets on land for me. Are you afraid that you and San San won't have enough to eat?"

But her father would not consent, "Brother, it is the only enjoyment left for me. Let me simply die a river ghost."

The team of boats is now far away, disappearing between the dark end of the embankment and the gray-black shadows of the shoals. Shui Xian returns to the shed. San San is still doing her homework on the bed.

"San San, has daddy always been drinking by himself lately?"

"Nope, I've found him some company."

"Who?"

"Ah Hua, the lunatic wife Hei Chou bought from Yunnan. She's really pitiable. She often asks daddy for cigarettes and money. When daddy is in a good mood, he gives her a few cents."

Shui Xian's heart gives a start. "San San, you always make trouble. She's a woman, and a lunatic too. What if something happens?"

"Come on, things are simple and straight in our Crescent Bend. Nothing will happen. With Ah Hua here, daddy will be keeping an eye on her fits, and he won't go gambling; he's also cut down on his drinking."

Shui Xian's slender eyebrows knit; she does not know why she feels a little nervous, as if she saw the shuttle-shaped scar on her father's face gleaming at her like the eye of a ghost. One summer she was selling fish with her father in a town near the Han River. A shrewish woman with her chest half open wanted to hitch a ride on their boat. Her father glanced at her chest and sang some wild tunes, and the woman shouted back angrily. The woman's husband and a few other local men jumped on the boat and stabbed him in the face.... When they got back, her father explained it away to Uncle Luo Er by saying that he had fallen on the boat and was hurt by the end of the anchor.

All of a sudden Shui Xian jumps up from the bed. "San San, you...."

IV. Song of Wilderness

Like the surprise attack squad that sped across the ancient battlefields with coins in their mouths to prevent from making any noise, the team of more than twenty boats moves silently over the dark river at night.

There are few stars above their heads. The sky and the river seem to have been dyed in black ink. Only the eyes of a goose hunter can tell, from the black surface of the river in front of them, which are sandbars formed by the rapid currents rushing by the shoals, which are the new shoals that come and go unexpectedly like the eyes of ghosts, and which are the old shoals where some farmers came on boat to spread wheat seeds that now have grown into seedlings. It is all up to the river god in charge of the flood season whether they could have any harvest.

On the river at night, the color black shows instead of white. The white garments of more than twenty men are glittering amid the twinkles of the water as if they were waves of the river. Ever since they set out, no one has uttered a sound. That is also the rule. All of them paddle cautiously, tight-lipped. The paddle dips into the water and draws lightly like the tail of a fish; its sound is muted by the roaring of the main current, and the shrieking of the river wind that cuts their faces. The spindrift, splashing at the bow, rushes against the straw wave absorber, then its noise too is smothered and dissolved. The small boats follow closely one after another after Luo Er's leading boat, in a formation like the half-open wings of a goose.

Luo Er's two night eyes, twinkling in the darkness like the will-o'-the-wisp, are searching for shoals in the middle of the river where the geese are sleeping. In the meantime he moves his two paddles in a seemingly careless manner. But his small square boat zigzags like a minnow, avoiding hidden shoals that may run him aground as well as the bottomless main stream of the Yellow River where the whirlpools are fearsome.

Suddenly he stops paddling and whispers, "Put on leather overalls!" So all the boats stop, and the men immediately take out from their cabins the leather overalls, which have shoes and legs and can cover them up to their chests. They put them on without any noise, knowing that their chief has discovered the shoal with geese on it.

They must row against the wind when goose hunting. So the team of boats keeps a good distance from the shoal, makes a big half circle around it, and situates itself to the leeward. The men all put away their paddles and slide into the water. Although they are wearing their leather overalls, the icy water in the cold weather pierces instantly to the bone. With the extreme caution with which they wait upon their women about to give birth, they lightly push the boats forward, inch by inch. The river wind blows hard in their faces and benumbs them very quickly.

Cripple Lao Ding's boat lies very close to that of Luo Er's. Luo Er could easily imagine, without turning his head, how his sworn brother is pushing his boat with his crippled leg. His heart remains heavy for a long while.

No sound comes from the boats or the men. A dead silence falls over the shoal there, too. If there is even a little noise, the ever-alert guard geese would discover it, and they would quack loudly to give the warning. Then the team's half night of toiling and suffering from cold would go unrewarded. These guard geese are being punished for the mistakes they made during the day, and in order to atone for their slips, they are stretching their long necks and searching the surface of the river around them. More troublesome is the lead goose, the smallest of all. It is pure white like a little swan--without a single colored feather. The cleverest of all, it stays awake almost all the time.

It is Luo Er among the flock of geese. And everyone knows that he must not shoot at it. Even if he does, he could never hit it. It is beyond any doubt that the river god will punish anyone who really shoots it down. Luo Er calls it "a goblin that has a lucky star above it," much like one hero praising another.

After who knows how long, the boats advance a few hundred yards toward the shoal, then fan out in groups of two or three.

The snow has just melted and the grass has just come out on the shoal. Nothing obstructs their view of the big, dark, bald shoal there. They seem to be able to see the sleeping geese now, whose bulging backs look like a mass of frozen waves. Only the long necks of the guard geese remain tall like oar-handles. They cannot risk moving closer, so the men follow their chief and stop. They stand in the water, bending their heads and crooking their backs. Then they turn around with extreme caution, keeping their upper bodies close to the water surface, and lighting the incense sticks inside their padded clothes. The sticks are wrapped with cattail wool and are as long as chopsticks. When lit, they are kept in the hollows of their hands so that no light leaks out. After all this is done, they hold their breath, straining their ears, and wait only for Luo Er's order to fire.

Even Luo Er feels that all his blood has lost its warmth, with crawling in water for so long. He senses that the crippled leg of his sworn bother beside him is trembling, and that the man is trying all he can to endure it with clenched teeth. He tilts his head in a majestic manner, and with his almost inaudible hiss whistles out the words, "Take off the fire cloth!"

The men seem to receive the order not with their ears but with their senses. At once they throw off the yellow oil cloth which covers the barrels of their guns. At the back of the barrel is a fire hole, and underneath that, a tiny iron dish with the fuse already on it, and the gun only needs the ignition from the incense stick to fire. Scores of eyes are now fixed on the sky above the shoal.

Then the thundering roar from Luo Er, "Aim--shoot!" As soon as everybody hears it, the flock of geese startles and rises in a black cloud over the shoal.

But it is already too late; the goose hunters are just waiting for them to fly up. They have pointed their sticks to the fuse, and almost at the same time more than forty dazzling fire rays spurt with a deafening bang from the twenty-odd boats. In an instant the shoal and the river are all shining red. Countless iron shots are whizzing toward the hundreds of geese that have just taken off. The lighted sky is shocked and it seems to have retreated to a much greater height. The few stars flee for their lives and hide themselves in the gray clouds which look like torn cotton wadding.

Amid miserable croaking, the geese drop like bricks to the ground. Seven or eight wounded ones fall directly into the water from mid-air; they beat their wings desperately in an attempt to escape death. Only the white lead goose shoots up into the sky like an arrow. It wails with quacks, gathers together a few lucky and stunned survivors, and flies high into the distance.

The men on the two dozen or so boats paddle a few times with sudden force and land on the shoal. And swish-swish, black shadows dash forward, picking up the fallen geese and throwing them back into the cabins.

Cripple Lao Ding limps in an attempt to get onto the shoal too, but Luo Er grapples him right away. Before Cripple Lao Ding can finish saying, "What's wrong with you? I can manage!" his sworn brother grabs him by the waist and throws him into the boat. Then he issues an stern order, "Shut up! Warm your legs with a quilt!"

"Brother Luo, can't you...."

"If you want something to do, dress the geese, and cook a pot of goose soup for all of us to get warm."

Luo Er turns and climbs up to the shoal. Cripple Lao Ding does not argue any more. He knows it takes considerable skill to light up the firewood and build a good fire in the stove at the back of the boat with the heavy wind blowing over the river at night. And after they have had the soup, the team will try several more shoals. At dawn, they have to come back again to collect the birds they missed in the dark.

The team of boats returns at daybreak. They have got nearly three hundred geese. Cripple Lao Ding has his share of a dozen or so. They are forbidden to drink when hunting, so the men rush for their wine bottles and gulp down a lot once they get to the shore. Then they crawl into their cabins to sleep.

Shui Xian finishes plucking out the goose down, arranges with Luo Er's son Si Bei to sell the geese for her when he goes to the county seat. Now she is cooking a fat and delicious goose, the only one they have left.

Her father wakes up in the early afternoon. After lunch, father and daughter use a net to go fishing in the boat behind the end of the dike where the water flows slowly.

On the vast and wild shore adjacent to the bank, a few old willow stumps have put on a fuzzy green. The sky is blue, the sun is warm, and the wind is no longer piercing. Far off, a woman is running toward them across the shore. There is a colored candy wrapper sticking to one side of her face, and she is holding a few willow branches, laughing, clapping, and hopping all the way. Shui Xian has already guessed that it must be Ah Hua, the lunatic, whom San San has mentioned. Though the woman is crazy, her skin is tender and white, and her looks are not at all bad.

She watches her father, who has already moved the boat toward Ah Hua. She takes over the punt-pole and is about to persuade him to leave. But Ah Hua has jumped onto the bow of the boat and stretches her hand before her father, "Ha, ha, ha, you give me money, find Xiao Jian, marry him...."

Shui Xian detects a faint smile on her father's face, and his shuttle-shaped scar becomes red again. He actually takes out a few ten cent bills and hands them to her. Tossing aside the willow branches, Ah Hua waves the bills, stamps the cabin floor, and shouts foolishly, "Oh, I have money, take the train, find Xiao Jian...." While she is shouting she steps over the goose gun in the middle of the boat. Then she hops a few times, and sits down right on the barrel,

Shui Xian hurries to pull her up, but her father's face has already darkened. "You get up, Ah Hua. Never sit on the gun!"

"I want to sit, I want to sit, sit on the train, clinking, clinking, finding Xiao Jian and marrying...."

Shui Xian hurries over and tries to get hold of Ah Hua's arms. "Don't make trouble! If you do, you might fall into the river!" And she whispers into Ah Hua's ear, "Ah Hua, it's the rule of us fishermen that women have a lot of Yinqi[11], and so our bodies are not clean. If the blood during our periods offends the gun, there will be a disaster."

Ah Hua cranes her neck and jumps up. She pushes Shui Xian aside, stares at Cripple Lao Ding, and shouts "I don't have it, no, not at all. You look at it." As she says so, she pulls her trousers loose, which drop straight down to her ankles. She thrusts out her belly, white and gleaming with sweat, and her legs too, toward Cripple Lao Ding.

Shui Xian looks up and sees that her father is stupefied. He is standing there with his hands crossed; his coarse and dark face turns instantly purple, as if it had caught fire. The shuttle-shaped scar grows so red and bright that it seems about to split; his eyes, bulging as a water-bird's eggs, are fixed on Ah Hua's nude body. Even his neck is purple and swollen, its veins throbbing. Like a man possessed, he has lost all control.

Shui Xian is terribly frightened. Her heart beats violently then tightens up as if ice cubes were being squeezed into it; at once her back breaks into a cold sweat. Ever since her mother died, father has led a life of...oh, for seventeen years he has never been near a woman!

She makes a quick turn and deftly pulls up Ah Hua's trousers. Then she puts on a grave expression and says, "Ah Hua, from now on don't come near our boat! Let's go, I'll see you home."

With coaxing, threats, and the help of a neighborhood boy, Shui Xian manages to find Hei Chou and leaves Ah Hua with him. "Brother, keep an eye on her more carefully from now on. Don't let her come to our boat. With the wind on the river and the waves, we can't be responsible for anything happening."

Hei Chou's face, lumpy with scabies, shows all his frustrations. "Damn it! I've no way to control her. If you lock her in the house, she'll smash everything she lays her eyes on. It's very kind of your younger sister...." Before he finishes, he grabs a shovel and curses Ah Hua, "If you dare to make

---

[11]In Chinese philosophy and medicine, Yinqi means the feminine or negative principle.

trouble on other people's boats again, I'll break your leg!"

It is already dark when she returns from the village. Shui Xian finds her father sitting on the bow with his wine gourd in his arms. He remains still as if planted there. Even when she is leaving, he does not stir except to wave his hand. She crosses the shore and waits on the dike for a truck--then suddenly she hears from far away the husky and drunken howling of her father:

> Near midnight, on a moonless evening,
> The widower is thinking of his wife,
> With tears, oh, that would never dry;
> Man and wife in every family
> Are kissing each other dearly,
> There is only Wang Bao[12]
> Who is left to his loneliness.

The long-drawn-out voice is like the laughter of the waves in the river, but at the same times, it is as melancholy as the wail of a river ghost that was wronged and driven to death. Shui Xian can no longer hold back her tears. If not for her and San San, father's leg would not have been broken, and anyhow he would have found.... She sighs, feeling that there is one more thing for her to worry about.

V. Yellow Whirl Wind

Shui Xian goes to buy oilstone for her husband, Da Shun, to sharpen the hook; she gets some for her father too. When she turns back to the Crescent Bend, San San has just gotten out of school.

"Sister, you're back at the right time. Daddy is drunk again. Lately he's been getting drunk every day, and he's been singing those wild songs so loud."

"Really? San San, has that lunatic woman from the village come again these last few days while I've been gone?"

---

[12] A widower in a Chinese folklore.

"No."

"Where is daddy now?"

"He's lying in the boat. I'm worried to death. All the others are setting up the nets, but he.... Then I tell him that tomorrow is Sunday, I'll use the net to catch fish myself in spite of him!" San San is cooking in the shed and pouting, banging the ladle around.

Shui Xian goes to look for her father, carrying a bag of pork cakes that she has brought along. When she climbs the bank, she finds that her father's two goose guns have already been moved ashore, leaning on the stone embankment built for protection from the wind. On the boat, the cabin covering put up at night for her father to sleep there has not yet been taken off, and it now rocks and sways strangely.

"Ha. ha, ha, it itches, it itches...." A woman seems to be laughing there under the covering! Shui Xian trembles all over, and she jumps as if a big black carp were in her heart. Isn't it Ah Hua's voice? She cries, "Daddy, I'm back!" She sees Ah Hua crawling out of the cabin with some ten-cent bills in her hand, her hair disheveled, and her padded clothes half open. Then she goes up the bank and hops away, laughing foolishly all the time.

Shui Xian scrambles aboard and calls her father, but he does not respond. His back turns toward her, facing the other side of the boat, he snores away like a pair of bellows. He seems to be drunk and in a dead sleep. Shui Xian opens her mouth a few times, yet in the end fails to say anything. "God!" she sighs heavily and sits down on the boat; then she looks at her father lying on the wrinkled quilt with his body drawn together like a freshwater shrimp.

Shui Xian returns again the next day. Cripple Lao Ding is again drunk and sleeping in the cabin. Uncle Luo Er has gone to the county to sell fish. And so the two sisters go fishing on their boat.

The sky is blue and the clouds are white. Over the huge, dazzlingly yellow river, there are only a few gulls with black wing tips and white bellies crying and flying after the little boat. The girls steer around an old shoal, two new shoals, and a tall rock embankment, then move into a shallow bend. San San is punting the boat, and Shui Xian is fishing with the net. The reflections of their red and green padded clothes ripple in the water against the blue sky and white clouds. "Oh--" San San shouts with all her heart, grabbing the punt-pole and striking the water with it, beating up a circle of spray. Several yellow birds with small heads and narrow wings soar into the air from a wild shoal close to the bank, and a pair of water birds flap their wings and fly away with croaks.

"Silly girl, you'll frighten away the fish!" Shui Xian is smiling too, but she is also blaming her father in her heart: Old man, you must never get involved in any scandal and make your daughters worry about you. In the meantime, she takes out the tow board and beats the side of the boat with it to drive the fish to a designated place--bang, bang, bang... bang, bang, bang... bang, bang, bang... bang, bang.... All of a sudden she looks up and narrows her crescent eyes. From the other side of the embankment comes howling like broken threads blown over by the river wind:

> Moonless night...in the small hours,
> Oh, the widower...is...gloomy;
> He longs... for...a mistress,
> But she...won't...old or young...

The wind seems to change its direction, and what is left of the song is blown away. So are Shui Xian's smiles.

"Sister, tell daddy to quit singing these stupid old tunes. It's so embarrassing!"

Shui Xian does not say anything for a long time; her face remains blank.

"San San, could you stop going to school?"

"Why? Daddy agrees to it. I want to go to school in the city. I'll go to high school and college to bring credit to us fishermen!"

"But look at daddy. He needs somebody to take care of him, somebody to look after him."

"But daddy says he's in good health. He once had four bowls of rice and three bowls of goose soup. Isn't it enough that I'll work longer and harder later?"

"San San, I had a nightmare last night. The bodies of several women were floating over the river, their bellies all bulging like gunnysacks. One was being driven along by the water, and she got tangled up in some willow branches. Suddenly she became a river ghost with two heads and two horns, and she ran over the water after our boat with her horrible laughter...."

"No, no, I don't want to hear it. Again it's about a little ghost that crosses a river without having to take off his shoes. You're superstitious, just like daddy." Suddenly San San exclaims, "Oh, sister, look, the yellow whirlwind!"

Indeed, on the vast expanse of wild shoals near the bank, a huge ball of yellow is rolling over from a distance, whirling about with loud whistling sound. As it rumbles closer it grows bigger and bigger, with a thunderous noise, as if it had uprooted a mountain on a plain. Then, carrying with it a gush of chilly air, it plunges over the end of the dike and disappears.

Shui Xian's round and white face turns blue with terror. She mumbles, "What's happened?" She blinks and shivers, pointing with her finger to the wild shoal where the whirlwind has just passed. "San San, look, what's that?"

San San narrows her almond eyes. "Looks like somebody's lying there. Let's go and have a look."

They jump onto the shoal and run toward the thing. "My!" Both are scared to death.

It is Ah Hua. She is lying on her back; her red damask padded clothes are wide open; and her lower body is stark naked with half of her shanks already sunk into the soft silt. Her eyes seem to have been pecked out by eagles, and are now nothing but two black holes. The whole body is covered with a layer of yellow sand left by the yellow whirlwind. And there are large, messy footprints around it.

After she collects herself together a little, San San's tanned face turns black with anger. She cries out almost in tears, "Who was that brutal and cold-blooded bastard! Catch and skin him alive!"

Shui Xian opens her mouth and stares at the body as if dumbstruck, "My... God, who...who could have done this? Who could have done this...."

San San tugs her away abruptly. "Come on, let's hurry and report it to the police station at the ferry crossing."

San San punts the boat, darts around the embankment and shoots like an arrow toward the Crescent Bend, where the team of boats are berthed.

Then she throws down the punt-pole and is about to drag Shui Xian to get ashore. "Sister, let's hurry!"

Suddenly Shui Xian grabs San San; her face sweats as if she were having a heart attack. With hands trembling, she stammers, "Don't...don't hurry, we... got to...ask daddy first...."

"If you're afraid, I'll go alone!" San San breaks free angrily, dashes up the slope, and runs off.

Shui Xian rushes into the cabin of their boat and throws herself down near her father, who is still dead drunk. She cries and shakes him, "Daddy, daddy...."

He does not wake up. Looking around, she finds that the bag of pork cakes which she bought and brought over remains untouched. Only the wine gourd left on the wrinkled quilt is almost empty.

"Daddy, daddy, wake up, you wake up now...." Shui Xian shakes her father by the shoulder with all her strength.

Finally Cripple Lao Ding opens his eyes halfway, but is still very much dazed. His eyes are covered with a net of bloodshot veins. "What...what's happened?"

"Ah Hua is dead! Hurry...."

"Who? Who's dead?" Cripple Lao Ding is shocked. He struggles to sit up.

"It's Ah Hua, the lunatic! She's lying on the shoal, raped and strangled.

Who did it? Do you know? Do you know who did it?"

"Er? Ah Hua...is dead? Really?" Cripple Lao Ding opens his eyes wide.

"Yes, daddy. The police will be here in no time, and they'll find out right away. Oh, daddy, tell your daughter honestly who really did it!"

"How...could I know?"

"Daddy, you have to think straight right now. Any man who commits rape or murder will be shot! If he is one of us, all of us will get into trouble. Have you forgotten that on the Dao Ba River the year before, two of our men made a pass at some women on the shore, and they smashed our boats and beat up the two men? What's more, they forced all of us to leave there right away. Daddy, now it's a matter of life and death, please see things straight!"

"Shit!" Cripple Lao Ding bangs the side of the boat and struggles to stand up, but his leg fails him and he falls, "How ...could I..."

"Daddy, I beg you, is it really...." Shui Xian becomes so desperate that she starts to cry.

Cripple Lao Ding shuts his eyes and mumbles through his throat. The shuttle-shaped scar on his face turns from red to white.

Shui Xian fixes her eyes on him in terror. All at once she screams "Daddy!" and kneels down with tears running down her face, "Oh, daddy, your Shui Xian is kneeling down before you to beg you to tell the truth. If it's really you, we...we have to think of a way, to run away or what. If there's the slightest chance, I will do anything to be with you. But you have to tell me the truth!"

Cripple Lao Ding bangs his big head against his knees; his scar quivers; and his two coarse hands pinch his crippled leg desperately. "I...I only...I didn't...I haven't...." he howls. He grabs his wine gourd, pours and gulps down in a dreadful manner every bit of the remaining wine. Then, boom, he falls on his back to the cabin floor like a broken mast.

VI. Nightmare

That night, the superintendent of the ferry crossing police station arrives with two policemen; they wake up the heavily drunken Cripple Lao Ding and take him away.

Shui Xian and San San sit in the shed and wait, frantic with worry.

"Sister, daddy's been gone for a long time, why hasn't he come back yet?" Shui Xian does not respond.

"Sister, did you ask daddy? Is it true that he knows something?"

Shui Xian shakes her head.

San San can wait no longer; she leans on the leg of the bed and falls asleep. Shui Xian does not close her eyes; she sits there the whole night.

At daybreak she goes to look for Uncle Luo Er. "Uncle, I want to ask about daddy at the police station."

"You stay put, I'll go!" Keeping a poker face, Uncle Luo Er puts on his padded clothes and leaves.

"Uncle, you...." Shui Xian bites her lips in order not to cry.

"Daughter, don't worry. No one could ever slander my name. Whether it's government officials or anybody else, whoever dares to frame your father, we'll try peaceful ways before using force. If they press us too hard, our dozens of guns can shoot other things besides geese!"

Shui Xian knows that Uncle Luo Er would risk his life for her father. In the Fishermen's Commune at their home town during the year when every family's woks were smashed and people were forced to eat in the public dining-rooms, which later caused widespread deaths from starvation,[13] Uncle

---

[13] The famine occurred from 1959 to 1961 shortly after the establishment of the People's Communes, which destroyed the rural economy. The loss of life is attributable to the severe natural disasters during this period.

Luo Er became a political prisoner. But he showed no sign of repentance, so he was beaten black and blue and locked in a dark room. Her father was a member of the armed people's militia,[14] and he was standing guard outside the house with a rifle. At midnight, her father opened the door and called, "Luo Er, go for your life. I'll handle whatever happens to me here." Uncle Luo Er escaped with his wife and kids. The next day, her father became the man who got beaten up and prosecuted.

The year after her mother died, her father, holding San San in his arms, dragging himself along and hobbling, found Luo Er on a bend on the Yellow River. They embraced each other and wept together. Uncle Luo Er took out a bowl of wine, grabbed a sharp fish knife and cut his thumb, saying, "Old brother, if you believe in me, let's kowtow and become sworn brothers. From now on you're my elder brother by blood. Wherever we go, whatever is mine is yours." He built a boat for her father and bought him a goose gun before he could offer to pay for them. Later, he even arranged her marriage with Da Shun.

Uncle Luo Er is back. He does not mention a word about her father but tells her that a group of Hei Chou's cousins have surrounded the police station. With a grave face he issues a strict order: no one in the gang, women or men, young or old, is allowed to go near the village, not even San San who goes to school there.

Shui Xian collapses. San San helps her to her feet, and before she can reach their shed, Shui Xian throws up.

"Sister, how could they suspect daddy? No, it's impossible...."

Shui Xian remains silent, leaning against the leg of the bed. Her hair falls down her face, which is as white as that of a dead man.

Cripple Lao Ding returns at nightfall. He looks much thinner, and in addition to the scar there are a few bloodstains on his face. He does not answer any question put to him but goes straight to his shed and pulls out two bottles of Fu Niu liquor. He swallows half of a bottle and pours all the rest into his gourd. Then he flings the two empty bottles against a rock they use outside to protect the shed from the wind. Bang, bang, they are smashed to

---

[14] Militia organized by the communist government.

pieces. He limps down the bank, plunges into the boat cabin, and does not comes out again.

Also at dusk, two days later, Uncle Luo Er returns from the police station. He waves his hand and declares, "The case has been solved. It was done by an old widower over fifty from the West Village." He adds to Shui Xian, "Why didn't I think of it, a man ...for so many years...hasn't... near him...."

Shui Xian say nothing but drops her head, sobbing.

Uncle Luo Er hurries to explain. "Don't you be angry, what I said is if we'd thought of this long ago, it wouldn't have been like... but now...hell!" He frowns, swings his hand, and goes away.

Shui Xian and San San get on the boat in a hurry to tell their father the news. After hearing it, Cripple Lao Ding becomes a bit wheezy, and suddenly he laughs, "Ha, ha, ha." But his face looks more hideous laughing than when crying. Then he struggles toward the door of the cabin, where he vomits some liquor into the river for a while. Finally he falls down on the quilt and dozes off.

Uncle Luo Er comes again, shouting before he comes aboard, "Brother, come on over to my shed. We'll drink our fill tonight!" But when he sees Cripple Lao Ding, he waves his hand. "That won't do. Shui Xian, take good care of your daddy. Give him a pot of strong tea after a while." He looks at the drunken man and sighs, "Oh, Elder Brother, I've been such a good-for-nothing, I've brought you so much trouble all your life...."

Shui Xian's nose twitches and she turns aside quickly.

Uncle Luo Er also instructs San San, "Later on, don't let any women on shore come on board the boat, whether they're beauties or idiots. Do you remember?"

Uncle Luo Er leaves. Shui Xian says to San San, "You can go to the shed and catch up with the lessons you missed in the last two days. I have to go back early tomorrow morning. Let me take care of daddy here today."

So San San leaves too. From a few sheds on the bank come the shouts of men playing a finger-guessing game. Shui Xian pulls off her father's shoes and clothes, covers him with the quilt, and sits there blankly for no one knows how long. Gradually there is only the whistle of the wind left outside, and the roaring of the waves in the main current are reminiscent of the howling and wailing of a multitude of river gods and water ghosts.

It is late at night; the half moon swims among the clouds like a dazed silver carp.

Cripple Lao Ding is having a dream. A huge bald eagle weighing more than a hundred pounds stands on his chest and stare at him malignantly, making it impossible for him to move even one finger. A group of extremely thin and single-horned water ghosts are burning his flesh with torches.... He feels dead, as light as a feather, floating and flying on the cloud after his wine gourd.... The water ghosts catch up with him, shouting and crying. They stir his blood with broken paddles, making it as hot as boiling water.... He himself becomes a big water ghost, all nude, and is chasing a woman. He longs desperately to press her down on the shoal. He has caught her, it is his Rong Rong with two round breasts! She says to him, "Brother Ding, look at yourself, you scare me to death!" Suddenly it turns into Ah Hua who sticks out her white and sweaty torso toward him while laughing. He stretches out his hairy hand to hold and tear them like mad. He seems to have grabbed a woman's body, warm and slippery.... Oh, it is not right. Who is she really? But all his body is already too hot and bloated to wonder any more....

Cripple Lao Ding wakes up at daybreak. He opens his eyes and finds Shui Xian sleeping soundly by his side, her face a sign of utter exhaustion. His whole body instantly breaks out into a cold sweat. He hurls away the quilt and sees Shui Xian, all nude. He recoils in horror.

"Oh--" he wails dreadfully as if he has seen a ghost. He pulls Shui Xian by the hair and slaps her head and face with his big palm.

Shui Xian, awakened by the beating, is struck dumb. She crawls into a corner of the boat, clutching the quilt.

Cripple Lao Ding swings his hands, clenches his two big fists, and bangs his head fiercely against the side of the boat.

Shui Xian stares at him, terrified. She stays petrified momentarily, then she scrambles up and dashes over to hold her father's shoulder, "Daddy, don't, I was afraid...." She breaks into a wail. "Daddy, please hit me instead. Beat me to death! I'm... really...afraid...you may...commit... the crime! Oh, oh, oh, oh...."

Cripple Lao Ding, lying on his back, spills out a series of "ah, ah, oh, oh" sounds. No one knows whether he is crying or laughing. But those who have heard it on the nearby boats can't but be frightened out of their wits.

VII. Fire Boat

The huge river is swollen. People say that the floodgates of the San Men Xia Reservoir have been opened so that farmers down the river may irrigate their wheat.

The water raises the boats several feet; its yellow waves swallow the new shoals that look like ghosts' eyes, and batter and bite off the old ones like broken boats. The currents whirl with foam, carrying rotten straw and dead tree stumps, and rushing eastward with a roar.

It is hard to fish when the river is swollen. It is getting warmer too; the geese are flying north. Men in the gang cease to go fishing in the river; they are busy getting ready to move up north to the upper reaches of the Yellow River in Inner Mongolia.

Luo Er is busy renting the railway carriages to carry both the men and boats there. He leaves with live fish and fat geese and comes home pretty drunk. You have to pay for your journey, and the boats are as precious to the fishermen as women in their arms. They mustn't be jostled up and down by those loading-men.

Only Cripple Lao Ding does not bother. He always goes out on the boat at dawn and stays away till dark. No one knows where he goes or what he does there, nor do they ask. When they meet him, their faces show no expression, their eyes are cold, and they say nothing. People only see more empty liquor bottles thrown out of his boat.

FIRE BOAT

Shui Xian has not come for nearly three weeks. She used to come early and stay for a couple of days at this time of the year, helping her father putting things in order and packing them on and off the boat.

Today she finally comes. Her face is pale, and thinner; her crescent-shaped eyes have lost their twinkles, and now droop. She does not greet her father but goes straight into the shed. Her face looks dull and lifeless, as if she is critically ill.

When she passes, the men turn their faces, shake their heads, and go away. But the women can not control themselves any longer. They first whisper to one another, then some begin to grind their teeth, stamp their feet, and spit.

Rumor finds its way into Luo Er's ears at last. His face darkens, and he strikes the one who has just told him about it. His eyes narrow into deadly knives. "Damn, you son of a bitch! Who are you accusing of this? One word more, and in a year you'll be celebrating your first death anniversary!"

The man trembles. "Uncle, who would dare? If I hadn't heard the fights on their boat with my own ears and seen the two of them like that with my own eyes, who wouldn't be afraid of being struck by lightning? If you don't believe it, you...you ask around yourself."

Luo Er sets out to see Cripple Lao Ding right away. It is not until he comes to the top of the bank that he finds a lonely boat floating on the bend below his feet. His sworn bother is sitting on the bow like a dead tree, holding his wine gourd and remaining dead still.

He stands there for a long long time and in the end does not call out. He turns back with a face full of thunders and lightning, clenching his teeth till they crack. Dogs and chickens would have been frightened away upon seeing him like this.

By noon Da Yang Ma has prepared a feast with wine, and he literally drags Luo Er there to discuss their journey to Inner Mongolia. Luo Er throws away the cup and grabs a bowl, gulping down every drop of liquor in it.

Both are getting pretty drunk. Da Yang Ma squints and gazes at Luo Er with his small eyes, "Brother Luo Er, I haven't dared to ask you about one thing. I heard the women talk about your sworn brother and his daughter.... What really happened?"

Luo Er says nothing and keeps his head lowered, but all of a sudden he pitches the small wine table over.

Da Yang Ma's thin face grows white with terror; he slaps his own cheeks and pleads, "Brother, I've had too much. I deserve to be punished, I deserve to be punished!" He hurries to pick up the table, makes a large pot of strong tea, and puts it in front of Luo Er, "Brother, Brother Luo Er, please don't...."

Luo Er remains silent and still, his eyes cold and menacing.

San San comes in and asks, "Uncle, my elder sister is sick. She has a fever. Could I borrow your bike to buy some drug at the clinic?"

Luo Er bangs the table with his fist. "Get out!"

San San backs out quickly with fear.

Cripple Lao Ding appears, standing tentatively at the door of the shed. "Brother, why scare the child? Give me the key."

Luo Er does not answer or raise his head; he grabs the pot of hot tea and throws it all at Cripple Lao Ding--the tea splashes all over his face and neck. Cripple Lao Ding retreats a step to the side and stares at him, muttering, "Brother, you...." Before he could say anything more, Luo Er charges forward, and boom! flattens him with one blow. Then he jumps on him and keeps pounding him like crazy with his fists and palms.

Men and women of the team come, but no one says anything or tries to separate them. Only San San, scared to death, is stamping her feet and wailing.

Cripple Lao Ding neither fights back nor moves. Blood spurts out of his nose and mouth. Luo Er pulls himself up, stumbles a couple of steps away, and falls down like he has no strength left.

Cripple Lao Ding struggles to his feet; he does not wipe off the tea leaves or the blood on his face. San San, crying, runs over to support him, but he shoves her away with one thrust of his arm. Then he limps along toward the river.

At this very moment, Da Shun, his son-in-law, arrives by bike in a great hurry. He has come to ask about the journey to Inner Mongolia, but upon seeing Cripple Lao Ding, he lays down his bike at once and runs over to hold him with his hand. At the same time he asks again and again, "Daddy, what's happened? Who did this to you? Why?"

Sobbing, San San answers, "It's Uncle Er. I don't know why he beat him so hard...."

Da Shun, who is as strong as a big black carp, rushes toward Luo Er's shed, "Uncle Luo Er, what's wrong with him? Why did you beat him so hard? Why? Why?"

Luo Er sits on a stool sullenly and refuses to answer.

After being pressed hard, he closes his eyes and says, "Da Shun, if you're angry, just beat me up."

Da Shun finds Da Yang Ma and grabs him by the chest, "You tell me why they had the fight right after they came out of your shed!"

Da Yang Ma twists his long, thin face and pleads, "Let go, Da Shun. Even if I'm risking my life today, I've decided to keep my mouth shut!"

Two men of the Jiangsu gang come; one of them sneers, "Da Shun, one saw but *can't* tell, and a friend *doesn't* tell. If you're man enough, go and discipline your woman first. Why make trouble here with our chief?"

Da Shun loosens his grip. His heart is full of suspicion, as if there were a ball of fish bones sticking in it. Shui Xian has acted a little weird these days. At night, she is sometimes unusually enthusiastic toward him, clinging to him like a snake, kissing him, laying her head on his chest. But she has tears in her eyes. When he asks her about it, she always says there's nothing wrong. But sometimes when he is so hot and eager to make love to her, she will be so distracted, letting him do whatever he wants without any response. My god! Does she have a man here?

Da Shun advances toward the man menacingly. "You spill it out!"

The man says, "Who dares to say things like this? Ask you old father-in-law if you really want to know."

Pow! Da Shun is struck dumb. The strange events of the past several days and today's fight have in a flash made everything clear. He feels his blood roaring like the swollen river, clashing and battering his head and heart so hard that they are going to explode.

Like a hurricane he charges into San San's shed where Shui Xian is lying in bed, her face red and swollen with high fever. Seeing him, she is so frightened that she jerks up involuntarily. Her face instantly loses all its color; her lips tremble; tears roll down. She shakes her head repeatedly, "Da Shun, let's go right now, I...will...give... you... everything..."

Da Shun runs out of there as quickly as if he had seen a ghost. He jumps on his bike and rides madly toward the ferry crossing. When he approaches it, he hops off and plunges himself onto a sand dune on the slope of the bank. Yanking his hair with both hands, he sobs and howls, "Ah, ah, ah, ah...."

By sunset, Da Shun has drunk a great deal at the small wine shop at the ferry crossing. He pushes his bike to the crossroad in front of the locally-sponsored middle school and runs into San San, who has just been dismissed for the day.

"San San, I'd like to ask you a favor. I have something to do tonight and may not be able to return to Pan Ma Bend. Your three-year-old nephew would be left alone, and I'd be worried. Could you take my bike and go there now, and keep him company for the night? If your sister and I get into any trouble later, we trust you to take care of him."

San San is a little suspicious, but she still takes over the bike and rides away along the dams of the Yellow River.

It has gradually gotten dark. Near the Wild Slope Ferry Crossing, the shore is dim and gloomy; so are the river and the shoals. The opposite shore fades into a dark line. The panorama, spacious and serene, seems to have changed little for hundreds of years. But as soon as it is splashed with the rosy glow of sunset, the river sparkles with golden light. In the eyes of goose hunters, accustomed to the night, the dark yellow river stands out against the little red brick houses at the ferry crossing, the white-bellied gulls flying over the river, and the ancient willows with their fuzzy green branches. Whenever a little boat sails from the end of the dike in the distance, everything turns exceptionally beautiful. It lures the eye and charms the heart, and it would be so hard to give it all up. Then a certain feeling wells up which defies definition.

That little boat now approaching is Cripple Lao Ding's.

All the people in the boat team are having supper in their sheds. Da Shun walks down the slope of the bank and jumps onto Si Bei's boat. He snatches the punt-pole without saying a thing, and with several quick and vigorous punts heads straight toward Cripple Lao Ding's boat.

The two little boats draw closer.

Da Shun pulls out a wine bottle from his waistband, smashes its mouth on the side of the boat, and pours all the liquor on his goose down jacket.

Suddenly he is stunned. Cripple Lao Ding stands tottering on the bow, holding his golden wine gourd. He does not look in Da Shun's direction, but says in a muffled voice, "Da Shun, don't bother. Let me go and join Shui Xian's mom myself."

He holds up the wine gourd and pours the liquor on the oilcloth covering and the floor of the boat. Then he strikes a match and tosses it onto the covering. Boom! it catches fire instantly.

Cripple Lao Ding limps over to the paddle, and rows a few violent strokes. The boat follows a rapid current, turns round, and veers toward the river's mainstream where the waves are raging like boiling water.

"Hey! the boat has caught fire, the boat has caught fire!" Men on shore are shouting. Those in the sheds are running out and jumping aboard their boats. A dozen of them punt out toward the middle of the river in a hurry, with Luo Er ahead of anyone else.

The shadow of Cripple Lao Ding is now surrounded and engulfed by fire and thick smoke. His boat is burning and cracking; the fire is rising higher and higher, and the longer it burns, the brighter it grows. The fire has lit up large areas of the river surface. The wind whips up large swarms of sparks behind the boat, lending it a long tail of fire. Swish-swish--two storks from an old shoal near by are shooting into the sky with stretched necks; several water birds are croaking in great surprise and beating their wings, fleeing for their lives from the shoreline into the distance.

The fire shines on Da Shun, making him look like a dark, determined giant standing on the bow. He is holding his twenty-foot-punt-pole athwart, blocking the way for those who are hurrying to the rescue.

Luo Er says nothing but works his pole swiftly, and the water splashes high in front of his boat.

Suddenly people see Cripple Lao Ding hopping out of the cabin and standing on the bow. He raises his arms to heaven amid the tongues of fire, and roars in his dreadful and coarse voice, "Fire of heaven, oh, retribution! Ah, oh, oh, oh...." He lets out a series of mournful laughter that sound like the shrieks of ghosts.

The dozen boats stop; people are looking at one another as if frozen. Luo Er shuts his eyes; the muscles of his dark face throb, bulging out like whipping marks. Da Shun's pole also hangs down loosely.

The fire boat is burning more and more fiercely; it has been washed into the mainstream, and is being carried down the river amid the towering waves and whirlpools.

Abruptly a little boat dashes out of the team, shooting toward the fire boat like an arrow. A woman is crying and shouting desperately, "Daddy, oh, daddy!...." She is Shui Xian, now standing on the bow, her hair wild. Her sharp screams pierce the air and float above the huge river, tearing at the darkening sky and people's hearts.

The men on the boats bow their heads and seem to have stiffened.

"Ah--" There comes another thunderous howl. Da Shun waves his pole and thrusts it ferociously to the very bottom of the river. In an instant, his boat flies into the mainstream too. It runs after Shui Xian's boat, after the fire boat. "Shui Xian, oh, Shui Xian!..." The river wind carries back his manly cries.

Over the dark surface of the river, and amid the billowing waves of the mainstream, the fire boat is being swept farther and farther. And the two boats following it are also being swept farther, and farther....

Early next day San San comes back.

"Uncle, where's my daddy? And sister? And Brother Da Shun? Why haven't I seen them? Where have they gone?"

Luo Er says nothing. He places his left hand on the hull of the boat and grabs a kitchen knife with his right. Ka! he chops down and a chunk of his finger flies into the Yellow River. "San San, with this finger as a proof, from now on, I'm your daddy!"

RECOMMENDATION

Xing Hongliang

Right at this moment the company's conference room is filled with cigarette smoke. However, the Party secretary, his two deputies, and three members of the Standing Committee, who have gathered together, remain in complete silence while puffing out the smoke as if it were the only thing they could do. How Xiao Tao, the secretary, would like to have two pipes extending from her nostrils out the window.

Today's meeting is for recommendation. Its topic is simple and clear: to recommend a young or middle-aged healthy and competent cadre. He will be first publicized as a model official, and then promoted to the leadership position of the Bureau. To be more exact, one of the seven leading cadres here will strike gold and become the First Deputy Bureau Chief, who is likely to take over the number one position later. All of the seven leading members of the company arrived at the meeting on time except Xiao Du, who was hospitalized due to a medical emergency. The meeting began at eight in the morning, and by now two hours have passed. There is nothing in Xiao Tao's notebook but a few introductory remarks by Qiao Dianlong, the Party Secretary. All Bo Le's[1] seem to have become dumb.

As a matter of fact, everybody is perfectly aware that anyone who speaks first will get burned. Since no one has the nerve to recommend himself, the best policy is to keep your mouth shut and wait for others to mention your name. Unfortunately, you have no control of others' mouths. Without superb tricks, you simply can't pry them open. And today's meeting is just as delicate and subtle. Under the circumstances, the one in the most advantageous position is naturally Lao Qiao, chairman of the meeting.

"Please be at ease, and say whatever you want."

---

[1] A lord of the Kingdom of Qin (770-476 B.C.) who had an exceptional knowledge of horses, thereby was able to choose from the herd the "winged steed," the best one that could cover a thousand li (about four hundred miles) a day. Here it refers to the recommendation of the best official.

Lao Qiao's piercing eyes sweep through the whole conference room while he urges everyone else again. It seems that his sharp eyes can penetrate the minds of all, which imperceptibly become a psychological pressure. The inexperienced would have fallen into a panic and got licked. But all the participants of today's meeting are veterans who have survived countless meetings and conferences. They have weathered countless similar situations, whether exciting, ceremonious, solemn, serious, silent, embarrassing, or troublesome. Each participant has had a history of almost twenty years in attending these meetings, and had long since learned all the tricks. Therefore they all bide their time and sit tight, waiting for the fish.

"The Bureau is pressing hard for our decision. Better have it earlier so we can send in our report!" Lao Qiao lights a cigarette again and urges, "Lao Lu, why don't you take the lead and say something."

"Eh, no, no, I...I haven't thought enough about it. Better listen to the others first." Lao Lu begs to be excuses and goes on puffing out smoke.

"Damn, the old slime!" Lao Qian gets so angry that he curses in his heart. After careful consideration, he picked Lu Bingkun to speak out first. Not long ago he chose this guy all by himself as Deputy Secretary, the no. 3 position in the company. Though under Wang Tunan, the first Deputy, Lu Bingkun is in charge of several very profitable factories. Lu used to show great respect and gratitude to him, yet at this critical moment Lao Lu, who always addresses him with the official title and flatters his health, strength, and great capability, shuts his mouth tight and shows no sign of recommending him at all. He is simmering with rage. Humph! A deputy for just a few days wants to be promoted to the Bureau leadership! Wild ambition!

Well, isn't is hard to speak through another man's mouth, and now you've met with a rebuff! Wang tunan, the First Deputy, is gloating over Qiao's slip and smiling secretly on the side. He thinks to himself that this Qiao Dianlong should have enough sense to step aside. And then with only Deputy Secretary Lu left, whose qualification and record of service are not to be compared with his....He might as well use Lu to clear the way for him.

Just as expected, Lu begins to fight back. "Lao Qian, the Bureau puts so much emphasis on age, I guess it must have a far-reaching significance..."

RECOMMENDATION

When Lu was promoted to be a Deputy, Qiao Dianlong had time and again recommended him as a young and capable cadre. What Lu has just said is to remind Qiao of his comments and not to be too forgetful.

Then he smiles to the remaining members of the Standing Committee. "You young comrades must have more accurate understanding of the directive from the Bureau. Lao Qiao, how about listening to them first?"

Trying to squeeze the ducklings! What a slippery fellow. Qiao Dianlong gets angry again. But it is hard for him to oppose the idea, so he has to add, "Well, yes, let everybody talk."

Wang Tunan certainly knows why Lu makes age the issue here, so he takes over in a hurry, "In my opinion, what Lao Lu said is a little one-sided. Health and age are certainly important, but it wouldn't be proper to consider them only while paying no attention to one's abilities! My suggestion is to take account of both sides. If we select, we have to select somebody who is really competent. Anyway, we can't have a Bureau Chief who needs to rely on other people's shoulders."

"That's correct, correct. What Lao Wang has said is correct!" Qian Dianlong immediately expresses his support. "Of course it won't do to line up people simply according to their years of service, we must also give credit to qualifications and record of service. They are the most important!"

Lu Bingkun smiles to himself, thinking Qiao Dianlong really acts silly as he has just been fooled without even knowing it. What Wang Tunan said is not an eulogy of Qiao's record of service but a selling pitch for himself. As for relying on others' shoulders, it is of course a vicious reminder of his own modest words at the time of his promotion. The purpose of Lao Wang's cross attack is none other than to take advantage of his own record while making up for his weakness in age.

"Lao Wang, you got me wrong! I fully agree with you on this point! Ability is certainly the prerequisite. But it has to be subject to public scrutiny. It's not right to slight the modest gentleman; and it's even worse to favor the Old Granny Wang who bragged about her watermelons.[2] After all we must

---

[2] A well-known figure in a Chinese folklore, who exaggerates the quality of her commodities.

not stick to the old way, but consider ability as the criterion."

Lu's response is smart; Wang's retort is just as shrewd. "Sure, sure. Recommending a person of virtue is not the same as finding somebody with a sharp tongue. We got to see his real stuff."

"Let's first hear what others have to say," Qiao Dianlong cuts in, thinking that, with what has been going on and the fight between Lu and Wang, he could safely thrust the cushy job of Bo Le onto those ducklings.

So the six eyes of the three secretaries fix on the three younger members of the Standing Committee. The atmosphere becomes tense instantly, the pressure rising to the breaking point. Anyone who refuses to declare where he stands risks defying the heaven and the winged steed. Nevertheless, they really find hard to say anything. With the three secretaries forming a tripartite balance of forces, locking in an unyielding confrontation in which each one is scheming to grab the nomination, anyone who makes the recommendation would greatly upset and provoke the other two. What intelligent person would bring trouble on himself by saying something stupid or put himself to a thankless task? Naturally the three younger members, very nervous and uneasy, do not know what to do. They really feel a little envious of Xiao Du who was hospitalized and is now far away from the battlefield. Sometimes it is lucky to fall ill. After all, why are they destined to be Bo Le's? What does it mean to be young and middle-aged cadres? Are they old men over fifty? Isn't is a joke! The three are tender in years, but they do have quick tongues. When pressed hard, they become less reserved and more querulous. Then they will talk with much less caution. So a bolder one among them blurts out:

"A man is considered to have had a long life when he reaches the age of seventy; he retires at sixty. How should we define the 'young and middle-aged?' Wouldn't it be necessary to ask a linguist to define it for us?"

That meets with instant approval. The three Party secretaries are stunned, their eyes wide open. The four sides on the battlefield have come to a draw at last. So those Bo Le's begin to meditate anew, making critical choices in their mind.

"Eh, this, I don't think is necessary. It's not appropriate for us to quibble over this point too much. Let's decide on a preliminary list of names!

RECOMMENDATION

We can no longer put it off!"

Qiao Dianlong has actually gotten confused, missing the mark in what he has just said. As opinions differ so widely, how could they possibly agree on such a list? Consequently the others do not feel like giving any heed to his empty talk; they resume their smoking with lowered heads, puffing out rings in great numbers. As to Xiao Tao, she fixes her stare on the clock, hoping sincerely that the meeting will soon come to an end so she can be relieved from the smoky battle formation. The newspapers often carry articles saying passive smoking is even more dangerous. If it goes on like this for much longer, she is afraid that she will get lung cancer.

Seeing that his words draw no response, Qiao Dianlong feels a little embarrassed. Such an impasse can last forever! The higher authorities are to blame, insisting that we must make the recommendation. Do they know how troublesome it is? Bureaucracy in its worst form! All his life he has chaired numerous meetings, but he has never encountered such a thorny, really uncomfortable situation. Nevertheless, he is an expert on meetings and is not going to be intimidated by the deadlock. He quickly takes out a book of documents from the drawer. "I think we'd better study the document once more to further clarify our minds."

The motion receives favorable response at once, which sounds like a violent thunder out of nowhere--the only thing your hear is the booming sound of the window panes of the conference room. It is as if a long repressed dry thunder had found a way to explode at long last.

So all begin to study the document and offer comments. Everyone joins in, expounding the principal guidelines for being a Bo Le to recommend men of virtue. Suddenly the atmosphere becomes lively, and the speeches cover all sorts of subjects under the sun with exceptional skill and ease. In addition, all show a perfect understanding in their superb bursts of eloquence, full of pearls of witticism and fountains of aphorism.

The guidelines are fully expounded pretty soon. And without further ado, they all automatically shift into a digression from the main topic. But however impassioned they wording has become, nothing is added to Xiao Tao's notebook except for a few synonyms and repetitions. The variation and digression, which lasts for more than one hour, brings little progress to the major topic. But with six Bo Le's, there is no winged steed whatsoever. The name of the man of virtue is still up in the air. It is Xiao Tao who first notices that the clock has chimed twelve o'clock, reminding them that if they do not hurry to the dining-room, it will close soon. After the Secretary nods his approval, she is the first to flee the conference room.

The meeting in the afternoon goes smooth, due to the news Xiao Tao brings. While having lunch downstairs, she received a call from a friend in the hospital, who told her that Xiao Du had been moved to the section for cancer patients with nonstoppable stomach hemorrhage. He is in very serious condition and the doctors are trying their best to save his life. The news spreads far and wide, and finally reaches the ears of the six Bo Le's. After verifying it with Xiao Tao, they know that the girl who called her is a nurse working in the section for cancer patients, which means the news is real and Xiao Du does have cancer. That is a surprise, but is within their expectation. Xiao Du went to have his barium-meal radiograph in the hospital last month, and polyps were found in his stomach. They have told him to pay special attention, but did not expect them to worsen so quickly, and now a strong, healthy, and active middle-aged man has been reduced to the verge of death. What a pity!

Xiao Du is the only engineer with special expertise among the company leaders. During the Cultural Revolution, he was unheard of, but his talent began to show itself in the Economic Reform. He volunteered to take over several factories that were about to go bankrupt, and succeeded in turning them around through cooperation with other companies and join ventures with foreign investors. What's more, each of these factories is now making a lot of money. People say he is the key star that can snatch a business from the jaws of death. This fellow also knows all the tricks for making himself popular: he donated his contract bonus, four hundred thousand yuan in all, to the country, without leaving even a penny for himself, thereby emerging as a man of great ability whom everyone knows in the Bureau.

All are very active from the very beginning of the meeting in the afternoon. And the topic is of course Xiao Du. First they talk about his illness, then his achievements. He is sick because of these achievements, and the latter seem more outstanding because of the former. The more serious his sickness, the more conspicuous his achievements grow. This is why newspaper always have articles about dead heroes. If they were not dead, how can we know they were heroes? Now since Xiao Du is going to die, his merits certainly stand out more clearly before these Bo Le's.

People have always been extraordinarily merciful toward the dying. Naturally it is not necessary to mention some of his shortcomings or some very controversial measures he once took. China is a country of etiquette, and its custom always is to praise the dead. Has anyone ever mentioned someone's dark side in his memorial speech? So all join in the eulogy, painting a lively picture of a second Jiang Zouying or Lu Jianfu.[3] They unanimously agree that Xiao Du is full of dedication, and has both professional expertise and management experience. And he is the type of cadre who, with his knowledge and abilities, can open paths for others to follow. Therefore he is the perfectly worthy of the titles of "man of virtue" and the "winged steed."

Xiao Tao has by now filled a thick notebook; there is enough material in it to be published in the *People's Daily*. Now who else should we recommend? So the accord is reached with no objections, and the recommendation materials are to be sent to the Bureau Party Committee immediately. We got to get it done right away before the hospital issues the formal notice that the patient is terminally ill. Otherwise there could be some inconvenience. And we also have to publicize his merits in a hurry. The people are now sick of newspaper articles publicizing dead heroes only. But right now we are lucky that no one has got wind of it--the "rumor" that Xiao Du is dying of cancer should not be taken seriously. So they make an instant decision: publicize Xiao Du's meritorious deeds within the company (the range to be further extended upon approval from the Bureau), calling on the cadres and workers to learn from him. At the same time, it is decided that all Bo Le's will visit him in the hospital after the meeting.

Xiao Du's face looks sallow. Lying in the hospital bed with pipes in his stomach, he is in a deep, dazed sleep, unable to wake up. His wife's eye sockets are red with grief. The Bo Le's decide not to disturb Xiao Du so as to let him rest more. But they feel they should say something to console his wife. So they say one after another, "A stomach ulcer is not necessarily cancer, and it is common to have a polyp in the stomach. It is not serious." "Xiao Du is not well mainly because he has lost too much blood. Once the bleeding is stopped, he will be all right. Please do not worry too much." Finally, on behalf of the company, Secretary Qiao urges that she take care of herself,

---

[3] Two middle-aged scientists who died prematurely mainly because of overwork and poor living conditions.

adding that Xiao Du fell sick simply because he has been working too hard, and the leadership is responsible for not taking enough care of him, and so on and so forth. Xiao Du's wife listens silently without denying the diagnosis of stomach ulcer or mentioning the word "cancer" even once. It looks like the doctors have taken pains to keep it from the family. His wife is muddleheaded enough; she doesn't know what kind of trouble her husband is in, even after he was moved to the section for cancer patients. But that's just as well, as they can leave the mistake uncorrected and make the best of it. They now have an excuse in case the Bureau blames them in the future. Besides, the most important thing is that they have made the recommendation, yet the road up for men of virtue remains open. Soon the position of Deputy Bureau Chief will be vacated, and all will have the opportunity to fight for it once more. The choice is very much to everybody's liking. On the way home, everyone feels that today's meeting has come to a perfect ending and that all their decisions are well- considered. Everything is so appropriate that all remains absolutely flawless and simply wonderful.

Beyond anyone's expectation, Xiao Du leaves the hospital and comes to work a few days later. He looks healthy, not in the least like a man who is going to see Marx.[4] By now all come to realize that it was a misunderstanding. Due to a shortage of beds, the doctors moved Xiao Du to the cancer section so they could stop his hemorrhage with intubation in bed. The nurse who had just come to her shift mistook him for a dying cancer patient, without asking. So there it was. Now, not only has the bleeding stopped, his polyps were also removed with an endoscope by the well-known medical expert Dai Xiaoguo, who happened to be on his case. And so he has escaped the pain of an operation, and is almost completely cured of his ulcer, which is healing quickly and will no longer bother him. He really looks like a man in high spirits after getting lucky. No wonder this guy has recovered so soon.

So the Bo Le's are feeling extremely upset. The fellow got so lucky that he could even take full advantage of his illness, and cancer at that! What an opportunity this is! You may not have one like this in all your life! This guy can turn a misfortune into a big win! How could his nomination convince anybody? This is too outrageous. Once again all Bo Le's have the exactly same opinion, saying it was only because of his cancer that they recommend him in the first place. Their praise for him was nothing but a kind of encouragement. In fact his achievements were the result of their unified

---

[4] To die, a common saying among members of the Communist Party.

efforts, while he alone is clearly responsible for his controversial measures. His donation of the four hundred thousand yuan was but a gesture. If he had not handed it in, how could he have kept it without serious troubles? Though he had special expertise, it is now not in vogue to promote professionals to the leadership positions. Better let him concentrate on his professional work. A man like him, too dynamic and inclined to act rashly, is probably not fit for the position of the Bureau Chief. So it is absolutely necessary to reconvene the meeting of recommendation. Only then can the whole process be termed prudent and discreet.

However, there is practically nothing they can do about it, as the formal letter of recommendation has already been sent out. What an injustice! As a consequence, their bellyfuls of resentment fall on Xiao Tao. The girl has been too irresponsible. How dare she be so perfunctory and make such a deadly mistake in such an important matter as recommending a man of virtue! So they reach a unanimous decision: Xiao Tao is to be transferred to a factory that very day as a warning and a punishment.

Xiao Tao, upon receiving the notice, feels so wronged that she sobs and cries. As she collects the odds and ends in her desk and hands over her job, she is arguing all the time that she was wrong to bring about the rumor, but that is just a personal error. It is up to others to believe it or not. And as she was not authorized to investigate it, nor did she make any formal report to the Party Committee, the punishment is not fair. To say that she is young and rash because of all this is grossly unjust. What's more, since the leadership has been to the hospital, why should she alone bear the responsibility?

While she keeps on talking, a bundle falls out from inside her desk. It would have been all right if she had not seen it. She is instantly shocked out of her senses, and her face turns white. It seems that the bundle is the urgent dispatch that had to be sent to the Bureau as early as possible. The formal letter of recommendation, the materials, and the decision to publicize Xiao Du's meritorious service were finalized and sealed by Qiao Dianlong, the Party Secretary, himself, then he gave them to Xiao Tao to be sent out at once. At that time she was busy copying another urgent document, so she put the bundle conveniently in a special drawer for it, and planned to mail out everything in it right after she finished copying the thing at hand. Who could have expected that the bundle would slip into the crevice between the drawer and stay there without her knowing it? And it is recovered in the presence of every leading cadre. There is no way to hide the fact even if she wanted to.

RECOMMENDATION

She feels she is really finished this time! What excuse does she have to avoid being accused as unreliable in handling things? At once she buries her head in her desk and wails desperately. Misfortunes never come singly; this time she cannot possibly escape the disaster of being transferred.

But unexpectedly, this misfortune proves to be a stroke of luck, too. The delayed urgent dispatch has saved her. Upon seeing the recommendation materials, the three secretaries' eyes brighten up instantaneously, and their faces are showing smiles. Not only do they not accuse her, they show her extraordinary kindness, announcing that they are willing to allow her a period of time to improve her performance. They discipline her casually for the rumor, and of course make no mention of transferring her job.

As neither the materials nor the decision is sent out or announced, the false alarm is over. They decide to continue the meeting of recommendation the next morning.

OLD ACQUAINTANCE

Han Shaogong

Mr. Yu came back to his home town from abroad twenty years later, which was some news in the small city. The provincial government had called beforehand, saying he was a patriotic overseas Chinese and had inherited tens of millions of capital and assets in Hong Kong and America. Now that he was coming back for a tour, the local authorities must give him a warm reception. The county government had held a special meeting to discuss it. And the no. 5 building in the county guesthouse was remodeled immediately afterward. They changed the carpet, killed mice, put out plastic flowers and Nescafe to show off the highest living standard of the county. The police posted a new sentry outside the building so as to prevent crowds of curious bystanders. It was said that a young man mistook the hustle and bustle for a local sale of hot exported commodities. He squeezed in with oily sweat all over his head, but was pushed past the security line by people behind him, forcing the policeman to try his electrical club. With one sharp shriek, the young man fell down with his whole body trembling all over, and a patch of gray showed on his face. There were two lunatics in the county seat, and nobody knew why they had the habit of throwing stones or dry manure at cars and trucks while singing the local opera. The drivers could do nothing about it and had gotten accustomed to it long before. The police had been commanded to keep them in jail temporarily in order to keep them from assaulting the car of the overseas Chinese. Because of this order, the kids were deprived of their enjoyment and fear, and had to be reconciled to watching the killing of a pig or the fight of ants. For days they seemed to be lost and disheartened.

Mr. Yu swished in in a luxurious sedan. The body of the car was unprecedentedly long, and unprecedentedly black and bright, like a huge black eel stealing silently and secretly through the streets and into the big and secluded courtyard of the guesthouse, which gave the people in this small city a shock without knowing why. The man who crawled out of the belly of the black eel was dark and thin. He looked like a middle-aged man, but his hair was long gone. His head, with its deeply sunken temples, gave the impression of tightness and solidity. He was wearing a loose, creamy yellow jacket for young men and a pair of flat cloth shoes that had gone out of fashion even in this little city. What attracted more attention was the empty left sleeve, hollow but full of cold and evil wind. It had become a motionless and expressionless burden, swinging along with his steps. When he entered the restaurant of the guesthouse, a waitress accidentally broke two plates with a loud bang; a truck outside the gate broke its tail lights while backing; and a pregnant saleswoman in the small store of the guesthouse unfortunately had a miscarriage on the very day. No one could tell whether all this was related to that empty sleeve. The bigwigs of the county came to see him in the guesthouse, and as usual they shook hands and exchanged greetings, and as usual there was the feast with white eels from the stream, white-faced civets from the mountains, plus roast piglet and such like. The several county leaders kept the guest company with wholehearted devotion to the public interest, and their stomachs suffered from the painful test. An assistant county commissioner played the host, showing him round the marble factory and the arts and crafts factory. When they entered the marble factory, there was an earth shaking bang from a nearby workshop. Everyone was terribly shocked and looked around except the guest who did not turn his head back or even blinked his eyes. Escorted by the assistant commissioner, he listened to an introduction by the director of the factory, which emphasized its serious financial situation because of lack of capital. He seemed to be aware of what was implied in this sort of introduction. He showed his sympathy by taking out a ball-point pen and very quickly signing an agreement of intention with the county government to invest in the factory. In addition, he showed interest in the county's resources of kiwi fruit. The assistant commissioner's face widened into a smile and became red and bright in spite of his stomachache.

The security personnel safeguarded the millionaire as well as his wallet and sneezing, but he often left them behind to do things by himself. According to their report, he always went for a walk in the back streets along the river. It was a narrow stone street with a high wall of gray bricks close on one side. There were spots of moss near its foundation. He always walked round from the grain mill to the river dock. And he took pictures of ordinary wall foundations, rocks, and small trees. No one knew what he wanted them for.

Every day he went to buy tofu from an old woman at the Little West Gate. He did not eat it, but put it in a water bucket. Now the bucket was already half full. The old woman who sold tofu there was almost blind; only her left eye had a little vision left. After investigation, it was discovered that she lived alone, and that she used to be a concubine of a certain military officer in the Nationalist army;[1] later she left him to make her own living. She had been selling tofu for more than thirty years now. Why did Mr. Yu always go there to buy tofu from her? Did he have some special relationship with her? Outsiders had no way of knowing. Several times, the assistant commissioner wanted to sound him out indirectly, but thought better of it and switched back to the topic of kiwi fruit.

Mr. Yu was not talkative. When he was pleased, his protruding eyeballs were very bright, so bright that they seemed a little menacing. But he just glanced from this side to the other, and then from the other side back, listening to others silently. His smiles were very faint and he looked very cautious. The thick cigar between his fingers was rarely lit. When there was nothing to look at, he would fix his eyes on a certain spot in the air before him, and his emotion, if any, seeped beneath the skin of his face, and what remained was a face of blankness.

The assistant county commissioner was afraid that he felt lonely. "Would Mr. Yu like to tour the Bai Gong Ferry? It is a ruin of historical relics."

The millionaire shook his head, "I've been there."

The assistant commissioner tried to guess his hobby, "Would you like to see some tapes?" he asked. "From Hong Kong, Taiwan, we have them all."

The millionaire smiled faintly. "Not interested."

"Well... is there anything else you want to do? Our small county used to be poor, but there have been big changes in recent years. It's no longer like the old place where you once lived. We knew nothing about your situation then, what's more we were unable even to fend for ourselves. I was sent to be reformed in the labor camp at the South River Iron Mine. Have you been there? It has become a huge mine! These years the production of timber, bamboo, fruits, and oil-tea camelia has boomed. If you want to do something or buy some local products, just let me know!"

Mr. Yu's eyesight turned round with his head and upper body. He stared hard at the assistant commissioner.

---

[1] The army led by the Nationalist government defeated by the communists in 1949.

"Really, whatever you say. And don't stand on ceremony. Aren't we fellow townsmen?"

Mr. Yu let out a breath lightly; he was about to say something, but stopped short. He stared at his cigar and nodded his head as if he had something in mind, but still did not say it. At long last he collected himself and ventured cautiously, "I want to see a man."

"Who?"

"Peng Xibao."

The assistant commissioner had been a cadre in this county for more than thirty years, and had know all the men with a little reputation. He was familiar with all the farmers in its eighteen districts who had passed middle age. But he had never heard of the name. He made some inquiries and came to know that this man was from Xikou area, the same place Mr. Yu once lived.

"How are you related to him?"

The millionaire shook his head.

"Why do you... want to find him?"

The millionaire shook his head again.

The assistant commissioner became suspicious, but it was inconvenient to explore any further, so he told the county government office to find the man and made necessary investigations. The office soon reported that there was a man named Peng Xibao in the Xikou District. At present his family was in a very difficult financial situation. Last year he was hospitalized for six months because of pulmonary emphysema. Though a Party member, he had not paid his dues for two years because of one reason or another. The cadres of the area could do nothing about him. According to the local folks, he used to be most ferocious in tying people up and beating them. And Mr. Yu's maimed left arm had something to do with him. Furthermore, Mr. Yu's father was beheaded as a chief bandit, and it was Peng who executed him with a broadsword. Naturally, the beheaded had already been rehabilitated in recent years, classified as one of those misexecuted.

With this information the county government found it somewhat difficult to satisfy Mr. Yu's request. Could he be planning to avenge his father so he wanted to see the man? One department head of the county government banged the table and exploded angrily, "Damn, don't you push too hard, Yu! The Communist Party now invites him to stay in the guesthouse with wine and meat, and that's fair enough. Does he really want to become a member of the home-going restitution corps, carrying out class vengeance against the poor and lower-middle peasants?" But one assistant commissioner took exception to his striking the table, "You can't say things like that. In those years, class struggle was carried out to the extreme, and in some individual cases people were wrongly prosecuted and killed. These were mistakes, and we should acknowledge them. Still it would be better to avoid the meeting. Why touch the sore spot after it is healed? It only hurts everybody's feelings." Another director who had in mind the negotiation to solicit Mr. Yu's help to build a canned fruit factory in the county, said with much worry, "It's certainly better for them not to see each other, but could it affect Mr. Yu's opinion about our government?" .... The meeting went on like this until late at night. Finally a decision was reached: Let the government of the Xikou District make a formal apology to Mr. Yu, and on the other hand persuade him to give up his request to see Peng Xibao. These seemed to be the appropriate things to do.

The director who banged the table was still indignant about this compromise, and when the meeting ended, he waved his hand and threatened, "Now the Communist Party looks worse than the Nationalist Party, and those who joined the revolution earlier are no better than those who came later! The people have a lot of complaints. You just wait and see, there's more to come!"

The assistant commissioner relayed the decision to Mr. Yu, but out of his expectation Mr. Yu refused it flatly. He was easy to talk to about everything else. It was no problem when the county asked him to help invest in the canned fruit factory; it was all right, too, when a certain director asked him to help arrange his son to study abroad. For those who asked with ingratiating smiles for a cigarette lighter or nylon pantyhose, it posed even less trouble: take it if you want. Only he had to see this Peng Xibao since he had made the request. His thick and unlit cigar was already shaking slightly, and his eyes, which had been fixed on the curtain, were cold and stiff.

The county leaders met twice more, and had to comply with his request in spite of the possible consequences. The director banged the table a second time, then he went for a drink at the home of one of his longtime underlings.

The assistant commissioner had a talk with Peng Xibao before the meeting. Peng Xibao was still wearing a pair of broken overshoes in the scorching weather; his clothes were torn on the shoulder; and his hair stuck together in patches. He would wipe away his running nose every time after he said a few sentences, and he was absent-minded, looking here and there all the time. When Mr. Yu was mentioned, he seemed to have forgotten who he was altogether. He only said that he would meet with anyone the leaders wanted him to, and he said it even with a kind of excitement. The assistant commissioner thought that he might as well remain the way he was so he would not get nervous.

The assistant commissioner invited him to drink a cup of tea, and gave him a cigarette with the filter tip. He did not know why there rose in his heart a little sadness and pity, as if he were not taking him to see a guest at the moment but throwing him coldheartedly out of the city gate to be beheaded.

The assistant commissioner led him to the guesthouse. When they approached the no. 5 building, Peng Xibao suddenly became terrified. Sweat poured out all over his forehead, and there was fear in his eyes. Upon closer examination, the assistant commissioner discovered a ball of green under his forehead; and Peng's face was as pale as if he had been steamed alive, put in a freezer for several hours, and then pulled out. He could no longer drag his feet along in his overshoes.

"Commissioner, I...my feet hurt..."

"It'll be over after you see him for a few minutes." The assistant commissioner knew Peng was not actually going to the execution ground right then.

"They hurt too much, I...I really can't go today..."

"You're imagining things. Refuse to go in at the door! Do you think I have nothing better to do than keeping you company with your foolishness?"

OLD ACQUAINTANCE

"I beg you, please, I really couldn't go."

The assistant commissioner wouldn't listen. He almost hauled Peng Xibao through the door, making him a target before the many strange eyes in the room. A wave of cold air gushed forward from the air conditioner, which made Peng Xibao start with a shiver. There were a few big, ferocious-looking sofas in front of him. A huge scarlet carpet sent forth dazzling light of blood and fire in the bright sunshine from the windows. The glassware and chromium-plated utensils all shone red; even the wall and ceiling were dyed a pale red, too. Peng Xibao was shocked by such a scene; his two overshoes did not dare to step on the huge scarlet carpet at all; and his knees trembled unstoppably.

There were many people in the room. According to the assistant commissioner, there need to be two or three times more people around to prevent any incident.

A pair of eyes had already fixed on Peng Xibao, and below them was a thick cigar which had always remained unlit but was lit up today.

"This is Mr. Yu. Peng Xibao, you sit down too...." The assistant commissioner tried hard to improve the atmosphere.

Peng Xibao appeared to get the hint. He muttered a smile and took a breath through his nose, "Is it you, Comrade Yu? Long time no see you, long time no see you. Are you still in the Agriculture Bureau? Your second son was driving a truck last time in the Town of Changle when I...."

He obviously mistook him for somebody else. The assistant commissioner poked him with his hand and said, "Mr. Yu came from Hong Kong this time...."

Peng Xibao opened his eyes wide and became aware of this correction at once, "I've heard he was transferred to Hong Kong. I know, how could I not know it! Cadre Yu, are you working in the Agriculture Bureau in Hong Kong or doing other business? Last time our village wanted to buy urea, I told them to look for you for help. Cadre Yu is the one who is most willing to help others...." He wiped his nose again as he prattled on.

It was already impossible for the assistant commissioner to cut in.

Mr. Yu never responded. His face darkened, and two piercing lights in his eyes flashed like bayonets in the sun. Slowly and deliberately, he measured from head to foot and from foot to head again the man he had wanted to see. Finally his eyes stopped at the Adam's apple in the man's neck.

The assistant commissioner realized quickly that that must have been where the head of Mr. Yu's father was severed from his body.

No one ventured to say anything. Mr. Yu nodded his head with satisfaction and moved sideways to survey the man's neck from another angle. His eyes were beginning to soften, and from these eyes exuded a relief that was both refreshing and relaxing. Suddenly they even glittered with delight as if he were enjoying a favorite antique or a delicate flower instead of a strange neck. And if he had cast his glance with a little more force, the antique or the flower would have broken or withered--which mustn't be allowed. To him the strange neck was so precious because he had to let his many years of yearning flow out at a leisurely pace from his eyes, which had to embrace and savor it with the utmost caution.

The glitter terrified the assistant commissioner, reminding him of the satisfaction in a butcher's eyes when he was slowly wiping his knife and contemplating where it ought to go.

"Mr. Yu, please sit...."

"Mr. Yu, they are all things of the past. It's the situation at that time, isn't it? Many things are beyond explanation. Let's all try to look forward. Come, have some tea, please."

Mr. Yu seemed to have just been awakened from a dream. He collected himself, wiped his face with his hand, and threw away his cigar with great force. Then he calmly said to the assistant commissioner, "Thank you. The quality of the water is important for the canned fruit factory; let's go and get a sample in the river today." He led the way toward the door without waiting for a reply from the assistant commissioner. Just as he was about to step out, he turned his head abruptly and shot a ruthless glance at Peng Xibao's face.

The steel-blue glance pierced Peng Xibao and shook him all over. At long last he realized who the man in front of him was, and immediately he uttered a loud, animal cry, "Yu, Yu Er, don't go away, I have four kids to feed...."

Mr. Yu's footsteps had already receded outside the door.

About two weeks later, the millionaire mailed a large sum of money from Hong Kong, and the county immediately broke the ground for its canned fruit factory.

Life in the small city remained tranquil. Only there were more cars and trucks coming and going, so the two lunatics could keep throwing stones and dried manure while singing the local opera.

CLASSMATES

Shen Rong

He decides to invite him over for lunch on Sunday. Zhou Wei, Assistant Director of the Education Bureau, issues an order of general mobilization Friday evening at home: wife shall be in charge of shopping; daughter shall take care of the cleaning up; and he will cook the dishes himself. But with their assistance, of course.

"I'm going to have a chemistry exam next Monday," his daughter protests mildly with a long face.

"Making such a fuss about it, who's the guest of honor?" his wife is also not without some objection.

"Wu Bojian, an old classmate of mine at the university. We haven't met for more than thirty years. Shouldn't we give him a warm reception?" Zhou Wei becomes enthusiastic, ignoring all the complaints from his wife and daughter.

"What big shot is he?" his daughter says with evident sarcasm.

"Big shot? He?" Zhou Wei laughs loudly. "Nothing of that sort. He was wrongly persecuted as a rightist in 1957,[1] and was banished to Xinjiang[2] for twenty years.

"What about now? Quite a few rightists of that time have become big shots." In addition to sarcasm, there is on his daughter's face a little contempt as well as a sneer that shows keen insight into everything.

"Jing Jing, what are you talking about?" Zhou Wei is upset. "Is your father a snob licking the boots of high ranking officials? According to your logic, well, what kind of person do you think your father is?"

"I'm just asking some casual questions."

---

[1] The year of a major political persecution against intellectuals in China who criticized the Party leadership.
[2] An autonomous region in northwest China.

"These can never be casual questions!" Zhou Wei's face is livid. "The way you asked them shows how you think. It reflects your opinion of our society, as if everyone fawns on high ranking officials. Is our society like this? Eh?"

His daughter puts on a long face and gives no answer. His wife comes over in a hurry to smooth things over.

"Enough, that's enough, could you please stop? She's just a kid. What does she know?"

"A ninth grader, she is no longer a kid! Her ideas are extremely intolerable, and it's because you always pamper and spoil her." Zhou Wei's anger has not subsided, and he turns to reprimand his daughter again, "Now we are fighting against capitalist democratization. You ought to have your thoughts cleaned up!"

His daughter gives him an angry stare with her black, round eyes, and is about to say, "I'm not a Party member. It has nothing to do with me!" But she holds back, seeing how angry her father is.

"Let's discuss the menu. What should we buy tomorrow?" his wife raises the practical question at just the right time and succeeds in diverting the topic.

Zhou Wei glares back at his daughter, well knowing that her silence means a kind of resistance. He is going to say something more to enlighten her, but a few words wouldn't work. If he blunders, her psychological rebellion would worsen, which would make it even harder to turn her around. So he gives up her ideological education for the time being, and turns around to discuss the shopping list.

"For cold dishes, the most crucial is to buy a smoked chicken. When we were at the university, Wu Bojian was crazy about smoked chickens. At that time, all of us were poor students and we usually went three months without being able to afford one. Only he had the money--not that he was from a rich family, he was a genius. He would publish an article in the newspaper every two or three months, getting some contribution fee. With the money, he would treat us to smoked chickens. Once he bought four chickens, and everybody fought for the legs and breasts, which really made our day. Well, what a guy! ...."

"All right, a smoked chicken," his wife writes it down.

"It's better to have a steamed fish for the hot dishes. I remember Wu Bojian loved fish. He was from the south, and was very particular about the cooking. He often said that you had to steam the fish to enjoy its full taste, because it kept all the original flavor. The hell with fried fish, sweet and sour fish, or fish in soybean or other sauces, they were all ruined. He...."

"Dad, I'm going to review my lessons," his daughter --with good reason-- cuts short his fond memories of his good friend.

"All right!" Zhou Wei has to nod, though disappointed. He then turns to his wife to give further instruction, "Go to the free market tomorrow, pick from the nice and jumping live carps and buy one."

"Buy live fish tomorrow? The lunch is for the day after, what if it dies?" his daughter makes one last stab as she goes out of the door.

"That's a problem." Zhou Wei is preoccupied with his live fish and has no time to attend to his daughter's attitude. "This guy Wu Bojian deserves to be called a gourmet. Once the fish is put on the table, he could tell whether it was killed an hour or two hours ago...."

"Okay, I'll try my best," his wife says cheerlessly.

"As to the soup, it must be good. Better be mushroom and duckling soup...."

His wife lays down her pen, "Sorry, you better take him to a restaurant!"

Zhou Wei is shocked. "To a restaurant now? Isn't it like offering yourself to be ripped off? And this is a reunion of old classmates-- mainly to have a chat. There are so many people in the restaurants, how can we talk there with that kind of noise?"

"If having a chat is what you mainly want, why prepare so many dishes?" his wife retorts. "Besides, I've never had this mushroom and duckling soup, I don't know how to make it."

Zhou Wei reassures her at once, "Haven't I just made it clear that you do the shopping and I do the cooking?"

"That's easy to say. As if you wouldn't sit cross-legged and keep them laughing and talking, leaving me alone in the kitchen," his wife begins to complain.

"Well, well, well, it's a rare chance and just this once," Zhou Wei narrows his eyes into a smile and says in a newly acquired consoling and ingratiating manner. When he sees that his wife still lacks enthusiasm, he presses hard with his persuasion, "It's because you don't know this guy Wu Bojian...."

"What else don't I know? He was crazy about smoked chicken, he loves live fish, and he's a gourmet...."

Zhou Wei laughs loudly, patting his wife's shoulder to be conciliatory. "These are all minor things. The most important is that he used to be the top student in our class. He could recite long paragraphs from Shakespeare's writings and could analyze clearly and logically the characterization of the protagonists in *Dreams of Red Mansions*. He was good at singing and painting; he had a good knowledge of historical relics as well as of history. He was scholarly and handsome. Let me tell you this: there were only a few who were as versatile as he was. Especially impressive is that he wasn't incredibly proud of his abilities. He didn't consider everybody and everything beneath his notice. He got along very well with his classmates...."

In her memory, his wife can hardly recall Zhou Wei speaking so highly of anybody. It is almost flattery. She knows him very well, having lived with him for so many years. He is not one of those who are jealous of people more talented or capable, but he never commends anyone rashly. He thinks pretty highly of himself. As a matter of fact, he is one of his university classmates who have "made the most of it." As early as eight years ago he was a department head; now over fifty, while names of men of the same age are dropped from the promotion lists one by one, he alone progresses-- promoted to assistant director.

Isn't he one of the best?

As they say, "However strong you are, there's always someone stronger."

Now there comes the best among the best. She would like to see what kind of genius Wu Bojian is.

"All right, mushroom and duckling soup." She finally jots it down.

"This lunch also serves as a practical lesson for Jing Jing." Despite his excitement, Zhou Wei cannot forget his daughter's rebellion, "I want to let her know that the leading members of our Party are not as snobbish as she thinks. We cherish friendship more than young people like her do."

What he has just said seems to have missed the target. Recently, when he becomes excited, he has often made such logically dubious statements. His wife has grown accustomed to it, so she ignores it and asks, "This classmate of yours, what kind of job does he really have now?"

Zhou Wei glances at her and answers casually, "What he does is not important. What's important is he's my old classmate, and a good friend. And that's enough."

His wife does not say any more.

On Saturday, his wife finishes the shopping according to their list, and his daughter, grumbling, almost finishes mopping the floor and cleaning the windows and doors. Early on Sunday morning, Zhou Wei marches into the kitchen with his wife and daughter, and starts to get busy with the initial preparations for the cooking. By now, his apartment is spotless, and the chicken and duckling are ready. All that is left to do is to wait for the guests patiently.

Two guests come on time at eleven. They were chosen very carefully for company. Of course, they were Zhou Wei's classmates at the university. One is an associate editor of a journal, and the other is a speech writer in the secretariat of a big government agency. Both hold the official rank of department head.

His wife, with her apron on, is left to her toil in the kitchen, braving the test of smoke and fire. Zhou pours the tea and hands out the cigarettes while chatting with his two old classmates. The topic is of course Wu Bojian.

"He was really a genius!" the associate editor exclaims wholeheartedly, holding the cigarette with his yellow, tobacco-stained fingers. "I like his prose the best, with its easy and plain style, but pregnant with meaning. Do you remember his 'Moon' published in the university magazine? It was really beautiful!"

"How can we forget!" the plump speech writer follows. "For this piece of writing of only a few hundred words, he received fifteen letters from the girl students. Well, as I recall the time when we were reading those letters together, I just couldn't help feeling jealous. Zhou Wei, do you remember you hid one of the letters and then tried to find that girl?"

"What a joker you are," Zhou Wei laughs uneasily, his big eyes turning round in the direction of the kitchen.

"You're not being honest!" the writer laughs. "After dozens of years of marriage, how could you still hide this act of disloyalty from your wife?"

Memories bring about a happy and exciting atmosphere. Things of the past are like preserved olives that are chewed once more and leave a pleasant aftertaste, then are cast aside again. By and by everything that can be chewed is exhausted, leaving nothing more to talk about. All of a sudden, a silence falls in the room; the air seems to have frozen, and the space is filled with a heavy feeling of void. Everyone there is at a loss what to do.

At twelve sharp, his wife pops in with eyes full of the question, "Why hasn't the distinguished guest arrived?"

Zhou Wei takes out his little address book and dials the newly-installed telephone. After hanging up, he says excitedly, "The receptionist in the hotel said there was no one in his room. He must be on his way here. He'll come soon."

To kill the time of agonizing waiting, Zhou Wei digs out his photo album. A few pictures of classmates at the university bring them another small climax of savoring their happy memories. The pictures were taken many many years ago. Because they used the 130 film and had no money to enlarge them then, the pictures are very small and full of heads like tiny ants. But the three of them still recognize each and every classmate without mistake, and are able to recall the funny stories surrounding the picture-taking.

"Look, Wu Bojian was waving his hand. I remember when it was taken, he was reciting, 'If it is for freedom, I would lay down my life and give up my love.' The camera clicked before he could finish the second line." Zhou Wei's big eyes glisten; he is indulging in the cheerful memories.

The associate editor, who has been swallowing nicotine through cigarette smoking, also proves to have a long memory. He hurries to add, "This photo doesn't have proper lighting. It was almost dark when we took it. It's all because of Wu Bojian, who couldn't distinguish between 'tian' and 'di' with his heavily-accented mandarin. He pronounced Tiananmen, where we were to meet, as Dianmen, so when everyone arrived, it was almost dark. What a guy!"

The pictures, which are but few, have been viewed, and the scenes they bring back have been fully reminisced, but Wu Bojian still has not come. The arms of the clock are pointing mercilessly to twelve forty-five. His wife has long since turned off the gas stove and joined the two guests in the sitting room, and now they are waiting silently together in rumbling hunger.

"What's happened? Could it be that he doesn't know the way?" the writer raises the questions first. A man who has grown fat always feels hungry sooner.

"Not likely. I told him clearly what bus to take, where to get off and everything," Zhou Wei said emphatically. "And how could a smart guy like him miss his way?"

"Did you say it was for lunch? Couldn't he have mistaken it for dinner?" the associate editor raises another point. He has been editing his journal for years and has become extraordinarily cautious.

"It's absolutely impossible!" Zhou Wei cries out. "I told him specifically to make sure he was here before twelve. How could he mistake it for dinner?"

His daughter, who has stayed in her room reviewing lessons all the time, is probably hungry too; she pushes the door open and comes out. Seeing that the elders are still sitting there and showing no sign of starting to eat, she goes back to her small room.

Only his wife sits there in silence, which mocks Zhou Wei more than hundreds of questions: where is your guest of honor? You keep me busy for two days for this genius who cannot even keep his promise?

Forced by his wife's silent stare, Zhou Wei calls again. The answer is disappointing: the man named Wu went out early and hasn't returned.

"Let's wait fifteen minutes more," Zhou Wei has made up his mind. "If he doesn't come in fifteen minutes, we'll eat."

Fifteen minutes passes, the guest of honor is still to come. Zhou Wei would prefer to wait another fifteen minutes, but his wife is more sympathetic to the two starving guests. So she takes the liberty to call their daughter out to help put the chopsticks in place, set the table, and bring out the dishes.

Zhou Wei, still hesitating, keeps looking at the front door. His wife says, "Let's eat while waiting!"

The two guests are already sitting at the table by themselves. And Zhou Wei has to come to the table, saying absentmindedly, "Come, let's begin. We can't wait for him any longer."

The smoked chicken, the steamed fish, and the mushroom and duckling soup are nonetheless elegant and delicious, but without the guest of honor, no one is in high spirits. It's even worse with Zhou Wei, who eats without tasting any of it. A meticulously prepared feast begins as well as ends in a joyless and gloomy atmosphere. Only his inconsiderate daughter eats to her heart's content the delicacies that are usually hard to come by, taking full advantage of the preoccupation which prevents her father from paying much attention to other things.

"This Wu Bojian, what's happened to him?" The associate editor is still full of questions after lighting his after-meal cigarette.

"Maybe he's still in trouble, and wouldn't want to see old classmates?" the writer begins to speculate.

"No. He was rehabilitated long ago," Zhou wei said.

"Is it possible that he has become a high ranking official and looks down on us," the writer goes further with his speculation.

"Not likely. I haven't heard he has become some high ranking official," Zhou Wei answers, but his voice reveals that he is not so sure of it.

The two guests take their leave with half-filled stomachs and an abundance of regret. The clock says it is already two in the afternoon. Zhou Wei, moaning and groaning, retreats to the bedroom and drops to the bed. At first he feels difficult to breathe, but then he falls into a sound sleep, leaving only his wife to deal with the greasy bowls and plates.

At two-forty, when his wife, almost done with the dishes and exhausted, is gasping for air on the sofa, she hears two vague knocking sounds at the door. She looks to the narrow doorway with uncertainty. There come two more indistinct knocks. She jumps up, still unsure about what it is. They installed a home-made music door bell not long ago. Though the sound is long and grating on the ear, visitors generally use it. She hesitates a little, then goes to the door and pulls it open.

There is indeed a man, an old man, standing outside. It is late spring or early summer, but the old man is still completely in his winter clothing. He wears an old gray Mao coat of Dacron khaki over a heavy, cumbersome padded jacket. His blue trousers are washed white and stuffed tight, probably by thick sweat pants inside. There is a muffler around his neck, too dirty to show its original color, but it appears to be light tan. Under the hat is a pair of dull and dim eyes wrapped in loose skin. Below his sunken eyes his lower lids hang down like small pockets as big as five cent coins. This old man is quite tall but crooked, and he looks so weak and senile.

"Who are you looking for?" the hostess asks with indifference. Obviously the old man has knocked at the wrong door.

"Please, please, does Zhou... Comrade Zhou live here?"

"Yes!" Her husband, because of his job, often receives some pitiable teachers. But they ought to go find him in his office. Why do they come to his home on Sunday? So, without hesitation, she tries to turn him away with an excuse, "He's not home. Please go to his office tomorrow."

"My name is Wu... I'm...."

"Wu Bojian!" Completely taken aback, she cries out the name which she has been mumbling for the last two days.

"That's...that's me."

"Why, it's you! Please come in, please!" the hostess invites him in with a loud voice, but the questions in her mind grow bigger. How could this man be Wu Bojian? How could he be the handsome and graceful old classmate Zhou Wei had commended so highly? She closes the door, still puzzled. Then she turns around and discovers that the old man is standing sideways in the hallway, keeping a distance of two steps from her. He does not follow her in, though the small, open sitting room is right in front of him.

"Please, please come in!" The hostess has to take a step forward to lead him into the room, then she looks back at the old man who is still standing at the door and urges him repeatedly to come in and sit down.

It is not until the third time that the guest finally sits down with much reluctance and great caution, as if in fear that his clothes might soil the sofa. He raises himself slightly before sitting tentatively on the edge of the cushion; his hands are still holding his unzipped old black handbag.

"Please sit down for a little while. I'll go and wake up Zhou Wei. He's just taking a nap." She turns to go.

As soon as he hears that Zhou Wei is taking a nap, the guest stands up at once. With the bag in one hand, he extends the other, trying sincerely to stop the hostess.

"Please do not wake him up. I could wait, or I could go out to take a walk, and come back an hour later."

"This is out of the question. Zhou Wei's been waiting for you all the time." The guest is terribly sincere, which makes the hostess feel apologetic, so she adds, "He's been telling me about you since the night before."

"That makes me even more unworthy of it. He's so busy with revolutionary work--I shouldn't have bothered him by coming here." He struggles in his crooked and weary body, showing extreme uneasiness.

The hostess is left helpless. The old man before her eyes, wearing shabby clothing and acting so contemptibly, is totally different from the image of a talented scholar that her husband had impressed upon her. At this instant, it is more appropriate to say that the hostess is even unsettled than the guest.

"Please sit down, please!" She resorts to taking a firm stand, forcing him to sit down in the sofa, then she runs straight into the bedroom to wake up her husband.

Zhou Wei jumps at the news; pulling his coat on, he hollers and rushes out of the door. "Wu Bojian, what's happened to you?"

Wu Bojian has already been standing there for a while. He nods at Zhou Wei with great respect. His head bends so low that it is more like a bow than a nod.

Zhou Wei is stunned. He stares at this strange man and cannot recognize him. Could it be Wu Bojian? His voice fails him and his feet refuse to budge. If his wife had not brought him a cup of tea, he honestly wouldn't have known what to do.

"Please sit down, and help yourself with the tea." Women are more composed than men at such critical moments.

Wu Bojian does not sit down right away; instead he recoils and steps back, mumbling garbled apologies which are a repetition of what he has already said: He should not have barged in at this time; he did not know that Comrade Zhou Wei was taking a nap; and it is indeed too imprudent of him....

By now Zhou Wei has more or less come to his senses; he hurries to ask the guest to sit down. Only after this does Wu Bojian sit down, still holding the bag in his hands. Zhou Wei's wife, seeing that it is not comfortable for Wu to sit with the bag, wants to take the bag and hang it on the clothes rack. Wu Bojian declines again and again, saying that she should not bother. He tries to find somewhere to put the bag down himself. First he tries to place it under the coffee table, but thinks it inappropriate because there are tea cups and an ashtray on the table. Then he tries to lay it down behind his seat, but that too is unsuitable. At last he bends sideways and puts it on the floor beside the sofa.

Noticing that Wu Bojian is out of breath from lugging the handbag, Zhou Wei wants to stand up, go over and hang it for him, but, without knowing why, he does not dare to make a move. He is afraid to hear Wu's words of courtesy. His wife pretends not to see anything, and when Wu sits down at last, she says simply:

"It's a rare chance for you to meet and talk. Excuse me, I have something to attend to."

"Please, please!" Wu Bojian again stands up in a hurry.

He does not sit down until the hostess hastens into the bedroom.

In the sitting room the two old classmates are left sitting face to face. After a long time, Zhou Wei asks politely:

"Wu, Wu Bojian, we arranged to have lunch together, why didn't you come?"

Wu Bojian mumbles for some time, then explains cautiously, "I, I was thinking, you must be very busy nowadays. I, I must not bother, I...."

"Oh, no! It's Sunday, what's to be busy with?"

"On Sundays, you may have... have a lot of work to do. I was thinking, it is better not to bother you...."

Where has Zhou Wei's usual eloquence gone? For a long while he does not know what to say. After a moment of "well, well," he says, "We're old classmates, you, why do you treat us as outsiders. We made preparations for the lunch and waited for you till two. There were also two other old classmates of ours here; they too were waiting for you the whole time."

"Really!" Wu Bojian's wrinkled face shows neither surprise nor pleasure but extraordinary caution and respect while his mouth murmurs only regrets and apologies.

"I am sorry, I am really sorry! I let them down, too...."

Zhou Wei's initial perplexity seems to have passed, and he grows hot when he thinks of the two days' preparations that involved everyone in the family, "I ask my wife to buy the smoked chicken and make the steamed fish, which you like most. I remember you loved to have live fish."

"Me? like it the most?" Wu Bojian repeats in a murmur, staring blankly at Zhou Wei's bright eyes, as if he knew nothing about his own connoisseurship.

"Yes, of course! Wu Bojian, what's happened to you? Have you forgotten? Once you bought four smoked chickens to give us a treat!" Zhou Wei raises his voice. He tries hard to relax his tense nerves, but inwardly he is experiencing a strong feeling that borders on sadness; he wants very much to remind the man before him of those smoked chickens.

"Is it true? I forgot; I am old."

The lethargic and indifferent response pours over Zhou Wei's heart like ice water. Looking at his old classmate and good friend in front of him, his heart aches. He is really old, at least twenty years older than his real age. Not only does his appearance--the thin white hair, the missing teeth, the crooked back, and the wrinkled face-- show that he is indeed an old man, his spirits are also gone. Not a trace of his past graceful bearing is left. The young, lively, proud and handsome Wu Bojian exists no longer. Sitting before Zhou Wei is only a dull and uninteresting old man.

"I called the hotel twice; they said you went out early. We thought maybe you missed the way," Zhou Wei gropes for something to say; he is afraid of facing the man in a silence like this.

"Actually... actually I came a little past one..."

Zhou Wei shouts before Wu could finish, "Why didn't you come in?"

Wu Bojian is surprised; he raises his head a little, and hurries to explain, "I, I was thinking you might want to rest in the early afternoon, so I walked around in the streets for an hour or so...."

"Why..."

Zhou Wei is going to continue, but he sees Wu Bojian stand up instantaneously with ingratiating smiles on his face. At a loss to figure out what has happened, Zhou Wei turns around and finds his daughter standing at the door, staring at the guest.

Zhou Wei raises his arm quickly and waves it again and again to urge the guest to sit down. Then he introduces his daughter, "Jing Jing, say hello to Uncle Wu!"

Jing Jing says hello and sneaks back to her little room right away. It is not until he sees the door closed that Wu Bojian sits down again in a seemingly propitiatory manner. Zhou Wei is not sure how he feels, angry or irritated; then an untold indignation surges slowly in his heart as if he were watching a glass object, which he himself has cherished for many years, being shattered right before his eyes. It is as if somebody had deceived him: How could a man have changed so much? Without even a trace left? Or did the disaster thirty years ago leave too much impact in the depth of his heart? Perhaps he is now still in deep trouble?

"You... where are you working now?"

"Now I, I work at the county cultural center, under the wise leadership of the Party branch, doing a little bit of work."

Zhou Wei frowns and asks again, "Are they nice to you?"

"Yes, yes," Wu Bojian answers, raising himself a little. "It is due to the great concern of the county leadership, recently, recently I was added to the list of committee members for the county's Political Consultative Conference. I have little talent and less learning, indeed I do not feel I deserve it."

Zhou Wei knits his brows. He can no longer find that old classmate and good friend in this faltering old man in front of him. Where is the old Wu Bojian in the past? Is time so cruel that it could not preserve a single spark deep in the soul of this man sitting opposite? Zhou Wei refuses to give up. He leaps up, takes out the treasured pictures, and hands them to Wu Bojian one by one. He also repeats what the three of them said before lunch when they were recalling the past. He once again talks on and on about how Wu Bojian was reciting lines from original plays of Shakespeare in the past, how he was commenting on The *Dream of Red Mansions*, the letters he received after the publication of 'Moon,' and so on and so forth. But alas, the timeworn man sits in front of him and listens respectfully with absolutely no response. His words seem to have lost in an ice abyss.

Zhou Wei is crushed.

Wu Bojian rises to say goodbye. As a matter of fact, ever since he first entered the door, he has sat just on the edge of the sofa, as if ready to leave at any time. Upon leaving, he offers very sincerely a host of apologies: "Sorry to have bothered you," "I am really sorry," an "I have wasted a lot of your precious time."

After the guest has left, his wife and daughter come out.

"Your old classmate is really funny!" his daughter giggles.

Lying collapsed in the sofa, Zhou Wei has no strength left to scold his daughter.

Her husband's silence makes her feel what a terrible blow this meeting has been to him. This time she comes out to rebuke the daughter, "Go and review your lessons! What do you understand!"

Her daughter grimaces and runs away.

His eyes closed, Zhou Wei sits down in the sofa for a very long time before he stands and says simply, "I'm tired, I'll go in and lie down again."

His wife consoles him, "Dozens of years have passed. Everyone has changed greatly, only we don't feel it ourselves."

A week later, the classmate who is the associate editor gives him a phone call:

"Hey, Zhou Wei, tell you some news. We are going to carry an article in our next issue featuring a very good exhibition of paintings by farmers from a county. The reviews from the artist communities are also pretty favorable. Guess who's been teaching all these local painters? Wu Bojian! This guy is really talented, having trained so many of them. He came to Beijing especially to open this exhibition. Hey, why don't you say something? You didn't expect this, did you? A talent is a talent--wherever he is, he's sure to blossom and bear fruit! It's a shame that the article says too little about him, only mentions his name. Could you find him again? We have to get together, and this time it'll be at my home. What do you say?"

After he hangs up, Zhou Wei calls the hotel at once. The receptionist answers impatiently:

"Those fellows from the country? They left yesterday."

FRUSTRATIONS OF THE YOUTH AH DE

Cen Zhijing

East of the crossroad there is a commercial street with all sorts of stores and shops for food, clothing, daily necessities, and everything else. Pass the crossroad and you will see an eating place which is not big but by no means too small, between Globe Leather Shoes and Times Beauty Center. It is De's Refreshment.

The owner is a young man over thirty, and his name is Li Mingde. Not only can he fry delicious and slippery rice noodles, or rich and crunchy cakes, he repairs bikes too, patching inner tubes, changing ball-bearings, putting on roller chains, and everything else.

Twenty years ago, Ah De was fifteen and a sixth grader at an elementary school. The Cultural Revolution was in full swing at that time. He very much envied his elders who signed up with the Red Guards and got to skip classes and join in the revolution. All day long they read Mao's quotations, distributed leaflets, held criticism meetings, and exchanged revolutionary experiences with others. But there was nothing Ah De could do, as he had been born at the wrong time. Amid the depressing boredom, he learned how to repair bikes. First he did his own bike, then he helped his classmates, neighbors, and friends. He was very serious and responsible in his repair job, and it was always free. Sometimes he even bought small parts with his own money. So all those who were familiar with him were eager to ask him for help.

During the first years of the Cultural Revolution, Ah De found his own pleasure in repairing bikes, and it did help him kill the meaningless time.

Then Ah De graduated from high school without knowing how.
Then Ah De became a worker in a foundry.
Then Ah De married a girl named Huizhen.
Then Ah De resigned his job in the foundry and opened the De's Refreshment with Huizhen.

During this period, Ah De never stopped repairing bikes for others.

Days went by one after another like this with nothing extraordinary happening.

Who could have expected that Ah De would become famous for helping others fix their bikes? Today, on its front page, in a special section called "Flower of Spiritual Civilization,"[1] the city's daily newspaper runs a feature on his meritorious deeds. It describes how enthusiastically Li Mingde has been repairing bikes of his own accord for the community since 1966, and has never received any money for it. The article also provides some statistics: "For twenty years more than five thousand bikes have passed through Li Mingde's hands," "he has saved more than six thousand yuan for the people." It ends with a gaudy note: "Li Mingde's noble character of seeking neither fame nor financial reward is unanimously praised by the people, who point out in one voice that the spirit of Lei Feng[2] is being incarnated in him...."

The writer of this article is Liang, a reporter for the daily newspaper. He is Ah De's neighbor and had often asked him to repair his bike, so he has the full authority to write the article.

On the day the newspaper comes out, Li Mingde buys forty of them at the newsstand. He keeps five for his own file and uses two for clippings which he puts in the frames and hangs in conspicuous places in the hall and the store. The rest he gives to his loved ones, relatives, friends, and neighbors.

The news that Li Mingde, the young man, has appeared in the newspaper draws a strong response from the society. The name of the Party secretary of the community where Li Mingde lives is He Le. As he comes to his office that day, he hears that Li Mingde, a young man who runs a private business in the community, has got his name in the newspaper, so he immediately finds the paper and reads the article three times in a breath. Then he gathers all the other leading personnel of his office for a rush

---

[1] Promoting "Spiritual Civilization" was a government campaign in 1986 to increase people's awareness of civilized behavior in the public.

[2] A young soldier in the army who was propagandized for his selfless hard work and blind devotion to Mao and the government in the 1960's.

meeting. He points at the paper and says to all of them, "The meritorious deeds of Li Mingde have been reported by the paper. It is the glory and pride of our community. It shows that we have contributed to promoting spiritual civilization. We have always shown concern for Li Mingde. Didn't we issue him the private business license? Didn't we lease him the store on very liberal terms?"

When the meeting is over, Secretary He calls in Xiao Liu at once, who is in charge of publicity. He tells Xiao Liu to go to Ah De's Refreshment with him and bring along the camera and flashlight. He is going to grant Li Mingde a personal reception.

This reception is conducted in a cordial and friendly atmosphere. Secretary He smiles and commends Ah De's achievements, and he encourages Ah De to carry it forward and do still better in order to make new contributions to promoting spiritual civilization in the community. In the meantime Xiao Liu is busy around them, taking pictures from all directions and angles.

After the reception, Secretary He tells Xiao Liu to develop the film as soon as possible and enlarge it to the size of ten by twelve inches.

Xiao Liu is very efficient. He develops and enlarges the film that very night, and the next day he gave the pictures to Secretary He. The secretary examines them one by one very carefully and picks out eight for Xiao Liu, directing him to post them on the community bulletin board with all speed. And each of the pictures is to be accompanied with a succinct caption. In addition, he is to write a report expounding how much emphasis Secretary He has put on the promotion of spiritual civilization and how the secretary has gone to De's Refreshment himself to grant Li Mingde a reception. It is to be sent to the daily newspapers, and of course, it goes with the pictures taken on the spot. Not too many, one or two would be enough. Unfortunately, the report never does get published--the only flaw in an otherwise perfect plan.

Secretary He begins to think. He is going to sponsor a conference on spiritual civilization and make Ah De the key speaker. All members of the community will be invited. As they come from all walks of life, it will surely have a widespread impact and achieve great publicity when they talk about it in their work places after the conference. Secretary He tells Ah De what he has in mind, but on hearing this, Ah De jumps up and cries:

"Secretary He, it won't do. Actually what merits do I have? If any, it's no more than what appears in the newspaper. Three sentences would say it all. How can it be used in a conference?"

Secretary He responds with a lecture, "What you've said is not right. How can three sentences include all that you've been doing for twenty years? I believe what the newspaper said is far from enough, and it is one-sided. Of course they are limited by space and it's impossible for them to carry a long story. But the conference is different; you can speak in great detail. If you can't finish in one morning, there's the afternoon and the next day. There's no limit. You can tell how you serve the people without thinking of reward, what difficulties you meet with and how you manage to overcome them, and how the Party Secretariat of the community has helped and supported you. How's that?"

"Secretary He, you know our store is small, and we don't have enough people. We have been so busy...."

"It's always possible to squeeze a little time every day. Write slowly, and we'll have the conference whenever you're ready."

"But I don't know how to write a report."

"It doesn't matter. Write a manuscript, then we'll discuss and revise it together. We can do it anyway."

"But I don't know how to speak at a conference."

"Can you speak at all? If you can, just do it and you'll know how well you can do it!"

Huizhen, his wife, is all for the idea. "Ah De, since Secretary He wants you to make a speech, it's not proper to say no. You just concentrate on your manuscript, I'll take care of the store!" When husbands become famous, wives share the glory. What else can he say? If he continues to find excuses, he will let Secretary He and his wife down, and they are so sincere and enthusiastic. Ah De braces himself and agrees to it.

Three days, half a pound of tea, and six packs of cigarettes later, Ah De finally finishes fifteen pages.

Secretary He reads it carefully and thinks there is room for improvement. Mainly, the section which covers how the Party Secretariat of the community helps and supports Li Mingde in promoting spiritual civilization is not concrete or comprehensive enough. It takes him three hours to inspire Ah De, and he provides nine suggestions for reference so Ah De can add them to his report. With Secretary He's hints and suggestions, Ah De struggles for two days more and completes the report at last.

The conference is held in the auditorium of an elementary school. The attendance turns out to be good and the atmosphere is rather warm, which pleases Secretary He. But at the same time he is not fully content. He feels that the scale and the social impact of this conference are much too limited. As a cadre with a quick and adventurous mind, he comes up with another new idea: organize a community speech troupe of about three members on the subject of spiritual civilization, not only to talk in his own community, but in other communities as well. Maybe they could even speak in the Memorial Hall of Dr. Sun Yat-sen[3]. And it would be more wonderful still if the TV station could be invited to report the news.

Soon, through Xiao Li's effort, the troupe of three is formed. It is headed by Secretary He. The troupe tries its hand in its own community, then marches out into other places in the city and leaves its traces in factories, schools, and the districts all over the city.

The troupe returns with fame and glory after thirty-five presentations, which take a month and half. It is the very first time the city has had a community speech troupe to tour all around and give speeches, so the whole thing is much appreciated by the authorities. Secretary He himself is commended by the department concerned, and the city newspapers publicize the event to varying degrees.

Li Mingde has become a rising star, and his name a household word.

For example, Huang, superintendent of the local police station, says time and again to others, "I said all along that the young man's nature was not bad,

---

[3] Dr. Sun Yat-sen (1866-1925) is the father of modern Chinese revolution and founder of the Republic of China.

but back then there were some who didn't believe it. Once, during the Cultural Revolution, he stole a brass basin from Lao Zhang who lived at no. 6 in Lotus Flower Lane. He took it to a recycling station and tried to sell it. I caught him. Some comrades wanted to throw him in jail, but I said we couldn't do that, and I let him go. Later I used to say him, 'Well, Ah De, from now on you'd better never break the law. Steal a needle when you're young, and you'll steal gold when you grow up. If you don't change your ways, you'll be in prison!' He received a good education. Isn't it true that for twenty years he has never done anything like that again? Now he appears in the newspapers and speaks on rostrums. A fine young man he is."

Superintendent Huang had been in public security service for nearly thirty years, and he was promoted to his present position the year before. The biggest problem his station now confronts is teenage crimes, the number of which has increased in recent years. It has given him a big headache, and he doesn't know what to do about it. That Secretary He asks Ah De to do a tour of speeches gives him a great inspiration. Right after the troupe completes its tour, he organizes a seminar to popularize knowledge of law, and invites Ah De to talk to problem youths, using himself as an example. Ah De is to tell how he changes from a bad boy into a good youth, as well as how the policemen educated him wholeheartedly, patiently, and painstakingly. On the first day of the seminar, Superintendent Huang specially invites his colleagues from the District Police Department.

Chairman Luo of the District Association of Private Businessmen often mentions Li Mingde before others, too.

The strongest point in Luo's work is his emphasis on discovering the talented. He believes that a leading cadre should not bury himself in his work; he's got to know how to find people with abilities. Like Bo Le,[4] he must know his subordinates well enough to assign them jobs commensurate with their talent. Only by doing so can one become a good leader. The difference between a marshal and field commander lies here. And so he has been watching the rising star constantly ever since Ah De appeared in the newspaper.

He attends Ah De's speeches. As he expects, Ah De is able to get to the

---

[4] See footnote on p. 45.

essential points. He presents theories and concrete examples, and he delivers his speech smoothly, which means he has brains. Chairman Luo comes to know further that Ah De has written the speech himself, proof that he is well educated and has literary talent, which is even more precious. Where can you find a man of both integrity and ability?

Chairman Luo becomes very excited; he plans to promote Ah De as his assistant. So he prepares to swing public opinion. First he gathers together the private businessmen in the district to study Ah De's merits, then he himself puts up a signboard, "Refreshment You Can Count On," in Ah De's store. He spreads Ah De's merits on every occasion and at all kinds of meetings. He even proposes, at a meeting of district and city APB chairmen, that Li Mingde be his assistant chair of the District Association of Private Businessmen. Because of his efforts, the motion meets with initial approval.

Ah De is becoming famous. Whenever he walks down the street, people greet him and mention his name. Ah De nods and smiles to them without exception. His nodding and smiling are so appropriate that his bearing becomes as stylish as that of a diplomat.

So more and more people ask Ah De to repair bikes, and he gradually finds it hard to cope with them all. His spare time in the evening most certainly does not suffice to meet the demand of this new situation. So he has to make use of his daytime, when his store is operating. Somebody even suggests that he put a sign reading "People's Convenient Bike Service" in front of his store, and provide wrenches, pliers, screwdrivers, and air pumps, all for free. The guy who has this idea says that it could kill three birds with one stone. First, with the tools there, people can do small repairs themselves, reducing the amount of work for Ah De; second, Ah De's reputation for serving the society wholeheartedly will spread even wider; third, it will attract more customers, so the store's business will improve all the more. After listening to it, Ah De nods his head and acts accordingly.

Yet the outcome is not as ideal as expected. The bike owners could certainly take care of small repair jobs themselves, but they still ask Ah De to do it for them when more complicated or major repair is needed. So the situation remains almost the same for Ah De. The store does not do better business, either. On the other hand, Reporter Liang writes another article, Li

Mingde's name appears in the newspaper again. And Xiao Liu of the community office comes to take some more pictures.

It has been two months since the opening of Ah De's "People's Convenient Bike Service," and it has received commendation from people from all walks of life. But there have also been a few problems.

Right across from De's Refreshment is a private bike repair shop. At first it did some business, but since the opening of Ah De's bike service, its business has dwindled and the customers are now few and far between. It is not strange, as everything in Ah De's bike service is free while in the repair shop there is even a charge for using the air pump. With Ah De's free service, people naturally would not patronize the shop. What couldn't they buy with the dozen cents saved?

The owners of the repair shop are two young men who get violently angry seeing all this. One day, pumped up by the alcohol of a few beers, they go up in a towering rage to De's Refreshment to make trouble. First they insist that Ah De should not compete with them and ruin their business, then they lash out, ripping down the sign for the bike service and trampling it. They also push a stack of bowls to the floor before they leave and threaten that if the convenient service continues its business, Ah De had better watch out, and so on.

Police Superintendent Huang, taking the case very seriously, handles it himself. He excoriates the two young shop owners and orders them to have the sign fixed and hung up again within two days. They are held responsible for all the property damages to De's Refreshment, and in addition to the apology they must make to Ah De, they must write and deliver to the police station an in-depth self-criticism.

By this time the alcohol is already gone, and the two young men begin to see things straight. They know that they are in the wrong, and as they see that De's Refreshment has the police behind it, what more dare they say? So they had to grin and bear it, paying for the damage and handing in the self-criticism.

Before the end of the year, the appointment to promote Ah De to Vice

Chairman of the APB is issued, and Ah De assumes the responsibility with great enthusiasm. Immediately afterwards, various titles come one after another: member of the Municipal Youth Association, member of the Research Institute on Self-Made Talents, member of the Provincial Council for Promoting Spiritual Civilization, adviser for the journal *Speech and Eloquence* and special editor of the newspaper *Law Education*, ... Ah De orders one thousand and five hundred name cards at his own expense; his many titles fill all the space on its back.

Gradually there are more meetings for him to attend. Notices of meetings come almost every day, as many as five in one day.

Busy, busy, busy. So busy that he feels dizzy and is unable to tell directions, and his speeches become inconsistent and confused. But it's worth it. Amid all this hustle and bustle, Ah De feels the value of existence in this world. He is excited and satisfied, his heart brimming with the kind of fulfillment he has never experienced before. Now he can sleep only four or five hours everyday but wakes full of energy. He feels that his every nerve is electrically charged.

Huizhen, his wife, is busier too. Since Ah De's social calender has grown full, he cannot possibly take care of the store, and the whole burden of it rests upon her shoulders. The workload is divided to the full among each of the store's personnel, and if Ah De cannot come, the others have to do his share for him. No one cared too much as long as the situation seemed temporary, but after it went on for a long time, the employees began to gripe.

It is Ah De who comes up with a simple solution: if there is a shortage of hands, why not hire one more person?

But Huizhen opposes the idea, arguing that the salary for this person would be eighty yuan per month. Because he gets two free meals in the store, they would have an additional expense of one hundred thirty or forty yuan every month. Now after the rent, taxes, employees' salaries, and utilities, the store has only a little more than four hundred yuan left. If they hire one more man, would they be able to survive?

Ah De asks, "Then what do you think we should do?"

Huizhen replies, "I think you'd better stop going to so many of those meetings, and spend less time on repairing bikes. Everything would be all right if you could do more in the store."

Ah De bursts out laughing. "This won't do. They invite me to attend their meetings, and if I don't go, they'd say I'm too arrogant to accept their invitations. And I have to repair bikes because my reputation depends on it. It's like my signboard, could we afford to destroy it ourselves? We could afford one more man anyway. I say let's not hesitate, Huizhen!" He pats his wife's head as if he were coaxing a child.

Huizhen can't help sighing, "Well..."

So the matter is decided. A few days later De's Refreshment adds one more employee, and Ah De can go on attending the meetings without a worry.

As usual there are meetings upon meetings. Sometimes an organization as unrelated as the Association of Potted Florists sends him an invitation. Ah De used to engross himself in his own restaurant business without knowing what was going on in the world. Now he realizes that there are so many meetings going on every day, and that there is no end of it. Sometimes they last one day, sometimes several. They are held in fancy hotels. The food is excellent, too. People need only pay a small fraction of the price. Sometimes you don't even need to pay, it's free! On the last day buses take them to the amusement parks, to rides like Mad Mountain Climber, Venture Into Rapids, Seven Star Flying Disk... all free. Where else can you find treatment as nice as this? As he attends more such meetings, his bearing and manner become more refined. He grows accustomed to applause and flashing lights; he has learned table manners and how to greet people, shake hands, do bottoms-ups, and speaking according to the rules of etiquette.

So Ah De is having a good time, carefree and joyous. He has gained more than five pounds, and has to go to the watchmaker's to loosen his watchband.

Only when he returns from a meeting or banquet in a good mood and sees his wife's face, which has become withered and pale from overwork, does he feel genuinely sad. Only then can he not help sighing secretly.

The year passes quickly. Every unit and department is busy with its summary of the year's work. The community office, the police station, and the district APB are no exceptions. All have had outstanding achievements and all have been commended and cited by the authorities concerned.

But things at De's Refreshment have not gone as well. Its business has declined, and for a month or two it can hardly pay the salaries.

Ah De and Huizhen take some emergency measures. First of all they fire an employee, the one who does not follow instructions very closely, thus saving more than one hundred yuan a month. Then they try to cut cost. Before the Spring Festival, they had planned to remodel the store by painting the walls with latex paint, now they use limewash; they have to give up their plan to put a fireproof surface on all the tables, and simply paint them instead; they establish the rules that the lights are not to be turned on till half past six in the evening and that the meat freezer is to be turned off at night till the next morning, so as to save some money on electricity.

These measures prove to be rather effective. Ah De reduces the expenses by nearly a thousand yuan, and he is greatly encouraged.

As far as manpower is concerned, Ah De is now able to work more often in his store. The reason is that shortly before the central government issued a directive against "mountains of documents and seas of meetings." Ah De does some calculation and discovers that meetings for this month is 56.78 percent fewer than those of the same period last year.

But the number of all sorts of social events is not dropping but rising. On May 1, the Labor Day, the community has a Volunteer Sanitation Day; on May 4, the Youth Day, the City Committee of the Youth League calls on young people from all walks of life to provide free convenient service to the people; on June 1, the Children's Day, the Children's Welfare Commission launches the Day of Donation for Disabled Children; on August 1, the Army Day, the Municipal Civil Administration organizes delegations to honor servicemen or the families of revolutionary martyrs.... These activities are all very worthwhile and significant, and there is absolutely no excuse to avoid them, but to participate in each and every single one would... would... would....

Because of the fewer hands and a new regulation concerning the employees' free meal benefit, the service in De's Refreshment is slackening. The bowls and chopsticks are not as clean as they used to be; the portion of food is often inadequate. The employees and customers often quarrel.

Furthermore, customers often complain about spoiled food; this happens from time to time because the freezer is frequently disconnected. After receiving letters of grievance from the customers, the Consumer Committee and the Health Department jointly conduct a surprise investigation and find that the trouble really exists. So they make the decision according to regulations: a fine of one hundred and fifty yuan, and removal of the sign saying "Food You Can Count On."

With the notice of the fine in hand, Ah De stands stupefied for a long time. "Huizhen, this time De's is finished, all finished," he murmurs in his heart.

Huizhen chuckles instead.

"What's wrong with you! They give us a fine and take away the sign, and you have the heart to laugh!"

Huizhen replies, "You'd do better after knowing the consequences. There is hope in it, so it means we're not finished yet."

Ah De blinks his eyes, not knowing the subtlety of her point.

Huizhen goes on, "Let me ask you who is the owner of De's?"

"Me, of course. What does that have to do with all this?"

"You're the owner but you don't stay in it all the time. You go to other places and find things to do that are none of your business. How can we go on like this?"

"But tell me what I should do. Shouldn't I go to the meetings when they invite me?" Ah De asks sincerely like a naive elementary school pupil.

"Don't go to those meetings that have nothing to do with you, those in which you could play no role, or those that invite you only as a showcase. Use your time to get down to your own business."

"Yes, this is the first. What else?"

"Then it's the bikes. There are places to have them repaired, and the people can afford the expense. Why must they ask you for help? They get several yuan of transportation allowance from the government every month, where does it go?"

"Would it be embarrassing to refuse when they take their bikes here?"

"It depends. When you're free, I don't object to your helping others, but when you're busy, you have to take care of your business. You just can't put the cart before the horse, do you understand?"

Ah De remains silent. He stares at the ceiling, thinking that you just can't look down on Huizhen, who can talk with reason, fairness, and proper restraint. She even knows a saying like "Put the cart before the horse."

"This is your second point. What else?"

"And... that's all. Everything will be fine if you agree to these two. And don't you worry that De's won't make it!" Ah De nods his head, and nods again.

He really mulls it over for quite a few days, and he finally thinks it through. Since he is doing business, he will have to devote himself to it. If he fails, he can't live on the many titles on his card. Oh my, to say things like this seems very backward and vulgar, especially for someone whose merits have been publicized in the newspapers, and who has given many speeches to promote spiritual civilization. A man like that should never think this way. But the facts of life compel, and there is something in what Huizhen says. Whatever happens, Ah De decides to become a little more practical.

He begins to say no to people who invite him to attend meetings or participate in activities that may or may not need him. He wants to spend most of his energy on De's Refreshment. Since the People's Convenience Service has already been established, he allows it to continue, with the wrenches, screwdrivers, pliers, air pumps, and so on still there. Anyone who needs some repair job done on his bike can use them. If he can't handle the job himself, sorry, he can push the bike to the repair shop across the street. Those who need help with their bikes become perplexed; they always raise their heads and look at the signboard, not sure if they have come to the right place.

As for his friends and neighbors, he cannot bring himself to say no. He has to save face. So he says yes to them when they come to ask for help and tells them to leave the bikes there. But he can only get to them, he says, when he has time. They usually have to wait for half a day at least, sometimes even takes one or two days. What's more surprising is that Ah De now asks them to pay for small parts worth only a dozen cents. He was not like that in the past! How could he do such a thing!

People start to complain about the changes in Ah De. But he turns a deaf ear to them.

He invites friends home to play Mahjongg when he is free. It has been a long time since he played it last, so he is a little rusty. First he loses all the time, but as he did know the game, he gets better and better after a few rounds and ends up winning back a lot of chips in every which way. He also goes dancing, doing disco to the strong-rhymed rock music. He has not danced in a long time; his limbs and hip joints don't feel as agile as they used to be, and his steps are always half a beat slower than the music. In addition, he likes to sing:

> Ali,
> Ali Ba Ba,
> Ali Ba Ba follows the bandits, how brave.
> ....

He can sing it almost as well as the authentic tape.

But people can never accept these changes in Ah De. Some even believe that it was only for his personal gain that Ah De once helped people enthusiastically. Now after he has acquired reputation, money, and official position, he shows his true face. Some predict that in a few days he will put up a sign, "Three Cents for Using Air pumps." That this Ah De, young as he is, should have learned the tricks and foresight to fish for fame and compliments, is indeed shocking. And after the shock comes indignation.

The newspaper's Public Service Department receives quite a few letters in succession from readers concerning the report on Li Mingde. In strong word, they accuse the newspaper of misrepresentation. The department relays these letters to Reporter Liang, who has been promoted to the position of Assistant Director of the Department of News Coverage, and a discussion follows. Liang looks very embarrassed after reading these letters, and explains, "There might be some misunderstanding in it. I'll verify and investigate it right away."

Reporter Liang finds Ah De and tells him about these letters from the readers. He also points out the possible consequences these public opinions may have for Ah De himself. But Ah De doesn't care. "The worst they can do is to dismiss me from the official post of Assistant Chair of the APB. It doesn't matter; on the contrary, life will be easier for me without it. I don't steal or rob, I haven't violated the law. And I make a living with my hands, working hard to make it--no, I haven't made it yet, and damn, my store could hardly survive--and I do something good for the society now and then. What's wrong with it? I have treated everyone fairly, haven't I!"

Reporter Liang blinks, unable to say anything for quite a while, as he knows more or less about Ah De's predicament. He remains silent for some time and smokes several cigarettes, and all of a sudden he says disingenuously that for a news reporter, the most deadly mistake is distortion of facts. Rumor has it that his name has been included in the list for promotion, if anything like this should happen, it....

Ah De is stunned on hearing this.

Secretary He also comes to have a heart-to-heart talk with him. He tells Ah De that his office is highly commended by his superiors, as it has actively carried out the policy of promoting spiritual civilization, and that the City Commission of Promoting Both Material and Spiritual Civilizations is going to award his office the honorary title of Advanced Unit.

Also comes Police Superintendent Huang who informs Ah De that he is planning to attend the Conference of Exchanging Experiences on Youth Education sponsored by the City Public Security Bureau next month. He has already prepared his speech, and two-thirds of it is about Ah De.

Chairman Luo hurries to his home the same night. He shoots at Ah De, "Li Mingde how can you say so casually that you don't want to be Assistant Chair of APB you think you can when you want or you can resign when you don't? for your promotion I walked my feet swollen talked my mouth dry but you said you'd quit how can I save face? of course my reputation is a small matter and I don't mind but you just couldn't let APB down because of this isn't it?" Then he shows Ah De a stack of final drafts. It was written by Chairman Luo himself, and it's detailed exposition of the relationships between Bo Le and the winged steed, with many examples which include the entire process of how the writer discovers and trains a young cadre Li Mingde. The article is going to be published in a certain journal of social science.

Even Xiao Liu visits Ah De's home with much worry. He says that there is going to be a big province-wide photography competition, and he has submitted one of his pictures showing Li Mingde wholeheartedly repairing bikes for the people free of charge. According to what has been disclosed, this photo will surely be chosen, and is a fine candidate for a prize. Furthermore it has been rumored that anyone who wins a prize in a major photo competition at or above the provincial level will automatically be accepted by the Association of Photographers. If you are accepted, though without a diploma of junior college, you will....

In each case Ah De has nothing to say.

He has never expected that he has become so vitally important, that what he does has so much to do with other people's destinies.

"Ah De, you mustn't listen to them. You go on like this and take responsibility for no one," Huizhen says to her husband.

"This time it's different," Ah De shakes his head. "I can't fold my hands and watch them die."

"Is it that serious, talking about life and death?"

"Almost."

"Ah, I understand. If you, the model, go down, they'll go down with you, isn't it?"

"Yes."

"You stick to the code of brotherhood. When others are in trouble, you'll do everything to help them in spite of all consequences, isn't that right?"

"Y...es."

"But has any of them ever volunteered to help you when you're in trouble? No, no one! If you go on like this, De's will have to close its door, Ah De!"

"I don't think it's likely. We just have to work a little harder, at the worst. Let's wait till we make it through this period."

"Don't be naive, things like this never end."

Ah De waves his hand and cuts her short. "Huizhen, please stop. I've made the promise, and have to stick to it. You have to make sacrifices for your friends," he says in a moving and tragic voice.

The news spreads and the people concerned feel happy and encouraged. "Ah De, you've done the right thing!" they say.

But Huizhen had become extremely irritable. Sometimes she picks fights with Ah De, throwing bowls and plates around; sometimes she weeps and cries before him with tears and a running nose. She has one purpose, which is to change his mind. At first Ah De does nothing but accommodate her. When she loses her temper, he hides himself, pretending to be deaf and dumb. He hopes that by doing so he could put some restrain on her outbursts. When she weeps and cries, he consoles her with words, pats her shoulders, or strokes her head affectionately. But the woman does not know good from bad and goes on pestering him. She simply will not quit before achieving her purpose. One day, after the whole thing has been repeated once too often, Ah De finally flares up. After all, he is not a saint, and he is not well trained in the art of enduring humiliations. He is a man, and a rather virile one at that. His anger, suppressed inside him for a long time, proves formidable, and he just stops short of hitting Huizhen with his fists.

Huizhen is not to be intimidated. Her little mouth curses him as sharply as a knife. They fling abuses one after another for a long time till they are gasping for breath, both believing they have won the fight.

Well, there have been enough fighting and cursing, so Huizhen goes back to pack her clothes in the bedroom. Ah De knows she is going to her mother's house, so he shouts in a vicious voice, "All right, you go. You think the sky will cave in without you?"

Huizhen is gone; the sky does not cave in. But De's Refreshment is about to collapse. Even with Huizhen working hard there, it was difficult to keep the job done. Now that she is gone, the store seems to have lost a leg; how can Ah De manage to handle all this? It runs better when Ah De himself works in it. But whenever he leaves, the store looks like a place where all kinds of rogues run wild. The employees all do what they like, chatting, taking a nap, or quarreling with customers.

De's Refreshment becomes notorious, and is very likely to go under. At last Ah De gives all the employees a long leave. As he puts up a notice on the storefront outside, The Global Leather Shoes and Times Beauty Saloon next door are opening their gates wide and welcoming the first customers of the day.

KITCHEN SMOKE AGAIN, KITCHEN SMOKE AGAIN

Ma Bende

By now the dusk has fallen. He pushes his bike wearily, climbing up the low and gentle ridge of yellow soil at last.

The Zheyang Mountain stands silently in the glow of sunset; the Old Man River is flowing as always. There is still the single ox cart rolling slowly on the dirt road toward the small village, and in the fields by the river there are still farmers drawing water with booms. That irrigation project crossing the ridge, once renowned as the Educated Youth Canal is sleeping meditatingly across the parched land, while those Root Trees[1] have already grown into useful timber in the muffled years.

In the slanting sunshine of the dusk, he gazes for a long time on the small village surrounded by green trees at the foot of the yellow soil ridge.

The village hasn't changed any, nor has the kitchen smoke. But their generation is no longer young. Nine years. He and his schoolmates gulped down with tears bowls of liquor made from dried yam in that big frenzy of returning to the city, and burned in a fit of madness their bed straw and reed mats, then fled the little village, all with the rejoicing of escaping hell. Later they became city dwellers. Now San Mao has become rich; Yan Jing is the head of a department; Lao Ba is a Ph.D. student at the University of California in the U.S.; Huang Wanping turns out to be a writer of some reputation among the educated youth, and he himself becomes the assistant engineer in an architecture firm. He has won an essay prize, published two pamphlets, and has deposited a medium sized contribution fee in the bank... in a few years history has paid back their generation everything it owed them for twenty years. But even if that is the case, what then?

The smoke, dispersing little by little in the village, sets off in him a myriad of emotions and memories.

---

[1] When the youth were sent to the rural area, they were advised to plant those trees to indicate their determination to stay there all their lives like the trees.

He remembers Jiu Er was pregnant then. Because of Jiu Er and that unborn baby, he had to postpone his departure for two days. These two days were so long yet so short. In the forty-eight hours when his destiny was decided, he stood across two worlds, the city and the village. His lofty and tragic marriage had suddenly become a burden. He hesitated and wavered between the two worlds, disconsolation gnawing at his heart. Finally the lure of the city proved too irresistible, and he clenched his teeth and left.

It was also dusk as the heat receded. When old Ma Zhijiu sent him from the village in an ox cart, Jiu Er stood silently at the village gate, following him all the time with her eyes till he passed the yellow soil ridge. He did not dare to look back. At that moment he was afraid to see the pair of eyes full of tears.

After the divorce procedures were over in the Gulou District Court, he parted with Guo Qianru.

All came to an end like this. Biking on his way to his office, he felt as if relieved of a heavy load, yet there was in his heart a kind of indescribable vexation and anger. Hard to pinpoint what it was. It had been there for a long time, causing him to bicker and fight with people on many occasions for no reason.

He came back home and found that Guo Qianru had already hired a truck to haul away all her furniture and belongings. Lastly, she opened the drawer loudly and took away his bank deposit book.

He stood by coldly, making no effort to stop her, nor saying anything.

"Humph! What's your good taste for!" When Guo Qianru was gone, his second younger brother cast a sidelong glance at him and sneered, "What's the use of your university diploma? For all these years, you haven't even got into the Party, you are incapable of moonlighting, but you dislike your wife for her vulgar ways... what is vulgar anyway in a time like this?"

"That's enough, Second Brother. Can't you let it go?" he replied.

He cast a glance at his brother and just went out.

"You high school students of the those three years[2] produce breeds of sages!"

He didn't want to pay attention to his brother; though only eight years younger, he belonged to an entirely different generation. His second brother had never experienced what he had gone through. Could he possibly understand the untold feelings of my generation?

In front of him, by the road at the end of the narrow lane, the same group of young men were again playing mahjongg. Everybody's face was full of iron clips; fits of loud laughter and boorish squabbles resounded through the sky.

More irritated, he went out of the lane by himself, wandering toward the broad street.

The street was just as noisy. After a whole day of hubbub, the city was still full of it. People were still busy after a whole day's hustle and bustle. Bike bells rang everywhere; peddlers shouted without stopping. The multicolored neon lights on the surrounding buildings, the glaring bill boards, the speeding cars, the heavily rhymed or soft music from Hong Kong and Taiwan--everything was showing off the prosperity of a metropolis at night.

When he was passing the Market, a Suzuki motorbike screeched to a stop in front of him. Raising his head, he saw his old schoolmate San Mao, with whom he had gone to establish revolutionary ties in Shaoshan[3] and later to the countryside. Two years of engaging in private business during which time he retained his government job without getting paid had made him extremely rich. Even his outfit and temperament had become strange. Not only did this guy wear a necklace and a ring, he also grew a beard like the Hazaks. A t-shirt with a 555 ad matching the Panamanian pants made him look rather in fashion.

"How about having a couple of drinks with me at the Weimeisi

---

[2] 1966, 67, and 68, when the Cultural Revolution was in its initial stage, and students were forced to drop out of school.

[3] Mao Zedong's birthplace, considered sacred by the Red Guards.

Restaurant?" San Mao said. "Tonight I'm having a business dinner, I've reserved a table...."

He shook his head. "No, I don't want to join in the fun."

"I know you're down, pal. Heard that you divorced your wife, haven't you? No good to be so pissed off. Money in hand, isn't it easy to find a woman again? Anytime you feel interested, I'll take you to the Yelaixiang Hotel in the west suburb, I guarantee you'll have a damn good time."

"San Mao, hurry up with your own business!"

With a wry smile he gave San Mao a push and left.

Passing the Crown Restaurant, he suddenly felt the urge to drink a little. In the past he seldom used to drink, but now he craved some excitement, and a strong one at that.

The place was clamorous. The stereo loudspeakers were blasting the popular Song of Ji Gong, and a crowd of people were playing a finger-guessing game and shouting. The waitresses, flaunting their lipstick and swinging their waists, were seating the customers without stopping. He hesitated a little, then walked straight through the main area toward a private section surrounded by a screen.

A man with sunglasses and a somber countenance was sitting there engrossed with his drink. He ordered two dishes and a bottle of wine, sat down opposite the man, and began, in low spirits, to drink all by himself.

The man with sunglasses looked him up and down, put down his cup at once, and slowly removed his glasses.

"Li Yan, how come you don't recognize me?"

He was stunned. The familiar face abruptly roused his memories from sleep, reminding him of the fanatical and abnormal times, and of an ardent youth with earthshaking heroism. It also made him remember the ice cold handcuffs, prison, and the desolate labor camp.

"Xitai! When did you get out?" he asked with great surprise.

"Out for two months," Lu Xitai gave a wan smile. "Ten years. Ten whole years. Like I've gone through the Cultural Revolution once more...."

"What did you do after you got out?"

"What can people like us do? I'm selling rat poison all day with my sunglasses on, like covering my face with a damn ragged hat in busy streets...."

He looked at Lu Xitai, for a moment unable to utter a sound.

"Haven't you got some official position?" Lu Xitai asked.

He shook his head.

"Yan Jing, that son of a gun, has made it," said Lu, "but what difference does it make?"

For quite some time, he gazed at the Red Guard chief who had piously led them a long way on foot to plant their red flags in the hometown of the Red Sun[4] as well as on top of the Jinggang Mountain[5] Scenes of the past, solemn, stirring, absurd, and laughable, flashed through his mind with all sorts of emotion.

Twenty years had passed, this generation of ours...he thought.

"Why don't you drink?" Lu raised his cup with a bitter smile. "Well, I forgot to ask, are you still in touch with that woman in the village?"

"No," he said.

"You were hot-headed enough then," Lu said, "Went so far as to marry a country girl. Luckily the show's over, or else you would have suffered all your life there."

"Not necessarily," he replied. "On the contrary, now I often regret that I fought my way back to the city. Those years in the village were really tough,

---

[4] Mao Zedong.
[5] Where Mao Zedong led the revolution in early 1930's.

but life there seemed pretty full. But now... sometimes I wish I could go back to the village."

"Looks like you're thinking of that woman in the village, aren't you?"

He nodded and then shook his head, "Perhaps, but not all."

Those Root Trees have grown into timber; from a distance they look luxuriant, like a green protective screen. Those are the twenty nine French poplars that once symbolized twenty nine absolutely earnest young students. Now these educated youth have gone off to distant places; what's left is a piece of green wood for memory.

He leaves his bike by the tree and heads toward a graveyard.

Old Donkey is buried there.

New dirt has recently been heaped onto the old man's grave. The tiny cement tombstone stands alone with bristlegrass and new cogongrass growing all around.

He stands before the grave for a long time.

An old hunchback suddenly drives a flock of sheep over from the wood. An old yellow dog follows closely behind, and upon seeing the stranger charges forward, barking loudly.

The hunchback roars with laughter. Li Yan has recognized it is Ma Zhijiu, and Ma also recognizes him.

"Why, it's you, kid!" Ma shouted, slapping his thigh with happy astonishment. "How come you're alone? Why don't San Mao and Lao Ba come along? They say you married a girl student in the city, isn't it? Why don't you bring her here for some fun?"

"We've divorced," he said.

"Why, how come?" Ma Zhijiu said. "That's the way with you city folks, marrying a woman's as easy as buying clothes."

A sheep suddenly veers into the corn field. Ma Zhijiu shouts at the yellow dog, who dashes out and drives the sheep back. The old man pats the yellow dog proudly, narrowing his eyes into a smile.

"See, sweeter than a wife," Ma Zhijiu says. "It's late, let's go back. We'll have a couple of drinks tonight, and might as well tell Xiao Huang to come over for dinner."

"Xiao Huang? Which Xiao Huang?" he asks in astonishment.

"It's the girl, Huang Wanping"

"What, is she also here?"

"She's been here for two days already," Ma Zhijiu says. "It's said she wants to stay longer; she wants to write a book. Every day she is invited for meals by this or that family, and until now I haven't got my turn yet. Today you happen to be here."

He does not say anything more but follows Ma Zhijiu toward the village.

Ma Zhijiu glances at him and asks abruptly, "Didn't you see Jiu Er at the Town of Xinji on your way here?"

He stops.

"She opened a restaurant at Xinji more than two years ago..." he giggles. "Now she had made a pile, perhaps more than this!"

Ma Zhijiu puts out a finger, chuckling somewhat strangely.

"Jiu Er has married again?" he asked.

"Yes, but divorced again the year before...."

"Divorced again?" His heart sinks a little, "Why?"

"Isn't it free and easy after divorce," Ma Zhijiu smiles mysteriously once more. "Otherwise how could a woman have lots of business for her restaurant...." More giggles.

"Did you mean...?"

Ma Zhijiu realizes at once that he has said a bit too much. He forces a smile quickly, "Nothing much, what I mean is that Jiu Er is now pretty smart." He chuckles again.

It's improper for him to keep on asking, but he feels puzzled and the whole thing weighs heavily on his mind.

After the relatives were escorted back to the village, he and Yan Jing stood for a long time before Old Donkey's grave.

Old Donkey died. This pitiable old man had ended his old life with a piece of hemp string only because he stole a few ears of corn from the production team. At the very moment when the two educated youth, newly arrived from the city and then on night patrol duty, first seized Old Donkey's arms, they despised him so very much that they brought him to the brigade office right away almost without thinking. Then Chang Chuan, the Party Secretary and a well known tyrant, called a public denunciation meeting the same evening. The next day Old Donkey, bound all over, was paraded through the street for half of the day. In the small hours of that night, loud and piercing cries came out of Jiu Er's thatched house. So there was one more new grave under the yellow soil ridge west of the village.

But how could all this have happened? In an advanced brigade which enjoyed a high reputation in the commune, that an old man should steal corn simply because there was nothing to eat in the family, and that there should be more families that had nothing left to eat! For days, after they had endured hunger till they were off work, commune members of several families went to beg in other villages without disclosing their names and without the brigade cadres knowing it.... All this seemed almost unbelievable, but it was real and was likely to happen again. Faced with the cruel realities in the country, the two young men, who had newly settled down there, were shocked as if they had been struck to the head.

"Damn, what bastards are we!" Yan Jing cried angrily. "Wasn't it just for a few ears of corn? Why in the hell did we want to catch him?"

He stood there looking at the new grave, his face pallid and lips almost bleeding from biting.

In the evening, he and Yan Jing started a donation. Twenty nine young people raised one hundred sixty-five yuan to console the survivors of the dead.

There were some cracks in the walls of the old, broken courtyard. The doors to the three low-thatched rooms were half closed; not a sound was heard from within. On a low side table made of dirt bricks, there was a dim kerosene lamp. Jiu Er, keeping her mother company, was sitting numbly by a spinning wheel as if stupefied. Both the mother and daughter remained motionless until the young people entered the house.

All of them gave him the hint to say something, but he stood before the old woman with lowered head, unable to speak for a long time.

Jiu Er looked at him dully, her eyes hostile. The old woman turned back her face and sobbed voicelessly.

He bent forward and held the two hands of the old woman, his eyes welling up with tears.

"Please forgive us, aunt," he said. "We grew up in the city from childhood, we had no idea it was this hard in the country... really, we didn't know you had nothing to eat. We should never... aunt, could you please forgive us young students from the city? From now on... from now on we are your sons. Really, we will take care of you all our lives and will never let you suffer...."

He could not go on but fell to his knees and threw himself into the old woman's bosom with tears all over his face. The old woman was moved to tears, and Jiu Er cried too.

It was late at night when they left Jiu Er's house. Walking on the narrow village road, looking at the low thatched huts in the shadow of the night, and listening to the drone of the spinning wheels from the windows afar, he suddenly had a solemn, raging idea.

"Damn, I must become the production team leader!" he cried in his heart. He could not believe that more than a hundred men and women should have nothing to eat from over three hundred *mu*[6] of yellow soil! He had to take over the solemn task: let the poor and lower-middle peasants live a good life.

Later he really became the leader. On the day when he assumed his duties, he stood on the big stone roller under the old scholartree and waved his arm enthusiastically, making a pledge to everyone in the village.

"I vow to change completely the backward state of our team within two years. If not, I, Li Yan, will never go back to the city again!"

He delivered his speech with great fervor, but none of the poor and lower-middle peasants clapped their hands, nor did anyone ever believe that he would stay in the country and suffer all his life. At the end of the year he married Old Donkey's daughter Jiu Er unexpectedly with lightning speed.

This kind of marriage, which was almost tragically stirring, quickly drew a great deal of attention from the County Office of Educated Youth. On the wedding day, officials from the commune and the county government were in attendance, and even a woman reporter from a state newspaper came, which published an article about him soon after. He was later chosen as a delegate to the State Conference of Activists Among Educated Youth. It was to be held in the state capital, which meant he could conveniently visit with his family, but he found an excuse and did not go.

"I've said I will never go back to the city without having changed the face of our team," he explained to Jiu Er.

All this moved Jiu Er greatly.

The poor girl growing in the country had never dreamed of being married to an educated youth from the city. In her mind, they were very mysterious and enviable. When these educated youth first came, she and the other girls of the village stood on the roadside with arms round each other's necks, measuring with their eyes their green army uniforms, new suitcases, canteens, tooth brushes, and paste. While Yan Jing took out an old accordion and passed by, one of the girls even exclaimed with admiration.

---

[6] One *mu* is about one sixth of an acre.

"Oh, look how rich the city kids are, so many things...."

Jiu Er heard this and giggled into the girl's ear, "Green eyed, aren't you? Why don't you get bold and have a date with one of them tomorrow?'

"Nope, it won't be my turn!" the girl retorted. "You're the one to choose first, being the prettiest of us all. You think they'll take a shine to me?"

"Well, let these sons of turtles be nuts about me till death!" Jiu Er replied. "I don't care even if they do like me, and besides, they'd turn up their noses at me for a bumpkin. They've been pampered in the city since childhood. Why should I want to serve them like a horse?"

"That's enough, Jiu Er," another girl cut in. "You would be extremely lucky if you could marry a young man from the city. Don't you see what they eat and wear?"

"Get lost. Who among us would be that lucky?"

Jiu Er smiled bitterly and sighed, and the other girls grew silent immediately afterward.

That evening, when they returned home and picked up a bowl of gruel, almost all of these girls lost their tempers with their mothers for no reason. Late at night, at least four girls were heaving deep sighs to themselves in bed. From that day on, whenever they had time, Jiu Er and the girls would visit the house where the educated youth lived, and soon they became very familiar with them. Almost all these pitiable country girls longed for one of the young students to fall for them, but no one but Jiu Er had her wish fulfilled. So during the unforgettable wedding night, she cried and cuddled in her student husband's arms, which quite baffled him.

Ma Zhijiu brings back two bottles of wine in high spirits, and dives behind the stove without coming back.

The old man is giving a dinner to the two young friends from far away.

He and Huang Wanping sit in Ma's cramped two room house, each feeling rather shocked. Neither has expected to meet in this remote village.

Two months earlier, they saw each other once at the May 1 Square in that distant city. She had just separated with Yan Jing and was looking rather depressed. He was also in a bad mood. They talked very little and then remained silent with bitter smiles.

It happened to be the day when the City Changjiang River Raft Team was officially formed.

With red flags leading the way, the band blared out marches, escorting a team of young heroes through the square. They paraded past the two of them full of power and grandeur, which excited the spectators more than a little. Li Yan and Huang Wanping looked for a long time at the departing red flags and heroes, thinking naturally of the bygone days of their youth.

"Well, we are old," Huang Wanping sighed.

"No, it's our hearts that are old."

After a while, to his surprise, Huang Wanping got a whim and suggested they join the raft team for the excitement of it. But he shook his head. He said if he had time, he would want to pay a visit to the place where he once settled down.

"Nowadays I really think of that place a lot," he said.

"How did you come earlier?" he asks. "What are you here for? To ponder your youth, or grieve over aspirations?"

"You're as sarcastic as ever," Huang Wanping says. "I also have no other choices: rejected by the Raft Team, and irritated in the city... what's more, I have always been writing about the lives of the educated youth. The little I know has long since been sold out. If I don't come here again, I'm afraid I'll be finished."

"No need to be modest," he says. "Haven't you just published a novelette? I've read it."

"That one is no good... what do you think of it?"

"Frankly, I couldn't finish it," he smiles. "Why do you have to moan and groan without end over our country experiences? I feel sick whenever I come across stories like that.... Don't laugh, I don't want to flatter you. I feel it's just too much. We lived in the country for no more than a few years, yet we keep on moaning and groaning all our lives as if we had fallen into hell. How would those old farmers feel, they've lived here generation after generation-- what are you laughing at?"

"I'm laughing at you, man, pretty sweet and still naive."

Huang Wanping asks again, "Do you know what Lao Ba is up to?"

He shakes his head, "No. We lost contact since he went abroad."

"Lao Ba is settling down in Los Angeles."

He is a bit startled. "Is that so? Won't he come back?"

"Absolutely not," Huang Wanping says. "It's said he has already married a Singapore woman who lives in the U.S. This woman is a whole fifteen years older than he is...."

"Fifteen years?"

"Fifteen years. I heard the woman is the widow of a millionaire and has a bundle. Lao Bao was probably attracted by it."

Smoking silently, he can hardly believe that this type of thing has actually happened to Lao Ba. He remembers when they were in the countryside, a girl student married an officer who was twenty years older and who headed the military area command, in order to return to the city in a roundabout way. It roused in Lao Bao great indignation and contempt. He cursed loudly, saying it was an absolute shame for us educated youth. But now, in order to stay abroad, he himself has married a woman fifteen years his senior.... Lao Ba, where are your manly character and dignity that you once had? And yet he quickly thinks of himself. What about you? Stop there, what damned right do you have to accuse others?

After a few drinks, Ma Zhijiu suddenly remembers that he has forgotten to invite the village head over to keep them company, so he dashes out with his crooked waist.

"Still the old way, after all these years?" asks Huang Wanping.

"Without a doubt. Probably the head is still the village god. Who dares not worship him?"

They sit face to face, and for the moment remain silent.

After leaving Ma Zhijiu's house, he hurries to see his ex mother-in-law in spite of the fatigue of the trip.

The old woman's hair has already turned gray. She comes tottering out of the door to greet him, clinging to a walking stick. Her trembling, skinny hands stroke his head and shoulders; her face is all tears with happiness. So many years have passed, the young man living in the distant big city still remembers her. The old woman is contented.

"Master Li, these legs of yours, do they still hurt with arthritis?"

The old woman addresses him in an affectionate way as she did before, and she inspects his legs with great concern. He looks at the old woman, a little choked up.

"A little, when it rains..."

"You silly boy!" the old woman grumbles. "If they still hurt, why didn't you write me a letter? Folk prescriptions can cure serious diseases. The liquor with snake slough and scorpions soaked in it works wonders...well, it's a shame, that summer I went out every night with a barn lamp for the slough. I caught quite a few scorpions, too. I was going to send them to you but we didn't know what government office you were working for. I asked Jiu Er to find out, she tried for a long while but didn't...."

His heart gives a quick beat, and a lump in his throat makes it impossible for him to speak out. He bends down into the old woman's arms in tears.

"Aunt, I've let you down. I felt too ashamed to write to you or come to see you all these years...."

"Son, you're talking nonsense," the old woman consoles him. "Why did you feel so ashamed to come back? If I say nothing, pay no attention to what others say. Really, all of you were kids who grew up in the city, so how could you put up with the hardships in the village? Now it was the government that sent you back to the city. How could I allow Jiu Er to be a burden for your whole life? Don't you mention it any more, let bygones be bygones. What matters is, you live a good life in the city.... Now son, weren't you married in the city long ago?"

"Yes," he says.

"Does your wife have a government job?"

"Yes."

"Is she nice to you?"

"Yes...."

"Well, that settles it," the old woman says. "You don't know how much I've worried since you left."

He looks at her and cannot find anything to say. After quite some time he asks about Jiu Er's divorce.

"Oh, it's all Jiu Er's fault!" the old woman says angrily. "She disliked his bad temper, saying he always beat her.... What does that matter? Who else would beat women except their men? When I was young and just married, wasn't I beaten a few times a month? But after several fights she wouldn't have it. And she finally divorced him."

"Why hasn't she remarried?"

"Let's not talk about her, not about her," the old woman keeps shaking her head. But she cannot stop herself, "The damned girl is good for nothing.

She's gone wild after living in the town for a few years, and all the townsfolks mock and laugh at her. Now she wants to build a house there. If it's not for my raising a fuss about it, she would have torn down this old house long ago. What's so good in the town? Without the restaurant there, the girl wouldn't have become such a no good. Well, that's enough, let's quit talking about her. Whenever I talk about her, I got so angry. I'd have nothing to do with her at all if not for my grandson."

It's obvious that the old woman has something too embarrassing to mention, which reminds him of Ma Zhijiu's funny chuckles. What has actually become of Jiu Er? He is eager to ask but finds it hard to, and this makes him all the more uneasy.

"Did Jiu Er take the child with her?"

"She did," the old woman replies. "The damned girl knows nothing about taking care of the kid. He's just about eight or nine, but she made him carry the plates and do the dishes all day long."

"How come, does the child go to school?"

His heart is sinking. In the city, children that age are the little suns in the eyes of their parents, while here in the country, kids run their own courses like wild trees. In his imagination, a little skinny boy is standing on tiptoe doing the dishes continually while his mother curses. There is an oppressive feeling of guilt in his heart. "That is my blood, my son!" he thinks.

He decides to go to town and see his son and Jiu Er tomorrow.

Today is the market day in the little town. It is still before noon, but the small restaurant is already full with noise.

When he first sees Jiu Er, he stops at the door very much shocked.

Nine years doesn't seem to have cost Jiu Er too much. She is wearing a creamy yellow, tight-fitting seersucker shirt, which is in fashion in the little town right now. A short, white embroidered skirt hangs from her waist, disclosing fully the contours of her plump hips. There is not a single trace of sloppiness characteristic of young country wives; instead an air of shrewdness, experience, and coquetry. She is flirting with a red-faced man, who is drinking, with her slender eyes blinking sideways; meanwhile the kitchen knife in her hand never stops making loud rat- tat sounds on the chopping board. Her whole face expresses happiness and contentment. No one could have guessed that she was once a woman in deep trouble. "Changed. Jiu Er has really changed," he thinks.

Immediately a kind of disappointment and uneasiness sweeps through his mind. He looks around, hoping to find the kid named Zhu Er. But what he sees is thin, dark-faced boy coming from inside with a stack of bowls. He is about to go to him, thinking it might be his son. But the boy turns back and with eyes wide open scowls in the direction of Jiu Er.

He too looks back, and blood rushes to his head--that red-faced man is still flirting with Jiu Er and his hands are busy.

The man is obviously a bit drunk. He holds Jiu Er by the waist with one hand and is about to feel her chest with the other. Laughing and cursing, Jiu Er twists her body and suddenly she turns and runs away. The man looks up and goes on laughing loudly with satisfaction.

Many follow him with uproars; some shout at the top of their lungs.

The red-faced man is encouraged. He grins cheekily and once again moves his head close to Jiu Er's face. Jiu Er becomes annoyed; she snatches a ball of the sticky mutton-filling at hand and flings it into his face with a loud smack. She chortles triumphantly, unable to stand straight. The red-faced man wipes his face with his hand awkwardly, but then leaps forward with a lightening speed, causing another round of uproars.

Laughing and taunting, Jiu Er reaches out to grab the man's ears and pulls him toward her chest. The man cries in exaggeration and seizes Jiu Er's neck, taking her by surprise.... There comes yet another big round of uproars.

The dark-faced boy is boiling with anger. He sticks out his belly and curses, "Fuck your mother!"

"Dame you, I'm your old man, don't you dare say that again!"

"Fuck your mother!"

The boy goes on cursing at the man, unafraid. Then he turns abruptly and runs out of the restaurant. There by the street, he squats down and begins to sob.

He has been standing outside the restaurant all this time, seeing everything. But Jiu Er never notices him.

Luckily, Ma Zhijiu and the old woman who is like a dear mother to him, are still there. There too are the old man and aunt who fought to have him over for dinner. Also the Educated Youth Canal, the Root Trees. the sad and lonely grave and tombstone of Old Donkey. There are still the warm little village, the endearing kitchen smoke, and the vast yellow land that has given rise to introspection.... Isn't all this enough?

No, I have no regret, he thinks angrily. He feels he has not come in vain.

FLUID PERSONALITY

Li Xingtian

The writer Fan Chong received the following message from a journal, "At present we have few stories about positive figures, please help."

So he took the train to the Town of Linhai. The town had long enjoyed a wide reputation as a model of the Reform, and Yang Hongshan, the general manager of its conglomerate, which was engaged in agriculture, industry, and trade business, was a pathbreaker in the Reform.

But Yang did not want to be interviewed. And Fan Chong stayed in the guesthouse for five days without seeing his shadow.

Nevertheless it was not boring to while away time like this on the seashore in summer. And Fan Chong did not stay idle these days. He walked in and around the town or joined in a chat with the townsfolks.

It was the morning of the sixth day.

"Comrade Fan!" Some one was knocking at the door.

Fan Chong opened the door and saw a girl. He recognized her immediately. It was Xiao Wang, secretary of the manager's office, he had tried every day to make an appointment with Manager Yang through her.

Xiao Wang came in and said, "Our manager has arranged to see you tomorrow morning." As she said so, she took out an invoice from a clipboard and added, "But you are requested to pay the labor fee for it."

"Labor fee?" Fan Chong was puzzled.

"It's our rule here. Any company that wants to use our personnel must pay the fee."

"But the manager..."

"He's no exception. He makes five yuan a day, three times more for other companies, so it'll be twenty yuan a day."

"Ah..." It was the first time Fan Chong came across such a regulation, but since he was eager to see the man, he said repeatedly, "All right, I'll pay, I'll pay...."

"You only need to pay ten yuan," Xiao Wang tore a copy from the invoice. "Tomorrow he can only be with you for half of the day."

Xiao Wang gave him the invoice with one hand and received the money with the other, then she left politely.

At eight o'clock next morning, someone was knocking at the door.

What Fan Chong saw was a man about fifty. He looked rather unsightly in his dark blue woolen western suit without a tie. The collar and cuffs of his white shirt had rings of grease on them. The man wore no socks but a pair of old cloth shoes. He was of medium size, a bit fat; he had lost half of his hair, but what remained was very black and stubborn. The muscles on his square face looked ferocious; his eyebrows were thick and his eyes bulged. The hair in his nostrils bristled, protruding outside. His wide mouth was full of sturdy teeth. He entered the door, coughing once as if there were no one around.

"I'm Yang Hongshan." He held out his hand.

Fan Chong felt Yang's weight while shaking hands.

While they talked, Fan Chong kept notes.

Suddenly Yang Hongshan interrupted him, "Don't write it down; it takes too much time." He took out a tiny recorder from his pocket. "Let's use this. When I talk, I like to see the other's eyes. I can't see your eyes as you bend down to keep notes."

Fan Chong thanked Yang for providing the recorder. And as he raised his head, he met Yang's eyes with a few creeping red lines, bright like fire, in the whites, which created a somewhat threatening impression.

"A tall tree catches the wind," Yang Hongshan went on with what they had been talking. "People in other places, seeing that the Town of Linhai has become prosperous, say that I must have stolen the money. They accuse me of being a villain, and call me a no good."

"What do you think of that?"

"I won't tolerate their calling me a no good, but I might agree if they say I'm a villain, because I do have some villainous habits and I have bullied others."

Fan Chong was astonished. He even thought of his future story: could a villain turn hero?

"Well, nevertheless, a lot of big shots from the ancient times to the present have been villains too. Wasn't Liu Bang of the Han Dynasty,[1] who killed the snake and led the uprising a villain? Wasn't Zhao Kuangying,[2] who later became the Emperor, a villain? Isn't Zhu Hongwu,[3] who burned the Hall of Victory Celebration, a villain?"

Fan Chong nodded again and again, thinking that Yang might have learned all this from the story tellers. It seemed traditional culture had played a role in educating the people.

"One who succeeds becomes the emperor; one who fails becomes the bandit!" Yang Hongshan let out a smile. "This I tell to you only. You are all right."

"Me?" Fan Chong grew suspicious, wondering how Yang Hongshan could possibly know he was "all right."

"I've done some investigation. You've been here in the town for five days. You've walked around eight times altogether, and have talked with twelve people. They say you are a decent sort."

---

[1] Liu Bang is the first emperor of the dynasty (256-195 B.C.).

[2] Zhao became the first emperor of the Song dynasty (927-976) after a successful military coup d'etat.

[3] The first emperor of the Ming Dynasty (1328-1389). It is said that he burned the Hall immediately after his victory in order to get rid of his powerful generals.

Fan Chong couldn't help shivering. Everything he did was recorded.

"At the beginning I thought they sent you as an advance party. Later we learned that you really were a writer."

Fan Chong remained puzzled.

"Especially yesterday, you paid your fee willingly and didn't put on airs. I have a feeling you are okay."

Okay! Fan Chong felt relieved that he had not been stingy with the ten yuan.

"Two months ago, there came a writer. When we asked him for the fee, he gave us a dressing down, shouting it was because he thought highly of us that he came for an interview. He gave us a tongue-lashing for failing to appreciate his kindness! Who needs your kindness? I, Yang Hongshan, am well known because of your kindness? What's so special about a writer? Why should I wait upon you? You can't use our men for nothing!"

"Yes, yes," Fan Chong answered repeatedly, eager to apologize for his colleague.

"I drove him away the next day."

Fan Chong believed the man standing before him would accomplish what he had promised.

"I asked my secretary to find me a novel of yours, and I've read it. I find that you are one of the writers who could say things for us common people, and that's why I tell you what I really think."

Fan Chong had never thought that a manager would ever read the works of a writer before talking to him.

"What do you want to write about?" he asked.

Fan Chong told him why he had come.

"Don't write about me," said Yang Hongshan. "It's not decided yet whether I'm good or bad!" But he did not seem so resigned to what he had just said, "But if you really want, there is something you can do for me."

Fan Chong had witnessed in these few days how a poor little village had been transformed into the present Town of Linhai. It was no exaggeration to say that Yang Hongshan had personally brought about all these changes. Now the town was too small for him to give full play to his talent. He had been trying to grab the county seat.

"I've heard you run several businesses in the county seat?"

"Sounds good to call them businesses," Yang Hongshan smiled. "In fact, nothing more than a restaurant, a hotel, and an electrical store."

"Oh, that's rare enough!" said Fan Chong with approval. "In foreign countries, it's common for farmers to flock to the cities after they go bankrupt; in our country, it's the farmers who go to the cities to invest."

Yang Hongshan showed great interest in Fan Chong's speech. He then poured out his views on the subject, expressing great contempt for government-owned companies.

"When there is time, I'd like to see your businesses in the county seat."

Yang Hongshan looked at his watch. "Let's go now."

The two of them left the guesthouse.

A car was parked in front of the door.

"Do we need the car?" Fan Chong hesitated. Since he had to pay the fee, it was likely that he would have to pay for the ride too. And that certainly wasn't going to be cheap. Besides, he couldn't get a refund for it.

"This is my company car." Yang Hongshan seemed to have read his mind. "Get in, it's free." And he pulled the door open to let him in.

They drove down the highway alongside the seashore and soon entered the county seat.

The first place they visited was the electrical store. It had a three-bay shop front with one manager and four salesmen, but business was brisk. The customers flew in and out without stopping.

"People can get the things here they can't get elsewhere," Yang Hongshan boasted. "We have more connections."

Fan Chong could see that this was so for many of the items for sale were name brands.

"We provide what others don't have, and even if they do have it ours is of better quality."

"Great, great!"

They went on to see the Linhai Hotel. It was a four-storied building with one hundred twenty rooms and two hundred and eight beds divided into three classes to serve ordinary tourists or accommodate conferences of about two hundred people. Close by was the Linhai Restaurant.

"The occupancy rate here is above seventy percent," Yang Hongshan explained. "We make one hundred and eighty thousand per year."

Fan Chong realized why he could afford the car.

As they toured the restaurant, Fan Chong was amazed that in a county seat there should be so many people dining out. They were sitting at every table; sometimes there were people of several generations, looking like a real family.

"From the patrons of this restaurant, you can see that farmers have money," Yang Hongshan whispered. "But some are forced to come." He pointed to a table with seven people, "Look, that's a young couple's engagement banquet; they've invited the cadres of their production team."

"How much would it cost?"

"From fifty to one hundred. With seafood, it'll be one hundred and fifty."

Fan Chong sighed to himself.

FLUID PERSONALITY

Yang Hongshan's eyes swept through the restaurant and dragged Fan Chong to the manager's office.

The manager, a man in his forties who looked rather dexterous, followed in.

Yang Hongshan picked on him. "Just now two customers ordered two bottles of beer. Why didn't you give them?"

"Eh..."

"Why there are two greasy spots on Waitress no. 3's white overcoat?"

"..."

"Why use white mushrooms in Mo Shu Pork instead of black ones?"

"..."

"Fuck your mother! Why don't you answer? Are you deaf and dumb?"

"Eh..." The manager stammered. "We just ran out of bottled beer. I bought some but there aren't enough to go around."

"Why haven't you thought of something? It's all right if other places don't have bottled beer, but it won't do here!"

"Yes, I'll try."

"Tell no. 3 to change her white coat right away. If I see her in greasy overcoat next time, I'll fire her on the spot."

"Yes."

"Don't think that you can save a little money by using white mushrooms. It'll ruin our name!"

"Yes, I'll tell the cooks right away."

"White mushrooms can be used in lotus seed soup. They're still good stuff."

"That's right. We'll add one more soup to the menu."

After losing his temper and giving directives, Yang Hongshan got in the car with Fan Chong as if nothing had happened.

Fan Chong wanted to compliment him for his resolute working style. "You're very strict with your employees."

"Even so, they still don't follow through."

"The manager of your restaurant follows your direction all right."

"If he didn't, I'd fire him!"

"Is he from your village?"

"He's my younger brother."

"A cousin of the family?"

"My younger brother."

Fan Chong could not pursue it any longer, remembering that Yang Hongshan had just boomed "Fuck your mother...."

They drove back to the Town of Linhai. Fan Chong felt there was much more they could talk about, so he suggested, "Manager Yang, let's go on in the afternoon."

Yang Hongshan sighed, "I can't be with you this afternoon. I have to face the investigation."

"An investigation?"

"The Tax Departments, the Procurator' Offices, and the Courts of the local district, county, and town are conducting a joint investigation against me!"

FLUID PERSONALITY

II

On the previous afternoon, Fan Chong had seen a group of about a dozen people entering and leaving the guesthouse. After hearing what Yang Hongshan had said, he realized that they had come for the investigation.

There was no sign of worry on Yang Hongshan's face, but Fan Chong became nervous.

After his brief encounter with Yang Hongshan, Fan Chong felt that he had found a naked soul, and he was determined to stay with the man.

What a shame that he could not join the investigation team or attend the interrogation session in the afternoon!

He closed the door and took out the recorder that Yang Hongshan lent him. "I won't tolerate their calling me a no good, but I might agree if they say I'm a villain, because I have some villainous habits, and I do have bullied others. Well, nevertheless, a lot of big shots from the ancient times to the present have been villains too. Wasn't Liu Bang of the Han Dynasty, who killed the snake and led the uprising, a villain? Wasn't Zhao Kuangying, who later became the emperor, a villain? Isn't Zhu Hongwu, who burned the Hall Of Victory Celebration, a villain?"

Fan Chong trembled. These emperors who rose from the greenwood were so similar in so many ways! How come Yang Hongshan could mention them so easily? Was it only because of the story tellers who spread these stories around?

This train of thoughts excited Fan Chong all evening. It was past ten, but he still did not want to sleep.

Someone knocked at the door twice.

Fan Chong opened it and Yang Hongshan stole in and closed it behind him.

Fan Chong felt that what Yang Hongshan was doing had a certain degree of secrecy about it.

Yang Hongshan sat on the edge of the bed, fixed his eyes on Fan Chong, and said, "Please keep something for me." He then closed the half open window, took from his pocket two tapes, and handed them to Fan Chong. "I told my secretary Xiao Wang to record it in the next room when they interrogated me in the afternoon." Having said this, he smiled treacherously.

"This..."

"It's very simple. Just use a wire running from under the sofa to the next room."

Fan Chong thought to himself, "Isn't that bugging? But why does he want me to keep them for him?"

"It's no secret," Yang Hongshan whispered. "What I want is to keep a file and find a witness." He put the two tapes on the bed and rose to leave.

"Could I listen to these tapes?" asked Fan Chong.

"Of course," said Yang Hongshan, turning round. "You can even make duplicates." He then left the room as nimbly as a cat.

Fan Chong was nervous, knowing that the members of the investigation team lived in the next room. If he got involved, what could the consequences be....

But all this carried with it some mystery, and the story was fascinating. As a writer, he wanted to know it first hand. He closed the door and windows and played the tapes very low on the recorder Yang lent him.

A stern voice: "Yang Hongshan, we, twelve of us, come from four departments on the district, county, and town levels. You made us wait for a day and half before seeing you. You really put on airs!"

Yang Hongshan's voice: "If I haven't been suspended from my duties to stand trial, I have to carry the responsibilities of daily operation as a manager. Is there any decision to relieve me of my job?"

A moderate voice: "No, no such decision. Comrade Hongshan, the

FLUID PERSONALITY

leadership has been very cautious about your problems. It is to avoid any error that a very... very discreet team is organized. We are not going to come to any rash conclusions."

A dignified voice: "Discreet doesn't mean you don't have serious problems. Look, these are letters of accusation against you, one, two, three, four, five, six, seven, eight, nine, ten! See? A stack half a foot thick!"

Yang Hongshan's voice: "Not many, just a few. I've heard that the District Party Secretary has got a big gunny sack full of them."

"You'd better have a more serious attitude."

Fan Chong could not distinguish the following voices, as the sentences followed one upon another.

"Confess how much tax altogether you've evaded in the last two years."

"Personally I never evaded any tax, not a cent."

"How about your conglomerate?"

"The only thing I know is that in 1985 we paid three times more in taxes than the previous year. As to tax evasion, I can't say."

"Can you guarantee that there has been no tax evasion?"

"I can't."

"According to evidence from various sources, your conglomerate has evaded more than twenty thousand yuan in taxes."

"I didn't handle tax matters myself. I don't know."

"How many times have you committed bribery?"

"What is bribery? I'm not clear about the definition. If gifts are bribery, I've given many of them, from the Party Secretary of the Province down to the accountant at the bank. Want me to list their names?"

"You have a very dishonest way about you!"

"Well, you don't want to pursue the problem of bribery?"

"Talk about your illicit relationships with women!"

"My wife has borne me three kids. I've nothing to confess other than that."

"Don't you have two female secretaries?"

"I don't have two female secretaries. The conglomerate employs them."

"What do they do?"

"One is responsible for letters, market information, and reception. For example, if twelve of you come, she's the one to arrange your visit. The other has the specific responsibility of reporting to me about absenteeism and job discipline."

"Are they under your charge directly?"

"I'm the manager. If they weren't, should they listen to you?"

"Have you done anything impermissible to them?"

"Both of them are here; you can ask them."

"It never works for people to have a pact to shield each other."

"That's only your accusation. I'll sue you if you bring a false charge against me."

"People have told us that you are a local despot."

"What? Why do you quit asking me about illicit relationships?"

"Don't you know it's a violation of law to beat and abuse another person?"

"Yes."

"Then why do you beat others?"

"They don't work hard, so I beat them."

Laughter.

The preceding waves of interrogation were repeated again and again. Some of the questions were easy- going, others were harsh. And Yang Hongshan flared up quite frequently.

After he finished the tapes, Fan Chong realized that the characters in his former stories had been too simple. Men were so complex in real life. Stories about Yang Hongshan had often appeared in the newspapers, and many leading cadres had praised him, but his resume consisted of tax evasion, bribery, womanizing, and investigations....

So the sky was not so clear.

The next day, Fan Chong got up very late. Because Yang Hongshan was under investigation, he could not visit him, so he went out for a walk in the streets by himself.

Originally there had been a small village here. Now it was expanded into a garden town. To the east there was an industrial area with a knit factory, an electrical parts factory, a popsicle factory, a building materials factory, and a truck repair shop. Chinese parasols and white poplars were planted around each of them; and in front of the gate of every factory were situated two huge flower beds. The green trees cast shadows; and the flowers were blooming. Everything was swept clean. Fan Chong saw a truck coming out of the repair shop. As it drove past him, the smell of gasoline floated in the air, but no dust rose from the clean streets.

He walked casually to the south of the village, and the first he saw was a chicken farm and then a dairy farm. He knew that every family here could drink fresh local milk. Adjacent was a vegetable field where two old men were working.

"Aren't you busy, grandpa!" Fan Chong greeted one of them.

The man stood up and smiled at him. "Yeah."

"How much can you make from one *mu*[4] of vegetables in a year?"

"I'm responsible for planting and harvesting only. There are others who take care of sales. They decide how much."

"What do you have here?"

"Tomatoes, peppers, eggplants...."

"Sure, these vegetable are all pretty much in season."

"The technician chooses the produce. He's done research on what'll be in season."

"How about your income?"

"Basic salary plus bonus. Both of us are fifth-level employees."

Fan Chong felt it was very strange that they designated responsibility even in vegetable fields. He guessed that it must be effective, so he said, "Isn't your Manager Yang smart!"

The man nodded, "Sure, he's the man. Without him, there wouldn't be today's Linhai. We do well because of him."

"Is he pretty tough?"

"Tough? You got to be like that. Spare the rod and spoil the child!" Ha, people here liked it.

Fan Chong explored further, "Would it be hard for a manager to avoid mistakes?"

The man blinked. "There are three hundred and sixty days in a year. Anyone can have troubles of one sort or another. Show me your ten fingers--

---

[4] About one sixth of an acre.

they're not all of the same length!"

"I've heard that the authorities have sent people to investigate him."

"That's common nowadays."

The other man, who had been working silently on the side, cut in. "It's because they saw that people in Linhai have fared well for a few days. Several years ago when we were dirt poor, we didn't see anyone come here to investigate anything."

"The authorities are not afraid of people getting rich, but they have to do it in an honest and lawful way," said Fan Chong.

"What's lawful?" the man sneered. "Look, aren't we making money by our honest labor? But could you depend on it at a time like this? Now tell me, can you accomplish anything without making some connections or going through backdoors?"

Fan Chong sighed, not without understanding, "If they arrest Yang Hongshan, would your conglomerate continue to do well?"

"Kill the leading wild goose, the fuck it would!"

Fan Chong did not know what to say.

III

Fan Chong was thinking hard the whole afternoon. He picked up his pen again and again, but dropped it each time. He was a writer with a sense of responsibility and would not put anything down on paper carelessly if he had not clarified it in his mind. He read through a set of information materials that Xiao Wang, the secretary, had given him: fifteen percent of the village's labor force was engaged in agriculture and husbandry; twenty-five percent in industry; eighteen percent in the fisheries; thirty-eight percent in service business; four percent in administration. The total output in 1985 was two point four times more than that of the last year. The average income per person reached one thousand eight hundred yuan.

The afternoon slipped away without his knowing it. Fan Chong glanced at his watch and got up to get some supper at a diner. But he saw four men standing at the door.

One of them greeted him, saying that they wanted to have a chat with him. He was picking his teeth with a match stick. Fan Chong consented.

The four men entered the room; two sat on the chairs while the other two sat on the bed. Fan Chong sat on a square stool.

"I heard you're a writer. It is an admirable job--the engineer of the human soul," he said, still picking his teeth, apparently because the stuff stuck in between his teeth was tough to get out.

"Oh," Fan Chong murmured modestly, then began to pay a little attention to the appearances of the four men. The one who kept picking his teeth was in his forties and had long hair, a straight nose, and a square mouth. He wore a white shirt and gray trousers--a cadre at first glance wherever he was. Another was a little younger, with a flat face and long hair hanging down to his ears. His body was wrapped tightly in his clothes, making him look like a fashionable man about town. The other two, both in their fifties, looked ordinary.

"We are team members on a special case under investigation," the tooth picker said, throwing away his stick and introducing everyone with a smile. "This is Lao Liu from the Office of the County Party Secretariat; this is Lao Zhang from the District Procuratorate; and this is Xiao Zhao from the County Tax Department."

Xiao Zhao from the County Tax Department added, "He is Assistant Director Wang from the County Party Organization Department."

"Wang Shujian," the tooth picker volunteered.

They had a casual after-dinner chat, talking about Zhu Mingying's[5] going

---

[5] A popular female singer in the mid 1980's.

to the US, and Huang Zhongying's[6] doing business....

"Hum, let them fool around! I really don't know what'll become of it all!" Assistant Director Wang said rather indignantly. "Speaking of their conglomerate of agriculture, industry, and trade, it looks hot, but deep down it's absurd!"

Fan Chong sensed that the topic was useful to him, so he quickly pursued it. "What do you think of Yang Hongshan?"

"This fellow," Assistant Director Wang waited a moment. "People have told us that it would be no injustice to tie and drag him out to be shot before prosecution! This man has committed every crime in the book, and nothing will quiet them down unless we punish him."

"But why is it that not long ago he was said to have made quite a contribution to the Reform?"

"All because of you writers who blew it out of proportion. Whether or not there was a grain of truth in it, you simply made it up!" Fan Chong blushed.

"You writers should be careful to see not only the makeup on the face, but also the rear ends of those people. And catch the tail there!"

Fan Chong discovered that Assistant Director Wang's voice was the stern one in the tapes, and so a sense of respect and fear rose in him.

They went on chatting for a while, and Fan Chong tried repeatedly to stand up. They realized that the writer had not had his supper yet, so they apologized and left.

After they had gone, Fan Chong looked out the window and saw that the diner had already closed. He remembered there was a small eating place selling dumplings, so he decided to go there.

On his way, he saw a man and woman coming out of a narrow lane in front of him. He recognized the man instantly, by the dark blue suit, as Yang

---

[6] A well-known female movie star who later becomes a writer.

Hongshan. The woman was slim and wore a dress with purple flowers. Judging from her figure, she should be Xiao Wang, his secretary. The two were deep in discussion, so they did not notice that there was some one behind them. As they walked they whispered into each other's ears.

"Don't say anything when they ask you."

"Yes."

"I'll send you away in a car at eight tonight."

"Yes."

"If they keep me late here, you make your own decisions."

"All right."

"After you get there, call me at the office at ten every night."

"Yes."

Yang Hongshan gave instructions; the secretary responded. As he was not far from them, Fan Chong heard everything clearly.

It was not right to eavesdrop, so Fan Chong deliberately slowed his steps. Who knows, he might step on a dry twig and make a noise.

Yang Hongshan turned his head and stared at Fan Chong strangely. Fan Chong felt embarrassed.

"You go now." Yang Hongshan waved to the secretary, and Xiao Wang left. But he waited on the roadside for Fan Chong to come over.

Fan Chong had to go up to Yang Hongshan.

"What are you doing, Comrade Lao Fan?"

"I'm going to have supper at that eating place at the outskirts of the village."

"Let's eat together at my place."

Fan Chong turned and looked back again at Yang Hongshan's red and hot eyes, feeling it would seem timid of him to avoid suspicion. So he forced himself to follow Yang Hongshan, thinking that you can't catch tiger cubs without entering the tiger's lair.

Yang Hongshan lived at the second in a row of newly-built, two-storied houses. Another five families lived in the same types of houses close by.

"They were built with the same design and at the same time," Yang Hongshan pointed to the other four. Entering the house, Fan Chong looked up and down. There were two large rooms facing south with a hallway in between, each about two hundred and seventy square feet. On the north side were a smaller room, a kitchen, and a bathroom. Add the upstairs and it had to be over nine hundred square feet.

"County Secretary Song came to my house and said my place was better than his," Yang Hongshan said with a little pride.

"Sure, sure," Fan Chong answered. "There are five in my family, and we have only two hundred eighty-eight square feet."

In the house were a woman in her fifties and a girl of twelve or thirteen.

Yang Hongshan made the introduction. "She is my wife, and this is my third daughter."

His wife seemed older than he was. And as she knew that her husband had brought some one along for supper, she hurried to prepare the meal.

Yang Hongshan opened a wine cupboard. "Look, Lao Fan, what do you want to drink?"

The cupboard was a feast for the eyes, full of various famous brands of wine and liquor, including, on the front row, two bottles of Maotai liquor.[7]

"A little Maotai?" Yang Hongshan reached for the bottle.

---

[7] A famous and expensive liquor.

"No, no, I can't drink liquor."

"Then have some beer." As he said this, Yang Hongshan pulled out a cardboard box from under the bed and took from it two bottles of beer.

Fan Chong walked around in the two rooms and noticed quite a few foreign-made products: A Sony television, a Sanyo refrigerator, a Toshiba washing machine, and, on the wall, an imported quartz clock.

A lot of good stuff. But Fan Chong felt that there was something missing here. What was it? Books! There were no bookshelves in the house.

--Liu Bang and Xiang Yu[8] never read books!

After reciting this line from a poem, Fan Chong's eyes were attracted to the several books on the head of the bed. So there were books after all! He went over and found that, scattered there were *Basics of Commerce, The Third Wave, Romance of Three Kingdoms, A Modern Translation of War Strategies and Tactics by Sun Zi, Questions and Answers about Basic Knowledge of Law*.

So he did read.

"Come here, Lao Fan!" The dishes were already on the table, so Fan Chong hurried to sit down.

His wife and daughter were eating in the kitchen, so their table-talk was more casual. "Lao Fan, I know at a glance that you're a kind person."

"How can you know that?"

"No one, good or bad, can escape my eyes! Look at my eyes."

Fan Chong avoided his menacing, bloodshot eyes, "I'd like to know how you judge what sort of people are good, and what sort of people are bad."

"It depends on the heart. If it's good, then he's a good man; if not, he's

---

[8] Liu's contemporary and a mighty general, who fought against Liu but finally failed.

bad."

After they finished the two bottles of beer, Yang Hongshan took out two more.

"Lao Yang, do you mind if I ask how you feel about yourself?"

"My value is fluctuating. In our village, most people listen to me, with only a few exceptions; in that investigating team, they've letters of accusation against me a half foot thick."

"But it's you I'm asking. What's your own judgment on yourself?"

"I've said that I won't accept it if they call me a no good, but I'd agree if they call me a villain."

The memory of Yang and his young secretary whispering to each other a moment ago reappeared before Fan Chong. He glanced to the kitchen, and did not have the nerve to be too blunt. "Lao Yang, we just couldn't afford to have a sex scandal."

"Ha, ha!" Yang faked a wild laugh, as a cover-up. Then he changed the subject. "Did the investigating team go to your room just now?"

"How do you know?"

"In a tiny place like this here, nothing escapes me."

Fan Chong could no longer hide. "There were four people there."

"What did they say?"

"They said--"

"I know it, you don't have to tell me. They must have said that I, Yang Hongshan, am wicked in every way! ... Well, some men are made for carrying the ball, and some only blow the whistle. I've been trying to carry the ball forward, but they keep blowing the whistle behind me."

"There has to be somebody to blow it, otherwise the game would be a mess."

"But whoever struggles for the ball gets the whistle; those who don't never get caught."

Fan Chong nodded his head repeatedly out of appreciation for this brilliant metaphor.

Four bottles of beer were now empty. Yang Hongshan looked at his watch and remarked, "Oh, I've got to attend to some business. We'll talk later."

The two went out the door.

Yang Hongshan left quickly in the darkness. Fan Chong felt he had had a little too much, so he took a walk toward the outskirts of the village.

The moon had risen; its soft light trembled on the fruit trees on the slopes. The trees seemed to be wrapped in a misty layer of silk, which added to his melancholy.

A whooshing sound came from the direction of the town. Fan Chong followed the sound and saw a black car driving down the South Street. Its lights were not turned on till it reached the town limits, then it sped away.

--"I'll send you away in a car at eight tonight." Fan Chong did not have to look at his watch to know what time it was. Their whisper sounded again in his ears.

IV

Several more days passed. Fan Chong did not think he could meet his editor's demand. On his trip to Linhai he failed to dig up a "positive figure." But he had become more interested in Yang Hongshan than ever before. He knew he was "the man."

What is "the man" like? Like Faust, he closed his eyes and looked into the darkness far away, and even recalled the poem:

With the new impression,
My organs of sense become confused.
I offer all my heart and liver,
Reveal, reveal thyself, and I'll die content.

Fan Chong's imagination flew even higher.

When Emperor Liu Bang of the Han Dynasty visited his home village at the peak of his power and might, a man pointed at him, saying, "Liu the Third, you still owe me money for the dog meat!"

Zhao Kuangying, who led the mutiny at the Chen Bridge, once cut off his sworn brother's head while intoxicated.

Zhu Hongwu, when he was a child cowherd, once stole a bull from his landlord, killed it and ate its meat.

Who among these emperors-on-horse, who had fought all their lives, hadn't made some mistakes? And still they all established their mighty reigns.

Yang Hongshan had said they were all villains, too.

Obviously, Yang Hongshan also belonged to the group of "villains" who rose from the bottom!

The word *Mang* in *Book of Songs*[9] meant farmers: "Stupid and deceitful farmers."

As Fan Chong traced his protagonist's roots, he heard someone laughing outside the window.

"Ha, ha, an instant victory!"

He looked out and saw approaching the sweaty faces of Assistant Director Wang Shujian and four cadres, who had left a couple of days ago.

---

[9] An anthology of folk songs and poems compiled about 3000 B.C., it is the first literary work in Chinese history.

"I know he can't get away from me!" Assistant Wang clenched his fists and waved them emphatically. "So she wouldn't confess even after you caught her?"

"She would say nothing," one of the four responded. "It wasn't until we gave the Hua Xing Trade Company the third degree that they spilled it out."

"How much altogether?"

"The conglomerate sold them electrical products worth thirty five thousand yuan and got fifteen tons of steel."

"All right. This alone is enough to make him a big fish!"

"It seems there's more still."

"Let that girl tell us more."

"She has said nothing, not even a word."

"She's a confidante of Yang Hongshan. She knows a lot of secrets. Don't let her go."

"We brought her back and handed her over to the town. She's already been isolated from others."

The five men passed by the window, and before Fan Chong there rose a patch of dark cloud.

What would the secretary say? Yang Hongshan, oh, Yang Hongshan, you've made your own bed! You bring disgrace and disaster on yourself when some of the shameful scandals are exposed. No one ever gave you the right to commit crime!

Fan Chong had originally planned to take a walk after supper outside the village. But now without knowing why, his feet led him toward Yang Hongshan's house. He argued stubbornly with himself all the way: I never went there to tip him off.

A few people were standing in front of Yang's door. Yang Hongshan was shouting loudly, "No way! Fire him, that's final! It's no use for anyone to plead for him!"

Fan Chong approached and saw a young man standing with his head lowered. A middle-aged man and a woman were also there. The man spoke to Yang Hongshan with an ingratiating smile, "Mr. Manager, be kind and have mercy on him this one time. He won't dare do it again."

The woman also smiled and pleaded, "He's too young to know it; he wouldn't dare next time."

Yang Hongshan waved his hand. "No! Do you think that I, Yang Hongshan, was in trouble, and my regulations wouldn't count? He's fired--that's final!

"How about a fine instead?" said the middle-aged man. "Just don't fire him."

"It has to be carried out strictly according to the factory regulations," Yang Hongshan waved his hand. "No more talk. Go away."

The middle-aged woman almost kneeled. "Brother," she said, "he's your own nephew. You can beat him and curse him too. But if you fire him, what is he going to do?"

"That remains to be seen. Right now I have to fire him!" Yang Hongshan's face looked as firm as a rock. The young man raised his head, his eyes flashing with disobedience. But when he met with Yang Hongshan's big bloodshot eyes, he lowered his head again timidly.

The middle-aged man, noticing that look in the young man's eyes, went up to him in anger and slapped his face. "You son of a bitch, kneel down before your uncle right now!"

His face red, the young man cried, "He can do whatever he wants! Don't be so cheap!"

"This is no longer the fashion," Yang Hongshan spread his arms out wide. "And it won't change my decision!"

"Fire me if you like!" the young man stamped his foot and turned to leave. "Today you fire me, tomorrow they'll fire you!"

"Fuck your mother!" Yang Hongshan cursed out loud. He wanted to run after him, but was stopped by the middle-aged man. The young man looked frightened and ran away.

Fan Chong watched on the side, thinking that Yang Hongshan really needed some self-restraint. He did not want to see Yang Hongshan beat and abuse others at a time like this, so he went over to mediate. "Lao Yang, what's happened?"

"He thinks my authority is now over, and won't do exactly as he is told!"

Well, the young man was a worker in the Truck Repair Shop. Because Yang Hongshan was under investigation, he went to see movies in the city without asking for leave. For two whole days, he did not come to work. His group supervisor criticized him, but he talked back. The secretary in charge of attendance reported it to Yang Hongshan, who at once gave the order to fire him. The middle aged couple were his parents, who had brought their son along moments ago to ask Yang Hongshan for mercy.

"Fuck his mother! Even if I, Yang Hongshan, fall, the regulations must not be changed!"

Yang Hongshan dragged Fan Chong into his house, placed a bottle of orange juice before him, opened it and put a straw in it.

With the lights off, the room seemed a little mysterious.

Yang Hongshan sat down in the sofa across from him.

"Haven't seen you for three days," said Yang Hongshan quietly.

"Yes. Why haven't you sent me the tapes?" asked Fan Chong.

"There's no one to do the recording," Yang Hongshan replied not without regret. "My secretary got into trouble."

Fan Chong's heart gave a start; he was about to say something but held back.

"She was detained by somebody and was kept in the town government."

Fan Chong tried to sound him out. "What happened?"

"I continue to violate the law!" Yang Hongshan lit a cigarette in the dark. "I'm afraid that they'd put me under house arrest and sever all my connections, and that will shut down my factories! Many of my businesses are run through the Hua Xing Trade Company. I shipped them thirty five thousand yuan of electrical products to be sold there, and they bought fifteen tons of steel for me. The steel was all purchased at the market price; I also paid an additional eighty yuan service charge per ton."

"Why do you have to pay such a high price?"

"If I don't, where am going to get it? Without the steel, how can my building materials factory operate?"

"But if they hunt down and seize--"

"No use for trying. I have it shipped here overnight. Besides, the money has already been sent out through the bank."

"What if they keep on pursuing this?"

"Let them! Investigating into this and that will cost them several months, and in the meantime my factory can operate as usual."

He was fighting for a way out in between, making full use of the time left.

"My young secretary is really something; she got everything done in one day after arriving there!" Yang Hongshan seemed to be very proud. But his voice suddenly became stern. "Damn! There are some who live off me while secretly helping others. Somebody listened in on her call to me at ten that night and informed the investigation team of it. Now everything is goddamned out in the open!"

Fan Chong realized why the four men left so suddenly.

"What have you heard from the team in the guesthouse?"

Fan Chong hesitated at first, but after being questioned repeatedly about this and that, he told him all he had heard and seen in the past few days.

Yang Hongshan snorted. "The lice don't make you itch as much when there are a lot of them!"

"Isn't it true that your conglomerate has a lot of problems?"

"All the raw materials for my factories are bought through illegal connections. Every purchase has a hole of thousands of yuan if they look into it."

"That'll be disastrous!"

"Is it my personal problem? Last time, when County Secretary Song came, I raised the problem to him directly. I told him if he wanted me to do it, I had to buy materials illegally. Once I got them, I could start producing and paying taxes, and the total output of the county would increase. If he said it was against law, I'd stop immediately, and he could reduce the risk of being implicated."

"What did he say?"

"Nothing. He just kept repeating,'drink, let's drink'."

"What does that mean?"

"What a bookworm you are! What else could he say or do?"

In China, people have a tacit understanding of so many things!

"If that's so, aren't you afraid of their investigation?"

"It's not that I'm not afraid. They can always catch me if they really want to. Who in the world hasn't got a little tail?"

The phrase reminded Fan Chong of Assistant Director Wang's admonition, "Catch the tail!"

FLUID PERSONALITY

"They came here to look into financial matters, but they'll most likely change their direction," said Fan Chong. Xiao Wang, the secretary, appeared suddenly before him and he added unwittingly, "Sex scandals are a most effective way to bring somebody down."

"Sure." Yang Hongshan would say nothing else.

It was already very dark in the house. Fan Chong could no longer see clearly the pair of bloodshot eyes, so he began to grow less scrupulous. "Lao Yang, about woman...."

"Yes, yes." He answered with only one word.

As they were in the darkness, Fan Chong continued to speak with the tone of an intimate friend. "If there is a woman," he said. "You can't wrap fire in paper."

"She'll never talk if I don't," Yang Hongshan said with curt finality.

Fan Chong remembered what the man in the team said: "She said nothing, not even a word."

"It was something beyond control," Yang Hongshan muttered in the dark. "My wife was recuperating after giving birth that year. It so happened there was someone who liked me."

Fan Chong was suspicious. His wife giving birth that year? His youngest child was already thirteen, and Xiao Wang, the secretary should be....

As Fan Chong calculated the age, Yang Hongshan changed the topic. "I've been thinking these days. Right now the authorities are looking for cases of financial corruption; they probably want to catch some people of reputation. If they pick on me, I have to go down."

A long silence.

Yang Hongshan continued. "But there's nothing wrong with the road to riches. Even if I, Yang Hongshan, fall, the road must not be blocked."

Fan Chong agreed.

"You have to write an article on us, putting in a good word for our conglomerate. Whatever happens, we must not allow them to destroy this conglomerate."

The product of his enterprise, and of how much sweat of his brow! Fan Chong nodded assent.

"A party needs discipline, and a country has its constitution. If I'm really sentenced to two or three years of imprisonment, I'll go and stay there. But when I'm out, I'll do it again; I'll still do it exactly in my own way!"

Fan Chong recalled a historical research which indicated that Chinese emperors of various dynasties were born north of the Changjiang River because people in the north had always been bolder and tougher. They dared to do things and face the responsibility. There had been more top scholars form the south, but they never succeeded in any uprising in spite of years of effort.

V

The land should have been ploughed, seeded, and harvested long ago, but thirty years had passed and it remained frozen.

All of a sudden there came the wind of spring. The land began to thaw, and the first to rush to it were the hungry and thirsty farmers. There was no road on the barren land, and the fertile soil was one vast expanse of mud. They struggled forward with one foot shallow and another deep in mud, jostling each other in the crowd. Falling down and climbing back up, and stumbling on one step after another, they finally broke a path.

Without a road sign to direct them or somebody shouting "left, right" or "quick march," those who were smart at choosing their own way got ahead.

"To say what you may not like, our Town of Linhai has fared well on nothing but speculation," Yang Hongshan had briefed Fan Chong on his own business experiences. "Abroad they call it opportunity, to be good at grasping the opportunity."

"It's very simple. A couple of years ago, electrical sockets were sold out in many big cities because large government-owned factories had ceased to manufacture them as they brought little profit. I thought the technique was simple, so I found a technician from the Northeast along with two experienced workers. All the apprentices were elementary school graduates from our village who had failed the middle school entrance examination. After only three months, my small factory began to market our product. I myself was the salesman. Within a year, we made tens of thousands of yuan! Now tell me who took advantage of whom? We did it to the big state-owned factories. We did what they wouldn't!

"From those thousands I made more. As the farmer got rich, they all wanted to build their houses. So I tried to buy steel through connections, and started a factory for building materials. And we organized strong laborers into a construction team. By doing this we made tens of thousands a year more!

"Things became easier when you had money in hand. Nobody could figure out why the government-owned restaurant in the county seat was in the red every year. I told them to let me take over and I'd pay them eight thousand a year! Well, what happened after I got it? After the eight thousand I gave them, there was twelve thousand left! It's like making the rope with borrowed hemp--I didn't spend one cent!

"To the restaurant, I added a hotel. As you've seen it's a factory with no chimneys. It has been making more money than the restaurant."

"There are more than enough opportunities. The question is who can seize and take good advantage of them!"

There was no doubt that Yang Hongshan held fast to these opportunities and he had been taking full advantage of them. His business snowballed. The village of Linhai had become the Town of Linhai; Yang Hongshan had become Manager Yang, coming and going in a car and hiring two young female secretaries.

With all that came a lot of accusations. And it was said that you could never do wrong to drag Yang Hongshan out and shoot him before he was even tried.

In addition, Yang Hongshan himself believed that he had made some mistakes.

"I think it's all right to take advantage of those good-for-nothings and idlers," he said, "But you can't eat off the country--for example, tax evasion. It hurts the nation, and one should be punished for it."

Hearing this, Fan Chong felt that the man did not lack a civic conscience. But Yang Hongshan explained from another perspective:

"A man mustn't drink his well dry. Anyway, the prosperity of Linhai depends on the Party's policies. If we don't have the open policy to begin the Reform, there's nothing anyone can do, not to mention myself. I was here ten years ago. What happened? I nearly went begging for food with a beggar's stick! Where had my abilities gone? It is the Party's policy that sets me free. Don't you ever smear this policy. If you evade taxes, those who oppose the policy would say that it doesn't work, that we have to turn back. And that means we'd lose everything!"

He had put himself in the same boat with the Reform.

"If they really punish me as an example and sentence me on certain charges to protect the authority of the policy, I'd accept it."

Fan Chong, the writer, now had a clearer view of his protagonist. He was still a farmer, but vastly different from those during the times of the Mutual Aid Group,[10] or the Cooperative,[11] or the Great Leap Forward,[12] when they boasted they could produce "five tons of grain per *mu*." It was no coincidence that he now wore a western suit. It was the new era that put him in it. China in the 1980's had produced a new type of farmer like him. They toiled like beasts of burden on the thawed land; breathing heavily, they were

---

[10] A form of collective farming in the rural areas organized in the early 1950's.

[11] A more centralized form of collective farming from 1955-1958.

[12] A mass movement from 1958-1959, which brought disasters to the Chinese economy.

FLUID PERSONALITY

not at all bothered by the mud on their wet clothes. However they were not fully prepared for modern civilization, and that was why Yang Hongshan lacked cultivation and was rude and vulgar in speech. He was probably involved in some sex scandals, too.

While the writer was lost in thought, there was a buzzing noise outside the window.

It was a girl's voice, "Don't you keep on saying this and that. Let's go to the hospital right now for the check! If I'm not a virgin, sentence me right there! If I am, I'll sue you for slander!"

Then a man's voice-- "It's what *You* yourself said!"

"I'll write it down with my signature for you."

"Don't do this, don't. Things will be cleared up," said another man.

"No way!" cried the girl. "You took me back and kept me in the town government. It is a violation of personal freedom. I'll sue you for sure!"

Fan Chong stood up immediately. Seeing several people surrounding the door of the room across from his, he squeezed his way in.

The two who had been quarreling were Assistant Director Wang of the Organization Department of the Party Secretariat and secretary Xiao Wang in the purple dress.

The Assistant Director pressed contemptuously, "You want to sue, whom could you sue?"

"You! You're the one behind all this!"

The Assistant Director pulled a long face, "Don't put on an act. You must confess everything honestly!"

"What do I have to confess!" The secretary would not hear of it. "Who's given you the right?"

"The people have given me the right!" Assistant Director Wang banged the table. "The Party has given me the right! You're not going to defy us, are you?"

"The Party gives you no right to spread rumors and bully the people!" She reached out to grab his chest, "Come on, let's go to the hospital and then to the court!"

Two others from the team were busy trying to quiet her down. "No, no," they pleaded. "let's talk, let's talk it over first."

But the female secretary would not listen. "It won't do. 'The Gang of Four' isn't in power anymore!"

Assistant Director Wang shouted back, stern in voice and countenance, "My, my, aren't you acting like one of the Red Guards!"

Each thought the other was acting like a Cultural Revolution radical.

A crowd of people had gathered there, making comments and taking sides. It was not till a noisy half hour had passed that the girl was finally persuaded to leave.

Fan Chong followed the spectators out, listening to their chitchat.

"He's slandering her--it's like dumping a chamber pot over her head!"

"There's no smoke without a fire. The authorities must have got something."

"To catch a thief, you got to have his loot; to catch the adulterers, you've got to surprise them both together. What does he have in hand?"

"The girl wants to have a checkup in the hospital to prove she's still a virgin!"

"Could it be done?"

"Yes, of course, the hymen."

"Check it out and sue him!"

"That's right. The girl has a fiancee. It'd destroy her reputation."

"Well, it's hard to say."

"A secretary is a piece of meat hanging over somebody's mouth. He'll lick it for sure if he doesn't eat it."

"Eating is not the same as licking."

And so on and so forth.

Two days later, the female secretary really went to have a health check in the hospital, and she took her fiancee along. The result showed the hymen intact. She filed a lawsuit in the county court, and completed her marriage registration in the town hall. A week later, secretary Xiao Wang got married.

On the wedding day, they invited fifty to sixty people for the marriage banquet in the guesthouse. The firecrackers alone blasted for a full five minutes, and the debris piled up half a foot thick downstairs where the investigation team was staying on the 2nd floor.

The debris half a foot thick did not drive away Assistant Director Wang's smile; he remained firm, coming and going with his chest thrust out. Obviously he had a ready plan hidden in there.

For a few days, Yang Hongshan seemed to be avoiding Fan Chong. Twice he failed to greet him when they met. When Fan Chong picked up his pen, he saw Yang Hongshan waving to him. It was time to write.

Fan Chong finished his story after three days of non-stop writing. He was planning to leave the next day. Before he left, he wanted to say goodbye to Yang Hongshan and give him back the recorder and the two tapes he had entrusted to him.

He crossed the street and found the door of Yang Hongshan's house. It was still the two-storied building, with the window panes scrubbed clean and flashing here and there in the sun. The flowers in full bloom competed for his attention; a few butterflies wove their way among them. It did not look as if misfortune had struck.

"Is Lao Yang home?" Fan Chong inquired outside the door.

"He's not," said Yang Hongshan's wife, coming out from the house.

"Isn't it true," stammered Fan Chong, "that he was released from his duty?"

"He won't stop anyway. He said if he did, the factories would suffer losses."

"Where's he now?"

"I'm not sure." Seeing that Fan Chong was about to leave, she hurried a few steps forward and grabbed him by the arm, "Comrade Fan, I want to ask you a favor."

"What is it?"

"Talk to Lao Yang and persuade him to quit."

"To quit?"

"We have enough to live on. Let's have some quiet and die in peace." Her eyes had lost their brightness, and there was a little muddy tear in each corner.

Fan Chong did not know what to say, so he agreed offhandedly. "All right, I'll try."

After he had taken a few steps, she followed over and whispered, "Comrade Fan, please don't believe those rumors. They are all made up on purpose to give Lao Yang a bad name." She looked around and continued, "All his life, he had only one woman outside the house. It happened when I was giving birth to San Ni, our third child. And he did not hide it from me. Besides this, he has never done anything wrong."

She knew about it, and she had excused him. Looking at the old woman's sincere eyes, Fan Chong was not sure whether it was weakness in her or kindness.

Two cars pulled off the highway and stopped in front of Yang Hongshan's house. Fan Chong's heart sank. He turned back to look at Yang's wife, whose face was full of apprehension.

Five people got out. One of them shouted, "Is Lao Yang home? Yang Hongshan, Yang Hongshan!"

His wife rubbed her hands on her clothes uneasily, her mouth trembled, uncertain how to respond.

Fan Chong noticed that there was something strange about all this, but he did not see anyone in police uniform, so he offered to answer, "Yang Hongshan is not home."

"Is he in the office?"

"I don't know."

"Go and find him quickly!"

From his tone of voice, the man seemed rather excited. Fan Chong guessed that it might not be an impending disaster for Yang Hongshan, so he said at once, "Yes, yes, I'll go and find him." And he went away with great speed.

When he found Yang Hongshan and accompanied him into his house, the five men were already drinking tea under the ceiling fan.

"Yang Hongshan, where have you been?" asked the one who had shouted a moment before.

"I'm under investigation, and that's where I was!" Yang Hongshan said with a long face.

Fan Chong smiled secretly behind the door. He found Yang in the Truck Repair Shop.

"Oh--" the man with the loud voice was a little embarrassed. "That is going to be over soon. Come, let me introduce to you Director Xu, member of the Provincial Party Standing Committee. This is Director Wang in charge of the Provincial Party Office; this is the Deputy Party Secretary of the District, and you know him, Director Qiu of the County Party Organization Department."

They shook hands in turn.

Fan Chong found a chair behind the door and sat down, trying to see what was really going to happen.

Yang Hongshan stood in the middle of the room for a little while, then hurried over to pick up the phone on the tea table. "Get me the office. Hello, is that you, Secretary Wang?" Then he lowered his voice. "Tell the guesthouse to prepare a lunch," he said. "On me. What? They are my private quests, eight in all." He put down the phone and asked the man who had talked to him, "Secretary Song," he said. "please go ahead with what you have to say."

Secretary Song asked Yang Hongshan to sit down and said with a smile, "Lao Yang, some of the policies have not been clearly defined at present. Director Xu is very much concerned about your conglomerate. He was attending a meeting in the district and heard that you were under investigation, so he's come specially to see you."

"Oh." Yang Hongshan nodded.

Secretary Song smiled at Director Xu. "Mr. Director, please go ahead."

Director Xu began, "First of all, we need to affirm that it is the Party's decision, and therefore legitimate, for Comrade Wang Shujian and the others to come to conduct the investigation here."

"Yes," Yang Hongshan nodded again.

Then Director Xu clarified the situation: in the first place, he stressed the significance of investigating allegations in financial and economic matters. Then he explained that there was no conflict between investigations and the Reform; what was more, they gave momentum to the Reform. He went on affirming the achievements of the agriculture-industry-trade conglomerate of the Town of Linhai, and at the same time he pointed out quite a few problems in its operations. Fan Chong, hidden behind the door, was very much surprised that this Director Xu knew the situation in Linhai like the back of his hand. And he spoke both clearly and logically.

At last Director Xu concluded, "We will give full credit to what you've achieved in the Reform, and we will protect your zeal and enthusiasm. As to those problems, most of them are what have been overlooked in the progress. We will discriminate among them and find the proper solutions. We will not keep picking on you."

"Yes, yes," several of them expressed approval and added, "We mustn't discourage the enthusiasm of the activists in the Reform."

"Errors are unavoidable if you do your job. Those who don't will never make any mistake. But where are the Four Modernizations supposed to come from if no one works? So we prefer those who are willing to work hard, even if they do make some mistakes. But of course, it would be better not to make any at all."

It was all very dialectical, and encouraging, too.

"Yang Hongshan, you're a hero!" Director Xu did not mean to flatter him. "Your contribution lies in finding a new way for the farmers to get rich together."

"Yes, yes!" the others joined in again.

"Here you have basically commercialized your products!"

"It is true that your conglomerate has gained a lot of experiences."

"Your experience in increasing job efficiency and improving personnel management is very impressive." Then the speaker turned to the others, "He is the general manager, and there are no departments or offices under him. The leaders of every unit report directly to him, so he can see everything as clearly as through a bowl of water. He employs the hard-working and fire the lazy. Our government-owned agencies and businesses are unable to do this."

"There's another thing that I think is excellent. Both of the secretaries are women. That's an advancement from abroad. It's said a young female secretary makes an office come to life."

"Because it'll make things easier in our country. With a young girl there, things are different."

"Ha, ha, ha...."

Yang Hongshan had become a rose.

Like the mercury in a thermometer, his personality shot straight up. And according to this measurement, Yang Hongshan was probably a positive figure. But without knowing why, Fan Chong somehow felt uneasy all over. He stole a look at Yang Hongshan, who narrowed his eyes a little like he was drunk.

Secretary Song was in a happy mood. "Why, isn't there a writer here who came to get his story? Tell him to write a good one!"

Yang Hongshan looked behind the door and pointed, "It's him."

"Ah--" The eyes of the five men fixed on Fan Chong, which forced him to stand up.

"Comrade Writer!" Secretary Song came over and shook his hand, "I'm sorry! It's your responsibility as a writer to help improve our job of publicizing. Welcome, welcome!"

Fan Chong could do no better than making a series of gurgling sounds.

Yang Hongshan did not want Fan Chong to say anything; he looked at his watch and suggested, "Oh, it's late, and time to eat. Please, every leading comrade here, please have a little something."

Director Xu declined at once. "No, no. We'll go back to eat, we'll go back to eat."

"It'll be too late to go back," Yang Hongshan pressed on. "I've already told the guesthouse to prepare it for us."

But Director Xu remained firm, "We have to set an example. We just can't criticize you and wine and dine with you at the same time."

"You leaders come to see me, and it shows you think well of me. Now this is just a small token of my regards, and it won't cost the company a cent. We can't cook, otherwise we'll eat here in my little house." Yang Hongshan was quite sincere, and he specially glanced at Secretary Song.

"Director Xu," replied Secretary Song, "how about having lunch here? If not, Lao Yang would become suspicious of our opinions about him again."

Reluctantly, the director agreed.

The team of men walked in front, followed by the two cars. There were eyes looking at them from every house. As they approached the guesthouse, Fan Chong saw Assistant Director Wang Shujian standing on the porch of the second floor. He stood sideways, his grave and dignified face expressing his worry for the welfare of the country and people.

WHEN I THINK OF YOU AT NIGHT, THERE IS NOTHING I CAN DO

FIVE SCENES AT CAVE DWELLING OF WEN FAMILIES

Chao Naiqian

BROTHER-IN-LAW

Early in the morning a donkey is braying outside the courtyard. Heidan says, "Damn, Brother-in-Law's come for you." A woman says, "Don't let him in till I put on my pants." Heidan says, "Damn, it'll be the same anyway." The woman blushes suddenly and says, "Or you can tell Brother-in-Law I couldn't go because I'm not well. Isn't it true that my period has come?" Heidan says, "It won't do. We Chinese never go back on our word."

Heidan comes out of the courtyard to greet his brother-in-law who then ties the donkey to the frame of the front gate. Heidan shouts into the cave, "Go and get a chicken for Brother-in-Law. I'll fetch a bottle of wine from the store at the commune."

"Brother," the Brother-in-Law says to Heidan. "I've brought a bottle of wine with me. How could I drink yours every time?"

"Damn, no need to say yours and mine between us."

Heidan's wife leaves the courtyard, lowering her head and avoiding looking at either of them. She is going to the chicken coop.

"No, no. A bull in our village died from a fall at night," Brother-in-Law calls to Heidan's wife. "I went to the house of the leader of the production team to borrow a donkey, and the bastard's woman was cooking the beef." He takes down a bag hung around the donkey's neck. "Here it is. Cook it some more if it's not done."

Heidan's wife takes the bag with lowered head and enters the cave, her eyes avoiding both of them.

While drinking, Heidan says to his Brother-in-Law, "It comes these days, how about waiting till it's over?"

"All right."

"But it's certain they'll deduct your workpoints for borrowing the donkey. What if you go anyway? Only wait till she's all right."

"Yes."

"Bring her back next month, I can't borrow a donkey here."

"Okay."

After finishing the wine Heidan says to his wife, "Put on some clean clothes. Don't let others laugh at us."

"No. I'll buy her a jacket and pants when we pass the commune."

Heidan sees his woman and Brother-in-Law off. They pass ravines and ridges in single file. His Brother-in-Law says, "Please go back. We'll go up the mountain." Heidan says, "Go up the mountain, I'll go back." After that he turns, hesitating. His Brother-in-Law waves his huge fist and strikes the donkey's behind, and its hooves strike out smashing, clumping sounds.

Damn. Go, go away. He asks for a thousand yuan less, like giving me a daughter for free. Damn, go, go away. Anyway only a month every year. Chinese never go back on their word. Heidan thinks this on his way back.

He looks around and sees his woman's turnip-like legs hanging down from the donkey's belly, swinging back and forth, back and forth.

Heidan's heart is also swinging back and forth, back and forth.

WOMAN

Weng Hai has finally got a wife, for which the villagers are quite glad. But according to those who listen outside on the wedding night, the woman refuses to let him do it. She has tied her red trouser strip into a dead knot and will not let it be untied. She does nothing but cry the whole night long.

Later it is said that not only does Weng Hai's woman refuse to take off her pants for Weng Hai, she will not go to work in the fields. When Weng Hai comes home, she doesn't even cook for him. She is still crying, crying for the whole day.

Still later the whole village is in uproar. "She could refuse to take off her pants at night, but it won't do not to go to work or cook meals. That is something she can never be allowed."

"Our forefathers have never set this rule in the Cave Dwellings of the Weng Families," they advise Weng Hai.

"What should I do?"

"Beat her till she stops it."

"Can I?"

"Ask your mom," says a man whose face is creased like a ploughed but unraked slope, and whose chin has a beard like the grass on a grave which has been half-gnawed by a goat.

Weng Hai asks his mom, who says, "Trees need thrashing to grow straight. All women are like that."

Weng Hai listens to his mom and beats his woman hard after he comes home. The woman's face is all black and blue.

According to those who listen outside that night, this works. Weng Hai does it once he is on top of the woman and says, "Fuck your mom, you think I'm fucking you? I'm fucking the two thousand yuan. Fuck your mom, you think I'm fucking you? I'm fucking the two thousand yuan."

"Weng Hai's father did the same to his mom that year," someone says.

Later Weng Hai's woman cooks meals for him.

Still later Weng Hai's woman follows him in a distance to the fields with a hoe on her shoulder.

"Hey, hey, black and blue."

"Hey, hey, black and blue."

The women in the fields twist their mouths, blink their eyes, and shake their heads.

LENG ER HAS GONE MAD

People do not know why Leng Er, who has been all right recently, goes crazy again, nor do they understand why he would suddenly become all right after he went mad for some time.

Leng Er's father has had a long history of asthma. It did not go away after he tried the herbs, so he wants to ask for some ephedrine from Leng Da, his elder son who works in the mine. His wife says, "Go there! He hasn't sent a cent for half a year. And bring back some cement bags." With much trouble Leng Er's father climbs up the cart sent to the mine to carry back the manure. And Leng Er goes mad the next day exactly like the last time, crying all day, "Kill him... kill him."

Lying on his back on the *Kang*,[1] Leng Er bangs on it with his big soiled palms like threshing harvested grain with a beater on the drying ground. After he gets tired, he gores the Kang with the back of his head and sits up

---

[1] A large bed for all the family, constructed with dirtbricks and used in rural areas of north and west China. It can be heated by burning a fire inside it.

straight, still crying "Kill him, kill him." When he gets tired of crying, he resumes banging. Leng Er's mother does not dare to leave him alone, so she stays with him.

Everything will be over if he really kills someone. He is possessed by a demon if he really kills. Standing by the stove, his mother is lost in thought. She thinks for a little while, then wipes her eyes with the front of her garment.

Leng Er often says, "Damn poor, can't even afford to have steamed bread made of naked oat flour. Always mixed with sweet potato." His mother says, "We want to save money for you." "Fuck, for how many years can you save two thousand yuan by not having oat bread!"

This time Leng Er's mother makes naked oat bread for him. Leng Er refuses to eat; he only cries "Kill him" and bangs on the Kang so hard that the dry dirt cover reveals itself through the reed mat mended with the cement bags.

The villagers suggest that if the barefoot doctor can't help, why not see a witch doctor. Leng Er's mother shakes her head; she knows none of them can offer any help. They did not cure her son last time.

Everything will be over if he really kills. He must be possessed by a demon if he really kills, Leng Er's mother thinks.

But the villagers do not remember which morning it was exactly that they ceased to hear Leng Er's cries and bangings.

Leng Er is sleeping on the head of the Kang, snoring like a pig.

"Is he all right?" someone asks Leng Er's mother.

"Yes."

"How?"

"He's all right."

Leng Er's mother leaves in a hurry.

Leng Er's father comes back on the cart for manure and says that their daughter-in-law would not give him money but only some cement bags and ephedrine. Leng Er's mother does not mention to him that Leng Er is mad; nor did she last time. Leng Er's father is not worried about how torn the mat on the Kang was originally, nor how it looks now. His only concern is the ephedrine. He says that swallowing two pills will satisfy his craving.

Leng Er's mother smashes the boiled sweet potatoes into paste, and with it Leng Er glues the soaked cement bags onto the torn mat.

Anyway it's better than killing somebody; anyway it's better than being possessed by a demon. Leng Er's mother, standing by the stove and thinking, watches Leng Er glue the mat on the Kang. She thinks for a while, then wipes her eyes with the front of her garment. She thinks for a while, then wipes her eyes with the front of her garment.

IN THE HAY STACK

Everything under the sky is silent. Granny Moon shines on the drying ground, making it bright and white. He and she make a nest in the haystack for themselves on the side facing the moon.

"You go in."

"You go in."

"Or let's go in together."

They climb into the nest together and topple it. The naked oats falls down, burying both him and her.

He stretches his brawny arms and props it up. "Never mind, it's good here," she says, cuddling in his arms. "Brother Chou, you sure do hate me."

"I don't hate you. The coal miners have more money than I do."

"I won't spend it; I'll save it secretly for you to marry a girl."

"I don't want it."

"I'll save it."

"I don't want it."

"I want, I want to."

He stops, hearing she is about to cry.

"Brother Chou," she says after a long time.

"What?"

"Brother Chou, kiss me once."

"Don't."

"Yes."

"I'm not in the mood."

"I want it."

Knowing she is going to cry again, he bends down his head and kisses her face. It is light and soft.

"No, it's here," she says with a pout. He kisses her lips. They are cold and wet.

"How does it taste?"

"Like naked oats."

"No, no. Want to try again?" She pulls down his head.

"Still like naked oats," he says after thinking for a little while.

"Nonsense, I have just had some rock candy specially. Try once more."

She pulls down his head again.

"Rock candy, rock candy," he hurries to say.

For a second time none of them say a word for a long while.

"Brother Chou."

"Well?"

"Or let's do that."

"No, no. There is Granny Moon outside, we can't do it. Girls at the Cave Dwelling of Weng Families shouldn't do this."

"Then wait till I come back."

"Yeah."

Again no one says anything for a long time. They hear only Granny Moon's footsteps and sighs outside.

"Brother Chou."

"What?"

"It is luck."

"Yes."

"We two have bad luck."

"Mine is bad; yours is good."

"Bad."

"Good."

"Bad."

"Good."

"Just bad."

He hears that she is really crying, and he himself is shedding teardrops that drip, pitley-patley, on her face.

GRANDPA GUOKOU

The villagers carry Grandpa Guokou back from the wild graveyard again.

Guokou is from another province and has no relative in the village. But everyone in the village calls him Grandpa Guokou. Every time he gets drunk, he would become everyone's grandpa, regardless of seniority in the clan. It is strange that the villagers really call him Grandpa anyway.

Guokou is the only one in the village who wants to drink every day and can afford it. His younger brother, Penkou, is a big shot in the province, and mails him twenty or thirty yuan each month, all of which he spends in drinking.

Guokou does not need any dish to go with his liquor, but he prefers it to be warm. His method of warming it is unique. He makes a pocket in the crotch of his trousers and simply inserts his liquor bottle there. After a couple of sips, it goes there. After a couple of sips, it goes there.

Guokou offers his liquor to others too, "Come, have a damn mouthful for Grandpa." He draws a deep breath as he says so, creating a hollow in his creased belly. Then his hand reaches into the crotch and takes out the bottle, which is warm. It has the smell of liquor, and another smell as well. Some dislike it and refuse the offer; others don't mind and hold the bottle high and swallow it as if they are blowing a trumpet. Guokou narrows his eyes into a smile and watches them drink with tipped head. His mouth closes and opens in turn as if the liquor is pouring down his own throat.

Once Grandpa Guokou gets pretty drunk, he would wobble to the wild graveyard, always humming the same lines from a folk song:

> When I think of you during the day,
> I climb over the wall;
> When I think of you at night,
> There's nothing I can do.

After he reaches the graveyard, he has a sound sleep on a big piece of rock and stretches out his hands and feet. And if it is not cold, he takes off all his clothes, despite ants and bugs crawling over him.

"Go! Carry your Grandpa Guokou back from the wild graveyard. Or he'll catch cold," the elders say to the young. So they would call out for three or five of them to go there.

People would tease Grandpa Guokou when he is a little sober, "Grandpa Guokou, do a tiger jump for us." He says, "I'm too old to jump now." "No, you're not old." They pull some grass and twist it into a rope, and Guokou sticks out his bottom and hold the rope in between. Then he bends down and jumps forward again and again. The grass rope, which does not fall, knocks against the bottle loosely hung from his crotch, and it makes everyone roar with laughter.

The villagers carry Grandpa Guokou back again. But after uttering one sentence, "Bury me in Widow San's grave," he no longer wakes up.

No one has expected him to say something like this. It strikes the villagers dumb.

ABORTION

Li Songjing

I.

Morning light creeps in through gaps in the curtain, shedding a few golden bars that tremble softly upon my feet, thighs, and breasts.

It is already seven; I have to get up. Moving my body makes me feel sour and lazy, and as I feel about, I know he has left. Humph, a big and strong man patrolling on a tiny Star motorbike is like raping a young girl--how pathetic. Traffic police are nothing but wanderers in police uniforms--my mocking often drives him to wail pitifully.

One, two, three, I struggle to sit up. My calves ache, and the joints of my lumbar vertebrae crack. I cannot blame him for these. They are the results of my demanding job. Ever since the fund of the public health care was cut down, the number of patients has decreased in all departments except for that of Gynecology and Obstetrics, which enjoys a stable market and brisk business. Day after day and year after year, the population that I have aborted is big enough to fill a few of Napoleon's divisions. Standing by the operating table seven or eight hours every day makes the veins in my calves curve and expand silently.

I put my clothes on, wash, and eat, then carrying my lunch box, I go to work.

As soon as I walk through the front gate of the clinic, Xiao Douzhou comes up to me and whispers in my ear, "Private section in the Tianxiang Restaurant at noon." I nod quietly, take the lunch box from my handbag, and go straight into the lab. I open the refrigerator, put the box in, which ordinarily holds my lunch. Once again a meal saved, I can't help showing a trace of satisfaction on my face.

"Doctor Xie, we have arranged six abortions in the morning."

Xiao Ru, the midwife, informs me of the amount of work for the morning once I step into the door of the department.

I frown and tell her, "Leave one for the afternoon. We have to stop a bit earlier at noon."

Xiao Ru nods to show she understands why.

I make myself a cup of jasmine tea, open the drawer, and take out a cigarette. I light it and begin to smoke. When I am half done, I smother it. As I am changing into my uniform, I tell Xiao Ru to call them in.

A young girl opens the door and enters, pretending to be nonchalant and experienced. Xiao Ru leads her into the operating room next door. After I finish changing, I go in too. While watching the girl take off her clothes, I ask indifferently, "Your age?"

"Twenty four." The girl tries hard to appear calm.

I catch Xiao Ru's eye.

"Get on the table!" I shout suddenly. The girl trembles in a shock, almost collapsing onto the cement floor.

"Relax, relax," says Xiao Ru malignantly, supporting her with her hands

The girl climbs up on the table, still trembling, then she opens her legs, looking like a lamb waiting to be slaughtered.

I begin to work. Once I open her womb, I ask again, "Why don't you keep your first baby?"

"We have no place to live after we got married..." I can hear the pumping sound from the arteries behind her ears.

"But your physiological development doesn't seem like that of a twenty four year old."

"..."

I slap her white and tender belly a couple of times with the rubber vacuum pipe, "Young girl, tell the truth now, where did you get your abortion certificate?"

The girl's face becomes as red as red paint. She turns her head aside and begins to sob.

Xiao Ru and I look at each other and smile. We have seen too many pregnancies before, outside, and without marriage, along with those of servicemen's wives. Having worked in the Department of Gynecology and Obstetrics for so long, we can see right through weather-beaten widows, not to mention teenage girls. If this girl would just tell the truth, it would be all right with us, otherwise we will subject her to our ridicule.

The young girl is still shedding tears after the operation. A little ball of fine creamy yellow hairs is floating in a small basin of bright bloody water. Xiao Ru shrugs and pours it down the sewer.

"It's over. Quick, put your clothes on." I pull off my mask, urging the girl who has drawn her body together in a ball and is still sobbing.

She dresses shakily, and is led to the outer room where I prescribe her some of the usual drugs. Knowing how futile it is, I still ask, "Want some days off?"

"No, no," she waves her hand in a hurry.

"But you have to rest for a few days in bed, understand?"

The young girl moves to the door step by step. When she reaches it, she suddenly turns and begs virtually kneeling, "Aunt, please do me a favor, and keep it a secret for me!"

"Get going, get going." Xiao Ru waves her away impatiently.

Today's young men and women are shockingly bold about sex. They dare to carry out their fantasies with no scruples whatsoever. If pregnancy occurs, they will ask everybody for help to find a back door. In case they fail, they will steal, cheat, counterfeit, or pay a high price for the certificate. They even exchange their bodies for it. In a word, there are a lot of bizarre tricks involved, and we became accustomed to them long ago.

"Next," Xiao Ru calls out again.

In comes a middle aged woman with round shoulders and a thick waist. She is short but has a loud voice; once she is in, her throaty cries fill the whole room, "I sell pork at a nearby food store. You doctors can come anytime to buy kidneys or pig heads; a short notice will do. My family name is Wu, Wu Dalan."

Xiao Ru gives her a signal to move faster.

Wu Dalan takes her pants off, and chatters on shamelessly, "At thirty they are like wolves, and at forty, tigers! That's true, really true. My old man loses his mind whenever he touches me!"

I try to kill boredom while operating on her, "That's your good luck. You don't want him to touch others."

"See if he dares!" she snaps. I almost laugh out loud, looking at her seriousness.

It is over; Wu Dalan jumps down from the operating table, "All right, thank you two doctors," she says. "I've got to go. I've got to hurry and take over the shift."

"No. You need to rest for fifteen days." Hers is a normal case, so she is entitled to the sick leave.

"Drop it, doctor. You know how much our monthly bonus is. This and this much." She sticks out her fingers.

Young girls do not dare to take the sick leave for fear that others might know their secrets; Wu Dalan does not want it because she is afraid of losing her bonus. I can not help feeling miserable that women's bodies are so cheap.

After the fifth, I give Xiao Ru the signal to stop. I take off the gloves, and wash my face and hands. While Xiao Ru is putting on face powder and lipstick, I finish the remaining half of the cigarette I left in the morning. There is never an end of candies and cigarettes in our department. The young fathers and mothers always leave them on the tables for celebration and out

ABORTION

of gratitude.

Xiao Ru is not done yet with her makeup. I wait patiently. Looking form behind her, every man would drool for Xiao Ru. She is tall and slim, and her black hair hangs down in a cascade which waves gracefully with each of her steps. But the front of her is disappointing. Actually, four-fifths of her face is all right with the only exception of her mouth. The jawbone is too big, the gums protrude, and her lips are a bit too wide and thick, reminding one of the Yangshao Culture[1] and earning her the nickname "Upper Cave Man.[2] Naturally her makeup-effort is mainly concentrated on her lips, which takes a whole five minutes.

Xiao Ru and I go out of the clinic at eleven forty. After a three block detour, we enter the private section of the Tianxiang Restaurant where Xiao Douzhou is waiting with a man and a woman.

Xiao Douzhou rises to make the introductions, "Doctors Xie and Ru, meet Xiao Du and his fiancee, Xiao Song. Xiao Du is a colleague of the nephew of Lao Li, who is a neighbor of my third aunt and lives across from her house."

Xiao Ru and I cast an indifferent glance at them, nod our heads, and sit down, with a mutual understanding between us.

Xiao Du lights the cigarette for me; Xiao Sung unwraps the candy for Xiao Ru. They wait upon us with the uttermost respect. Soon we start to eat and drink. At one twenty, Xiao Ru and I wipe our mouths, say our thank-you's, and turn round to go back to our afternoon shift.

At three in the afternoon, Xiao Douzhou accompanies the girl into our department.

"Take off your clothes," Xiao Ru says and helps her get onto the operating table, more polite.

---

[1] A culture of the Neolithic period, relics of which were first unearthed in Yangshao Village, Henan Province, in 1921.

[2] A type of primitive man who lived ten to twenty thousand years ago and whose fossil remains were found at Zhoukoudian near Beijing in 1933.

As soon as I switch on the vacuum pipe, the girl breaks into hysterical screams, "Doctor, I'm scared! Mom, oh, I'm scared!"

I have to behave more gently, "It'll be over in a minute, and it won't hurt at all."

I insert the pipe into the womb and move it about, and at once I detect something wrong. "Did you have an abortion recently?" I ask.

The girl is going to lie, but meeting my eyes, she stops short. I breathe in a little and wave my hand dejectedly, "Get up, the walls of your womb are too soft now. You can't have the operation."

I ask Xiao Ru to help her put on her clothes and send her out. Xiao Douzhou barges in right then and demands, "What's happened?"

"Quit doing this to us!" Xiao Ru gives her an angry look.

I too yell at her not without fear, "You really want us to get fired, don't you!"

Off work, I decide to take a walk through the food store, and find Wu Dalan standing at the meat counter with a knife in her hand. She is working briskly, and her face is rich with expressions. There is no trace of tiredness or weakness in her. A good, strong cow.

I walk over as if nothing has happened, "Master Wu, a yuan of pork."

Seeing it is me, Wu Dalan shows a smile, raises her knife, cuts out a lean piece, and throws it onto the scale. Then she blurts out casually, "Go, one yuan."

I weigh the piece in my hand. It must be worth more than a yuan and a half, so I hand her a yuan bill with satisfaction.

"Five yuan, four yuan is the change!" Wu Dalan calls out the price loudly and gives back the four yuan change. You can't help marveling at the ease with which she handles all this.

I take the four yuan in change; my face flushes abruptly but returns to normal soon enough. "Come to me if you need to," I say calmly.

"I will."

Both sides perform up to the standard.

Fried pork and pepper plus tomatoes and eggs. As soon as I finish cooking the supper, he comes home looking upset.

"Go ahead and eat, angel of the street."

"I'll have a drink first." He takes out the bottle without a word.

"What's wrong with you this time?"

"She even dares to speed through the red light on Guohua Road. I signaled her to stop, but she waved to me flightily and said, 'I'll stop if you can catch me'."

"Did you?"

"Hell no! She has a Suzuki 125, and mine is the little Star! How could I? Finally my walkie-talkie had her stopped at Post no. 5. Fuck, she turned out to be the daughter of the commissioner of our Public Security Bureau. I was so infuriated."

"She must be ugly."

He is stunned.

I continue mockingly, "Don't you forget your three exceptions."

"Don't be stupid. Eat your supper." He blushes.

Those bad guys in the traffic patrol team all set their own policies, which vary according to personal peculiarities. My husband makes three exceptions: no tickets on the second of January, no ticket on the first of June, and no tickets for pretty girls. I was a beneficiary of the third. I was quite pretty, so he did not give me a ticket when I dashed through the red light. But he did not let go, either. He was trying to find something to say, which shows clearly that he had malicious intentions. And that's how we got to know each other. I told him I was a graduate from a medical school; he said he had finished his courses at a vocational school. I declared there was no common language between us; he insisted since mandarin was the popular dialect all over the country, of course we had a common language. With his glib tongue, thick-skinned face, persistent begging, and solemn pledges he fought for my love. After a considerable length of time, my emotional defensiveness began to weaken. And on a dark, windy night, in his shed built as a shelter against earthquakes, he forced open my physical Maginot Line. After he had invaded me, he held me in his arms, explaining patiently the value of the hymen while I sobbed uncontrollably all the time. I was just like other women in my ignorance of the hymen, even though I majored in medicine. And when I saw that he was five- foot-eleven and powerfully built, we got married one month later.

Seven years into our marriage, we are still without a child. I do not understand it at all. Whenever I turn on the vacuum pipe and watch the surplus fine hairs of others being sucked out, an unspeakable emotion surges through my sense organs. I suffer from a long-drawn-out emotional distress and feel an undercurrent of hatred. Sometimes my lips turn purple with jealousy. While other women are so stably productive, I produce not a single hair. Where's the justice in it?

"Why do you look so distracted? Hurry up and eat. I have one more shift to go tonight," my husband reminds me by striking the rim of his bowl with chopsticks.

"Are they going to pay back with their own lives if people in your profession work themselves to death?" I flare up.

"Better to work myself to death. At least thank God I won't die of anger!"

He is now done with his supper. He lights his after-dinner cigarette, and puffs rings against the ceiling.

It is not easy to be a patrolman in this city. There are a lot of high ranking officials and celebrities, and their sons and daughters as well. There are also many senior officials from the central government to inspect their work performance. It is difficult for the patrolmen to handle their responsibilities. You can't be too strict with those in the leading circles; you can't be too harsh with ordinary people, either. If you offend those above you, you'd better worry about your promotion; but if you bully those below you, then you are sure to get a tongue lashing. A fifty cent fine will bring three days of cursing on your ancestors. The neighborhood committee once conducted a poll, and in the column of "Whom do you find most disagreeable?" more than eighty percent of the residents wrote "Patrolmen."

"I have to go." My husband puts on his huge police cap, buckles up his white Sam Browne belt, and goes out the door.

"Should I tell him the truth?" Looking at the shadow of his back, I lose myself in thought. The quartz clock on the wall keeps time without a sound; its shorter arm jumps forward stiffly.

II.

The clinic is like a sparrow, small but containing every organ in it: departments of traditional medicine, western medicine, orthopaedics, physiotherapy, gynaecology and obstetrics, home care, prevention and cure, and lab, etc.. The one hundred and ten people all work the way they prefer. There are seven or eight men in a big department, and one or two in the smallest.

Our department is neither big nor small; we have three.

Xiao Ru and I are responsible for outpatients and abortions. Doctor Shen is in charge of visiting the home patients in the surrounding neighborhoods before and after they give birth. Every day she comes to sign her name in the clinic, then she becomes the Goddess of Liberty with a medical bag, wandering here and there and doing whatever she likes. There are traces of her everywhere within the service area of our Dexi Neighborhood Clinic. She appears wherever there are or no patients. She knows a lot of back doors and has many connections, which gives her the nickname "Water Over the Foot," showing how smart the woman is. She has a sharp tongue and is capable of doing whatever is needed. She is past forty but short of fifty. She looks heavy but not fat. She wears eye shadow and lipstick. She tweezes her eyebrows and paints fingernails. Though over forty, she leads the clinic in fashion: jeans, leather jacket, bat tops, snow shoes, boots, and bra without buttons. When gold jewelry becomes hot, she has five rings on her ten fingers: two are real, two are imitations, and the last one is half and half.

Xiao Ru prefers food to clothing. She has only a kind of woman's jealousy of Doctor Shen's dress and trinkets, but shares none of her other pursuits. So she puts up a fight from time to time, "Doctor Shen," she says, "where do you get so much money?"

"I earn it myself."

"By taking off your pants?"

"Show respect to your elders. If we're talking about sex, a virgin like you better step aside!" Patches of green and purple show on her face, and her eyes narrow viciously.

Afraid that Xiao Ru might get hurt, I change the topic. "Don't you mind, she's only kidding. Seriously, isn't your old man just a conductor in the railway station? How could he afford to buy you fashionable clothes for all seasons?"

"There are tricks in buying."

Xiao Ru and I listen attentively.

"With three hundred yuan in hand, you could be in fashion all year round. Wear you spring clothes carefully, return them in the fall. With the money, you buy things for the fall. Follow the cycle and you'll dress differently every day. The key is your connections. Frankly, I've used my electric iron for three years, but I made Xiao Chen in the home electronics store take it back, then I bought a new one."

Doctor Shen is telling the truth, and we two look at each other in speechless stupor.

Xiao Douzhou comes by again, whispering in my ear and begging, "It's true the girl had an abortion four months ago. But she is pregnant again. You tell me what she could do? It's bad for a girl to have a baby. Would you

ABORTION

please do it for her?"

"Is the operation a game? If they have the nerve to do it, they ought to face the new life." A hidden feeling rises in me, making my fingers tremble and my earlobes numb.

"What? You want them to keep an illegitimate child? Don't you be ridiculous," Xiao Douzhou is getting mad, too.

"Why didn't they get married?" asks Xiao Ru, concerned about that most of all.

"It's simple. The parents on both sides don't approve of the marriage. First they won't let them have a room, and secondly they won't give them money. How could they get married!"

I am not willing to risk my job. The walls of her womb are as soft as mud and as thin as a piece of paper. Who is to be responsible for her life should something like perforation and massive hemorrhage occur?

"You're an expert in abortions in our district and everyone knows your reputation," says Xiao Douzhou, aware of what is going on in my mind and drawing closer to flatter me. Her face, full of pimples, looks like red beans in gruel. She was hired to replace her father and is now in charge of the pharmacy for traditional medicine. She often remembers to leave me something when she receives some traditional medicine in beautiful package. Once she gave me an electric pressure cooker. I was suspicious and refused to accept it. I said, "Isn't is too much to use this as the package of your medicine?"

"You don't understand. This is like the weasels digging holes--doing the same thing in different ways. The drug companies have unique ways to promote their products. If we help them sell ten boxes of unsalable drug, they'll give us a certain amount of money, you can buy anything you want with it. This is for our mutual benefit."

Looking blankly at the crafty girl, I was at least stunned, if not shocked to death.

"You fool, why do you operate for nothing on these women who don't have a certificate? A woman's reputation is the most important thing she has. You save that, and don't you think they should be grateful to you?"

Xiao Douzhou tries hard to enlighten me, but I still feel reluctant, "These woman are already in predicament. Who would have the nerve to rip them off?"

From then on I began to waver--a vacillation which originated in my soul. Later the waiting lines for the operation grew longer and longer, and getting the certificates became more and more a matter of formality. My conscience found peace in my social awareness that I was aiding the policy of birth control.

"Doctor Xie, for the sake of our friendship, please take the risk and do it. You can be sure it won't go unrewarded!" Xiao Douzhou is winking at me all the while.

"Wait till I finish this cigarette." I see no way out but give in.

"As you like." Xiao Douzhou leaves cheerfully.

My addiction to tobacco is worsening--I now have to smoke at least two cigarettes per day. In the past I could not bring myself to understand why men ever smoked. Now I realize that smoking is addictive. I have already known why I never conceive: the extremely low ratio of my husband's active sperm. I have always kept it from him, for fear that it might hurt his self-respect and masculine energy, or worse, I am afraid of the anguish that would come along with the knowledge. He is tall and strong, full of vitality and perfect confidence in his body. So he has never had the slightest doubt about his ability to father children. Recently, I have been able to nurse him with greater care only by keeping it secret. And I pray and pray whenever the darkness of night falls.

"Doctor Xie, let's begin!" Xiao Ru helps Xiao Song onto the table again, who mumbles in embarrassment, "Doctor, I'm not the one to blame, he..."

"Don't talk." I concentrate and begin the operation cautiously. A second abortion within four months. I have to keep calm in anticipation of the girl's miracle. I cannot afford to feel jealousy or resentment, nor can I hurt her. I must help and save her, with a broad mind like God's. The sucking of the instrument sounds like a remote wail. A ball of short fine hairs comes floating out. It drifts on the bright red water, peeping at the outside world intimately. Luckily, the operation goes smoothly with no accidents. I should be proud of my expert handling and invaluable experience.

After Xiao Ru sees her out the door, I discover fifty yuan on the corner of a table in the outer room. Well, that is why Xiao Douzhou winked at me. I think of it a little and tell Xiao Ru to give it back to Xiao Douzhou. "It's all right for them to treat us a meal, but no cash, not even a cent."

Xiao Ru agrees with me; we two know each other perfectly well.

III.

Today the electricity is cut. I grab the chance to wash my white overcoat. My views about the garment are rather odd: while others only consider it as the uniform of doctors, I believe its white color is the color of angels. And so I keep my white overcoat carefully ironed and spotless all year round, making it look graver and more dignified than the color black. And I never send it to the laundry.

After I finish washing the white overcoat, I have nothing to do, so I walk into the office, trying to kill time by reading a few newspapers. There is only one office in the clinic to administer all the organizations as well as all the departments, including the Party branch, daily operations, the union, the Youth League, and the Association for Woman. The director of the clinic is nicknamed Big Joker, and his assistant, Small Joker. The clerk is called Heart Four. When I enter the door, both Jokers are out. Only Heart Four is there, sitting and reading a magazine. His real name is Bai Feng, and he is responsible for logistics, security, personnel, political work, and public relations.

"Where are the big shots?"

"At a meeting, or gone out." Bai Feng raises his head and glances at me, then he buries in the magazine again.

He is a retired serviceman. I was told that he had been in service for six years. He was assigned to the clinic after his retirement, and was left with all the responsibilities that the two Jokers would not take. He has been here for only three years, but he has managed to offend just about all of his colleagues. The directors make him handle everything that may cause resentment, and as a result he gets into fights with everybody everywhere and becomes the scapegoat of the office. Once I gave him a piece of well-intentioned advice, which was to pay attention to his relationships with the colleagues. But he retorted without a care in the world, "They should pay attention to their relationships with me! Don't you call me Heart Four? Doesn't that play a special role in card games?" All retired soldiers are just as rude and unreasonable, and sooner or later they will lose all their friends and be dismembered and die a miserable death. This fellow has a little crooked talent, and has published a few short stories. His eyes are too small, but he has the habit of squinting at you. It seems that he has an eye on me. Once, I was going to call him on it, but I gave up the idea because I felt that it didn't really make much sense. I pick up some newspapers and am on my way out.

"Doctor Xie, sit down for a while," he says to me without raising his head.

I sit down, but he is still reading. Then he says without moving his eyes from his magazine, "I've heard that you smoke?"

"Only started three years ago." I dislike the topic.

"What brand do you prefer?" His head still bends over the magazine.

"'Courtesy'." I begin to feel irritated.

He puts down his magazine and smiles, "I'm sorry. Not that I'm impolite, the ending of this story is too damn good. Hey, I have Kent cigarettes here, want one?"

I glance to the office door and reply, "I'm not that bold around here."

"Anyway, we have nothing to do right now, so why don't we go to the Meile Bar? On me." He stands up and bows to invite me. I do not know why my face feels a bit hot, or why my voice sounds a little unnatural. "With no one on duty in the office...," I hesitate.

ABORTION

"Come on, nobody dies in our clinic, you don't have to worry."

I appreciate his frankness. What does it matter that he is a few years younger than I am? So I say, "All right."

We turn twice in the noisy and chaotic streets, walk up to the second floor of the bar, and sit down in a corner. Bai Feng orders coffee and a mixed wine that has three different colors.

"Here you are."

He really does take out his Kent and light it for me. I start smoking skilfully. All imported cigarettes have a harsh, sweet flavor, and the ashes are disarmingly white.

He plays with his lighter, takes a few sips of his wine, and raises his head. "Because you are tired doing your work?"

He is asking why I smoke, obviously.

I do not answer.

"Because of your problem in having a child?"

I refuse to answer.

He changes the topic tactfully, "I've published another story recently. It's called 'Cruel Love'."

The introduction of this new subject perks me up a little. I sip the coffee and begin to talk. "Do you understand love?" I ask him.

"All the best plots come from those who talk about but do not understand love...."

He talks about his story with dancing eyebrows and a radiant face, while I listen halfheartedly. There is something in it, and it seems a little better than what I have read before.

"You're not afraid of moonlighting?" I have heard envious people backbite him, saying things like "He doesn't keeping his mind on his job," or "He writes immoral stuff for money," etc.. "You don't want to be the Party Secretary of the clinic a few years from now?"

He puffs out a series of rings, watches them disperse slowly into thin air, and says, "Promotion is like writing stories--both require opportunities. A man who wants to be promoted may not get it. In some stories, somebody succeeds in climbing up by stepping on others' shoulders, but actually that's a fabrication. You tread on others, but you don't necessarily get what you want. Instead, what usually happens is both sides get whipped--as they say, 'The fish dies, and the net snaps.' Most of those who really climb up are people who look on at the fights without being involved, and then they come out to reap the profit. What prospect do you think I have as a scapegoat in the midst of all these deadly games? Besides, a post with the rank of an administrative official wouldn't wet my appetite."

Young as he is, he is really smart. I stare into his small eyes. "What's your plan for the future?" I ask.

"Try to become a third-rate writer," he says in all earnestness.

"You're a good-for-nothing."

I know that nowadays most retired soldiers do not have a particularly bright future. They either do odds and ends in various institutions, or work in factories or stores. The smarter ones have been working their heads off to obtain a diploma so that they can compete and land a place for themselves in their careers.

"Aren't you attending a vocational school part- time?"

"I am."

"What department?"

"Veterinary."

"What?"

"Since it's only for a diploma, it doesn't' matter what I study."

A mutual silence.

"I'd like to visit your family some day," he changes the topic again at last.

"Welcome to our humble abode."

"I heard your husband likes a drink. I'll try to beat him."

"You take delight in probing into others' privacy?"

"My job requires it. It's a hobby too."

"Any exciting news?" I ask a little wickedly, probably because the coffee has roused me. In the meantime I find I could chatter along pretty smoothly, which testifies to human hypocrisy.

"Of course, but it's highly classified."

"My lips are sealed," I say, justifying myself.

He turns his face, and watches the scenes outside the window. After a moment of consideration, he says, "Ok, I believe in your sealed lips. Well, speaking of Doctor Shen in your department, she'll hop in bed with anybody regardless of age or feelings; the only thing that counts is practical reward. Don't you see how she wears pearls and jewelry all year round?"

"She said she--" I am thinking of what she told Xiao Ru and me.

"Spending money carefully may be one of her talents, but it's not the only one. According to what I know, she has affairs with quite a few married men," Bai Feng says with a wave of his hand.

He sounds very serious, not like someone spreading a slander.

I get angry, "Why haven't you exposed and punished her?"

"Free trade. You can't interfere with that."

"You're a Bolshevik!"

"The Party's Constitution doesn't say we must bring to light people's privacy." He very calmly extinguishes his cigarette butt.

All of a sudden I feel wronged. Why am I myself not a Party member! I snarl, knocking the table with my finger tips, "And she, a doctor, has brought shame upon all intellectuals!"

"Whether doctors in clinics could be categorized as intellectuals is quite debatable. It's like elementary school teachers, folk artists, and the very best carpenters."

Immediately I realize that this fellow is more experienced and cunning than I have known.

"You're really a slime," I say, coldly.

"You're not exactly innocent, either. Does every woman you operate on have official approval? How do you feel about that?" From his small eyes a beam of light shoots into my pupils.

Stop. That's enough. If he knows about these illicit affairs between men and women, then he surely must have smelled things like my having lunch at the Tianxiang Restaurant or my receiving "medicine" with beautiful packaging in secret from the pharmacy. He hoards the secrets of others while looking on coldly, pretending to be deaf and blind. Such a man is both detestable and dangerous. He reads my thoughts apparently, and realizes that I am disgusted with him. So he stands up, pays the bill, and leaves.

IV.

"Why are you feeding me like a cat these days?"

"This is a folk prescription. Eating more salt- water fish helps in child bearing."

My husband spits out the bones and sneers, "A medical school graduate who believes in folk prescriptions!"

"I believe in anesthesia, not acupuncture, but it's true that acupuncture can stop pain," I defend myself.

"Why do you eat less than I do?" He reaches out like a child to tip my bowl.

"The prescription requires a ratio of three to one. You get three and I get one."

"But which of us has something wrong?"

"Not determined yet."

"Not determined, not determined. They don't even know how to solve a small problem like this. Medicine is lagging far behind electronics," he grumbles with resentment.

During the first years of our marriage, we pretended to be undisturbed, while making many excuses to deal with outside pressures. As time went on, however, all our high-sounding excuses became sheer jokes. When you still have no child long after the wedding, you cannot continue deceiving others as well as yourselves. Time waits for nobody, and we were panic-stricken. We had to have tests taken in a special hospital. I never told him the results; I always put it off saying that nothing had been determined yet. It was easy for me to take him in since he knew nothing about medicine. At the same time, I try hard to nurse him, hoping for a happy ending on the day when I can tell him of my pregnancy. Every day I secretly studied technical means of strengthening his vital forces, such as supplementing him with trace elements and supplying high protein in small doses.

I did not think Bai Feng meant it, but he really comes to my house with a bottle of Xifeng wine. After I introduce them, he and my husband exchange greetings. Less than an hour later, they are on intimate terms and become the best of friends. I whip up a few fried dishes and put them on the table to go with the wine; at the same time I remind my husband to drink less. He says yes over and over, bowing unctuously. But when he picks up the cup, nothing in the world can restrain him. I have been curtailing his drinking to the minimum for having a child. But this time somebody comes without being invited and offers him booze, which makes him feel so exhilarating that he loses his head completely.

After three rounds, Bai Feng asks my husband, "Want to play a game?"

My husband pulls up his sleeves instantly, "You're on. One more drink for the loser!"

Both of them have gone completely out of my control, and in the end their tongues cannot even work straight while they call each other brother, which was utterly disgusting.

"Help me...get ...a motorcycle ...license."

"Brother... no... problem."

A pair of drunkards have met each other much too late, and a thousand drinks would not suffice to make up for the lost time. They will not stop before they become totally intoxicated. I am glaring at them fiercely all this time, hoping they can exercise some self-control. Nevertheless, they ignore my existence, so finally I have to clear the table by force.

"Brother... come often... when you've time..."

"Please... stop...please... stop here."

Leaning up against the door frame, they say their goodbyes. The whole pathetic scene makes me sick. Bai Feng wobbles away, and looking at him from behind, I doubted he will ever become a writer. Even becoming a third-rate writer, I am afraid, is only a daydream.

My husband's drunken slurring continues till one o'clock that night. When he goes to his street post at six in the morning, his eyes are still vacant and blank.

At eight thirty in the morning, Bai Feng stops me at the door of our department. "Why haven't you told him?" he asks.

"Told him what?"

"That he is the reason why you haven't been pregnant. I knew everything from your eyes last night."

I grind my teeth, knit my eyebrows, and rap out in a low voice, "You've poked your nose into things too long!"

Then it starts again. Once again I begin to dispose of other people's "surplus commodities" that I have so cherished but have never been able to acquire. Xiao Ru, nearly crying, takes out two tickets to a dance at the Cadre's Club, "He doesn't like a girl who eats fat pork," she moans. "It's over again. Do what you like with the tickets."

She has had quite a few dates, but the relationships always fizzle as soon as they dine out. She's got an enormous appetite, and what's more, she never refuses anything, vegetables or meat. Her table manners also leave something to be desired. Add in her "Upper Cave Man" looks, no one can endure it all.

"My husband doesn't like to dance."

"Just for fun. Anyhow you don't have any child to worry about."

Instantaneously I become vicious, as if I have to strike back when somebody hints at my secret anguish. "How many men have you broken off with?"

"I can't remember." She wipes the corners of her eyes.

"Can't you wise up and see that you can only eat half full when dining out with your boyfriends? How many times do I have to tell you what they want is a wife, not an African refugee?"

"Oh!" she begins to wail.

I keep the tickets and call my husband, who says he has a shift at night and can't go. I say I will go find somebody else, and he tells me to do as I like. He never interferes with my freedom, especially these last two years. He often encourages me to spend more time doing things for fun or to go places for relaxation, because there's no child to take care of. He says when we have a child later, I won't be able to do these things even if I want to. But who can I get to go with me? There is no lack of dance partners among my old classmates, yet they are all married now and have children. Better avoid them as I still feel a little jealous. I decide to ask Bai Feng.

"Very much honored to be your partner."

"This is at someone else's expense," I say, explaining how I got the tickets.

At seven thirty that night, as he walks up to the dance studio, wearing a western suit and assuming an affected and pretentious manner, I size him up for a while longer. As a woman, I feel sorry for his eyes, which are too small. They make your heart ache.

Seeing that I dressed up a little halfheartedly before the dance, he lets out a sigh. "Heavy makeup or none at all, she always looks attractive. Madam, if you please."

As we do the slow four-step dance, he holds me by the waist and says without emotion, "You should have told your husband the truth earlier."

I look up at him, but he avoids my eyes. He is glancing with his small eyes at the female drummer in the distance whose very sexy breasts protrude conspicuously.

"Aren't you over concerned with my affairs?"

"I myself don't know why."

He is still looking at the drummer, and I feel a little jealous. So I thrust out my chest and move closer. "How old are you?" I ask him.

"Twenty-seven."

"A virgin?"

Slightly surprised, he turns his face about and at last our eyes meet for three whole seconds. "Absolutely."

"Why haven't you gotten married?"

ABORTION

"It's not like cooking dumplings that you've got to push them into the wok when the water boils. Aren't you over concerned with my affairs, too?"

We laugh, and in a quite friendly way.

During the quick trot dance, we swing around in great excitement. The band is good at knowing how to step up an appropriate mood. This is the first time I have ever danced with Bai Feng, but surprisingly our dancing skills are similar and we move well together. The faster we swing, the more harmonious the centripetal forces become. Our minds are frozen, and all distractions are forgotten. I cling fast to his chest; he hugs my waist tight. Round and round, one, five, twenty... the dim and hazy neon lights, the fluid music, and the simplified thoughts. When the music stops at the final climax, the world seems to have lost its sense of direction. I feel a rainbow somewhere is spinning out colored lights in a floating universe. My knees give way and I land softly in Bai Feng's arms. Explaining my helplessness, I murmur in his arms, "Sorry, my cerebellum lost its balance."

"I didn't think it was anything else." He plants his feet firmly where he stands, waiting for my cerebellum to regain balance.

How embarrassed I am at this moment.

After the dance, Bai Feng sees me home in the clear moonlight and night breeze. By now the biological clock of the city is ticking away at a more relaxed and gentle pace. It is a soft night, and the air is extraordinary clean. Rustling in the shadows of the trees and behind the flower beds, lovers intertwine like snakes.

When we are almost home, Bai Feng tries to persuade me again, "If you respect him, you'll tell him the truth. Men hate to be deceived."

I still worry about how my husband will react once the truth comes out.

He has come home from his shift and is lying in bed reading today's *Reference News*. He smiles and helps me take off my clothes. Then he fetches some warm water and gets the towel ready. While I am wiping my chest, he stares at me with agitation.

"Don't be disgusting." I cover his eyes in the mirror.

He is waiting for me.

Once the lights are out, he jumps over like a strong hunting dog. His eyes shine in the dark with excitement and he pushes like mad. He is always so piously hopeful for each and every time. Whenever my period comes a little behind schedule, he shouts and dances with joy. But time and again he rejoices too soon, and disappointment follows. I haven't told him why, and he does not realize that in our case we have to wage a protracted scientific warfare. He believes that the more often we make love, the greater hope we have. As a matter of fact, we actually have to do it less often in order to improve the quality.

"The ratio of your active sperm is too low."

Suddenly I blurt out the truth. I have to, because I need cooperation. Creating a new life is the most precise science of all; it does not allow the least bit of carelessness.

"What, what did you say?!" He jumps up as if from an electric shock and shakes my shoulders violently.

Now that I have begun, I explain to him in full the diagnosis of the special hospital, and tell him in detail the methods of treatment for the future. He stands frozen before the bed like an ice pole, as if stunned by a crushing blow to the head. After a long time he shouts, "Why didn't you tell me before?"

His voice is full of hatred. There is something to what Bai Feng said.

V.

The Darling Baby Toy Store is having a sale of kids' keyboards for eighty one yuan instead of the original eighty six. The five yuan discount has lured many customers. Nowadays if the price is right, there are men who are willing to risk their lives for you; and if the discount is big enough, there are women who will do anything to take advantage of it. A woman who is nine and a half months pregnant braves the crowd and struggles to the counter. As she hands over the money, she crashes to the floor with a piercing cry. Hearing the news, Xiao Ru and I rush to the spot, take some emergency measures, and accompany her to the Central Hospital for Women. To our great relief, the mother and baby turn out safe. The whole incident is quite moving at the time, but again it falls within our daily responsibilities. What turns out unexpectedly is that Bai Feng publishes a report, entitled "Baby Born on Counter," in the evening paper five days later. I find the paper and read it over; it makes me almost faint with fury. Bai Feng, exaggerating, heaps praises on us, especially on me, as doctors of high professional and moral integrity, kind hearts, expert medical skills, and an honest practice. According to him, we have always been serving our patients hearts and souls, and have always been perfect models for human behavior. What nonsense!

Bai Feng finds me and says quite proudly, "Doctor Xie, what do you think of it?"

"After I become the minister of Public Security, I'll shoot every single third-rate writer!" I growl in reply.

"You don't want to be famous?"

"I despise a literary scoundrel more."

Disappointed, he beats his head with his fist. "What a born loser I am!"

But I am the more miserable. As soon as you appear in the newspaper, you become the target of everybody else. Freezing irony and burning satire, uproarious laughter and false accusations, all come pouring over me in some subtle ways. The wind will surely break the tallest trees in the forest, so why should I be the tallest and get hit? In order to cool off the widespread jealousy against me, as well as to save my skin from their tongues-lashings, I have to go everywhere vindicating myself, insisting that I am not so noble-minded or worthy of so much respect. There aren't many employees in our clinic, yet their backgrounds vary in a complicated way. We have some people who used to be quacks before liberation, or medicare personnel in the headquarters of the puppet army during the War Against Japan. And we have ex- housewives who joined the work force in the 50's, and young men and women with some education who had gone to the countryside and returned to replace their parents upon their retirement in the 70's. We also have graduates from two-year colleges or medical schools, and retired soldiers as well. For half a century, time has brought every one of us together within the space of this small clinic. We influence, infiltrate, disintegrate, and betray one another. And in the end, we become distorted beyond recognition and definition. Spreading rumors, creating mountains out of molehills, making groundless accusations, and letting loose a torrent of abuses--these are the traditions of our clinic. Poking fun at each other, looking for scandals, making anonymous calls, and sending anonymous letters, are all our "native delicacies." I am not willing to die a target for everyone. In the first place I am not an advanced worker or anything like that. If I want to survive or live long, I have to breathe, eat, cry, and laugh like everybody else. Longevity is something you can hope to attain by getting lost in the crowds.

The most frightening word of all come at last.

"Let's adopt a child!"

They come like the cold, piercing wind from the mountain valleys, making me tremble all over.

"No! I won't. I have to have and bring up my own child."

I will not give up. Never! I am entitled to the full satisfaction of being a woman. I am entitled to enjoy the happiness of creating a life. I am entitled to show a mother's love and tie of blood. And I am entitled to experience the full life of a woman. I kneel down before the bed, begging him to brace up and rouse himself, and not to give up. But with spirit crushed and willpower gone, he looks at me dully and says, "I've tried scores of medical concoctions. Where is the hope in it?"

"It's in persistence. Constant effort yields sure success."

"Forget it, time waits for nobody. Right now we are young and strong enough. Isn't it the right time to adopt a child? Why do you have to be so stubborn?"

A husband is what he is; he can never understand his wife.

ABORTION

I go to work and come back home in depression. Whenever I see Bai Feng, I burn up inside, "All because of your advice," I tell him, "he knows the truth. Now he wants to adopt a child."

"Don't you agree?"

"You bet!" I almost slap his face.

Seeing my fury, he becomes a little embarrassed. He looks at my face and doesn't know how to console me in words. I quickly realize that it is not necessary to lose control over him. We are only colleagues, and I would be putting myself in an awkward position if I treat him in such a desperate manner. I calm down and search for an excuse, "It's said they've already succeeded in their experiments on artificial insemination in the South."

His small eyes open wide with surprise. "What do you mean?" he asks.

"Might as well try it when necessary." I feel the skin of my face is growing thicker little by little, as if it were the only thing existing in the whole universe.

VI.

Big Joker calls me to the office.

I am stunned when I enter the door. In addition to Big and Small Joker and Bai Feng, there are two policemen sitting upright at the desk. I glance at their uniforms and shoulder decorations and know their identity at once: security police. One of them is thin, the other is fat. The thin one has a young and pallid face; the fat one looks dark and coarse.

My heart can't help sinking, and all my brain cells go on full alert.

"These two comrades come from the Security Section of the District Police Department. They have something to talk to you about," says Big Joker, introducing us with a serious face.

What for? I make some quick guesses.

The fat one begins, "Is your name Xie Ning?"

I give him a nod.

"You are implicated in a case. That's why we have come to talk to you." His eyes fix upon my face like rivets.

I have yet to rob a bank or explode a reservoir. What case could I be involved in? But still I feel I have already been dragged into something, and a certain uneasiness rises in me.

"Do you know Zi Yue?" the fat one asks abruptly.

I shake my head.

"Do you know Xi Deqing?"

I shake my head.

"Do you know Wu Qinghe?"

I shake my head again. I shake till my cervical vertebra tires and aches.

The fat policeman loses his temper, "If you know none of them, how can they have abortions in your department?"

I relax a little, having guessed the trouble. "Are you talking about how abortions are done without proper approvals? Let me tell you then, they are done on references."

"Who refers them to you?"

"Many people. From the leadership of the clinic down to Old Liu who keeps night watch here to make extra money after retirement. All of them have referred to me pregnant women without the certificate."

Big and Small Joker look angry; Bai Feng frowns.

The fat man, experienced in such matters, is quick to respond. He avoids this line of questioning and lunges at my weak spots, "Have you fleeced them for doing operations without the certificate?"

I nearly faint on the spot. God knows whether I, Xie Ning, have ever fleeced anyone. But...

He seems to have seen through me. He throws his head backward and looks at the ceiling, then says with great poise and no emotion, "You want to tell us everything here, or go to the District Department with us?"

My heart beats wildly; my blood pressure is rising and the color leaves my cheeks. I look very pale. I really don't know what to do. I think at the moment I must look like those captured female criminals in the movies. The fat policeman, seeing that I have lowered my head and am not about to reply, snaps at the two directors, "We are taking her in now."

Big Joker nods and agrees to it at once. Small Joker looks right and left and remains ambiguous. Bai Feng cuts in flatly. "Comrade Xie Ning," he says, "you must be honest. Today these policemen comrades come only to talk to you. Simply tell everything and it's over. They don't have a warrant or subpoena with them today and that means they wanted to give you a chance. How about this, why don't you go home and think it over carefully today, and tomorrow you tell the two comrades all you know. What do you say?"

The two policemen are breathing audibly. It looks like they really do not have the proper documents. Times have changed after all. The law restrains not only common people but also law officers themselves. They do not act impetuously. After looking at each other for a while, they agree. "All right. You go home, Xie Ning, and think it over pretty well. We'll see you tomorrow."

Back in my department, I feel as dizzy as if the sky were whirling around. A shrill metallic noise explodes in my ears, and cold sweat oozes continually from my palms. I want to vomit, but am too weak. Ignorant of what has happened, Xiao Ru comes over and asks with concern, "Doctor Xie, are you all right?"

"Nothing." I mustn't collapse.

What should I do? The word "Fleece" flashes savagely before my eyes like the red tongues of fire. What is "Fleecing"? Should things like the lunch at the Tianxiang Restaurant be counted as "Fleecing"? I had done nothing more lavish than that. There have been countless such meals. Where should the line be drawn.... I feel I am plunging into the abyss, waiting with eyes shut for the terrible crash. What shall I say tomorrow, or, more exactly, confess...

After work, I ride my bike slowly in the streets, as terribly weak as a black carp dying for oxygen. All the passersby are hurrying on their way, while I am the only one wandering without a destination. A man wearing a large police hat waves to me, and I ride over numbly and ask him, "Why? Did I cross the red light?"

"I'm not a traffic officer." He gives me an angry stare.

I blink my eyes hard, and find that he is in a gray uniform and is probably a tax collector. I smile reluctantly. "Why did you wave your hand?"

"I was waving goodbye to my colleague," he explains with impatience.

I could neither laugh nor cry.

A man on a Flying Pigeon bike catches up with me from behind and brakes to a stop in front of me.

"I called your husband and told him you had to work some extra hours in the clinic, so you would be home a little late. Now, come with me," Bai Feng says out of breath.

I ask him with my eyes where we are going.

"My place."

Looking at his honest face and considering what he has just done, I turn my bike around and follow him readily.

"My old man got an apartment recently upon his retirement, so I took over this room," he explains, opening the door.

ABORTION

It is a medium-sized room, facing west; it has a large window and a wide angle of view. There is nothing fancy in it; only a single bed, a couple of electroplated folding chairs, a corner chest, a bookshelf, a desk, and a floor lamp--nothing else. Near the window stands a desk with a few pads of draft paper. A piece of calligraphy in free style hangs on the west wall. It reads, "Worldly wisdom is literature."

To save time, he cooks two bowls of instant noodles and hands me one, "Have some, please."

At the moment, little is left of my worldly desires, so how can I eat anything? I push the bowl away and sit there in a stupor. Bai Feng opens his cigarette box, and we each take one. I smoke hard and deep; he smokes slowly. When he is half way through, he says in a low voice, "Sister Xie, let's have a good talk."

The sockets of my eyes burns like the wires in an electric stove. The way he addressed me makes the whole of me feel much better. I sob for a while, and when I calm down I reveal to him, bit by bit and one incident after the other, all of the dark side of my work and mind, a side that has established itself after all these years. I have never refused invitations to eat, drink, or smoke cigarettes, but I have never gone beyond these sins. Heaven is above, and I can swear to my personal integrity.

Bai Feng has been listening quietly with the exception of a few occasional questions. When I have finished, he gets up to make me a cup of sweetened tea.

"Is that all?" He gives me the tea.

"Yes. You must believe me."

We look at each other; soon I see in his eyes that at long last he trusts me.

"What shall I do tomorrow?" I tremble to think of it.

Bai Feng lights another cigarette, puffing out rings of white smoke that rise up one after another in perfect order. He explains to me in great detail what I should do. "First, tell the truth. Second, don't be afraid of blackmail. Third, say nothing that involves the directors of the clinic. Will you remember?"

I am still shaking with terror. "What punishment they'll give me? How are they going to determine the nature of my offenses? Is what I've done considered 'Fleecing'?"

"Yes. But yours are not serious. As to what punishment you'll get, better not think too much about it. Just tell the truth tomorrow."

"I know nothing about these people they mentioned," I mutter nervously.

"They may understand that. Now go home," he urges. "Your husband will get worried if it's too late."

My fear has not yet subsided; I don't want to go, but I have to. I have one leg outside the door, but I step back, turn around and say to him quite shamelessly, "Could you... kiss me once?"

He looks at me warily.

"I don't mean anything more. It's just that I need courage."

He comes over, lifts up my right hand, and kisses it lightly.

After I arrive home, I tell my husband all that has happened during the day, from beginning to end. He measures me up with a strange eye; when I throw myself into his arms for understanding and sympathy, he jumps aside to avoid me and, as a present for me, he cries, "Degenerate!"

Nothing more is said that night.

The two policemen come again the next day. As they take me away, I see Bai Feng give me an encouraging nod.

The interrogation begins with questions and answers. I remember well Bai Feng's advice: be honest about what I know and don't know; tell no lies; do not refuse to talk. At a little past three, the fat one says, "You may go now.

Wait in your clinic for our decision."

I realize from the interrogation that some of the pregnant women whom I have operated on without certificate are prostitutes. After they were "detoured" by the police, they tried desperately to pull others down with them as their "cushions." They even dragged down people like me whom they never knew. The malicious thought, "If I die, you die too," blinded their conscience and made their lies more vicious. Apparently they did not know me, but said they had been on very intimate terms with me; or they had treated me to only one meal, but said they had also bribed me with three hundred yuan. As they say, "A bit of rat's droppings spoils a whole pot of gruel." It's also a kind of revenge for the criminals. Too vicious, and too dangerous. From now on, I shall never bother about other people's business. I swear to the policemen that I will abide by the law and behave myself at work.

As soon as I am out of the front gate of the District Police Department, the sun shines brighter, and I am filled with relief. From a public phone booth I call Bai Feng, "I'll wait for you on the second floor of Meiqi Restaurant."

I order steak, fish rings, salad, and grilled pork; I want to pay for all of it. After he arrives, I pile up his plate with the various dishes and we toast each other many times. My gratitude overflows into everything I say and do.

Bai Feng is sipping the Wangchao wine with his head bent low when all of a sudden he blurts out, "You have to do an operation without a certificate next Tuesday."

"Don't kid me," I glance at him, annoyed.

"No, I'm not kidding." He is avoiding my eyes.

"What are you talking about!"

"Our bureau chief's future daughter-in-law. I swear she's not one of these prostitutes."

I feel wronged and want to cry, to wail. I look at Bai Feng. There is already a cold tear in the corner of his eye.

I resume my work, and can see from their eyes that many of my colleagues are gloating over my misfortune. A scandal like mine that rocks the sleazy universe of our clinic would definitely set their tongues wagging.

Xiao Ru knew I was interrogated, and was in constant fear for herself as she has always been a star player in eating and drinking.

"I'm the doctor and the chief operator. The police held me responsible. There's nothing for you to worry about," I say, comforting her for a long time before she finally quiets down.

"Doctor Shen is going around and saying, 'It's a big mess, we have a madam in the clinic. The Department of Gynecology and Obstetrics has become the home base for prostitutes!' Xiao Douzhou too is saying to everybody she sees, 'I'd never guessed that Xie Ning took bribes too, but she has so little professional morality!" she tells me.

A violent anger surges in me, and its vicious force drives me out of control. I counterattack at once by spreading Bai Feng's story about Doctor Shen's illicit relationships, adding inflammatory details. To deal with Xiao Douzhou, I devise a wicked scheme. I steal away her underwear while she is in the shower and throw it into the boiler, which results in her having nothing to wear under her skirt. On her way home from work, a gust of wind blows up her skirt, and exposes to full view her plump white bottom on the seat of her bike, causing all shocked pedestrians cry out, "Stop her, stop her!"

Bai Feng approaches me just as I am taking great delight in my revenge. He says to me with the corners of his eyes dropped, "Now you should quiet down and find a book like *Principle of Girlhood* to read." He is speaking sarcastically.

VII.

My punishment is soon announced: an administrative demerit for not abiding by the abortion regulations, for protecting criminals, for accepting bribes in the form of feasting, and for vitiating the morality of the medical profession.

I tell my husband about it, but he does not even bat an eyelash. "You've made your own bed" is all he says.

A cold war. We stopped making love long ago. He does not get excited; I have no desire. Nothing more is said the whole night.

One day, he tosses me a color photo of a chubby boy.

"What do you think?"

"About what?"

"We'll adopt him later."

"No!"

At one stroke, I send the photo flying and run out of the room with my hands over my face. So much grief, anger, despair, and suffering is gushing out at once. In hysteria, I run to Bai Feng's place.

"I want to borrow your place for a while."

"Where am I supposed to go?"

"I don't care."

"I have to write."

"I don't care."

I collapse in the chair and wail till I lose my voice. Bai Feng hands me a towel and asks, "Is the war escalating again?"

"I don't know... where he found...a ... a child," I am sobbing.

"If love is eternal, it doesn't matter if you adopt a child."

"The love between us won't survive a single blow, I..." The pain inside me is beyond words. Huge teardrops slide down into my mouth through the corners of my lips, bitter and sour to the extreme.

Standing with his face to the window, Bai Feng is thinking hard to himself. Thick cigarette smoke from his nostrils rushes onto the glass and refuses for a long time to disperse. From behind, I could see that he is breathing heavily, and has a lot going on in his mind.

"Better go back and try one last time," he speaks to the window, but the sound waves deflect and knock hard on my eardrums.

My husband does not want a compromise; I won't retreat, either. I try to help him regain his self-confidence, but he says that's to waste time chasing an illusion. On the surface we are fighting for a child, but deep down we realize this is the end of our love. We fight more and more fiercely, covering more and more subjects until all our emotional conflicts are thoroughly exposed. At last he issues the ultimatum: if I do not agree to adopt that child, we will go our separate ways. The nature of the confrontation is finally clarified. With the child, he will put up with me; without the child, everything will be lost.

In utter confusion and seeing no way out, I walk over to Bai Feng's room again.

When I arrive there, he takes out from the corner chest a can of meat and a bottle of liquor. He pours the liquor into two cups, filling them to the brim. We stare at each other, and each of us gulps down a big mouthful. Strong and hot, the liquor chokes me. I suspect it's a homemade alcohol-and-water mix.

"I've had a miscarriage in love," I tell him numbly, full of sadness.

"I wish you good luck." He picks up his cup apathetically.

An sinful thought comes to my mind. Drunken and bleary-eyed, I size him up, who is younger than I, "You... show me how to play the game."

"First three drinks as a tribute to your master."

I raise my cup as if unflinching in the face of death, and gulp down three mouthfuls without a moment's hesitation.

"Why are you doing this?" he asks, grabbing my cup in surprise.

"Young man, today we'll do no talking but eat, drink, and enjoy ourselves." I hold a cigarette in my mouth, light it myself, and try all I can to lure him with my charming and seductive eyes. He is forced to lower his head, pouring and drinking the liquor by himself.

"Young man, raise your head and look at me."

"Sister Xie, don't incite me."

His frankness sets me loose. The alcohol in me has leavened my courage. I take off my coat and walk toward him deliberately. Then I grab his head and bury it deep between my breasts. I can feel his trembling and restraint.

"Afraid?" I insert my fingers under the back of his collar and stroke his smooth back.

"Yes." His head goes on caressing my breasts.

I bend down and kiss his thick black hair, encouraging him by my seductive silence.

Finally, he stands up, holds me with both hands and groans, "I want to commit the sin."

He throws me onto the single bed.

Our passion has converged; the fire of sexual desire is raging. I have opened a new world for him. He is so wild that his hairs stand on end, and his bones crack as he twists his body futilely on top of me. I welcome him as I welcome the sunrise, and guide him as a rider guides his colt. When he enters me rash and hard, I feel the thumping of his heart, and it makes my nipples itch and throb. A warm current flows into me from inside him, which transforms into a blissful weariness. And we fall asleep in each other's arms.

The moonlight is flickering and flowing like water when we wake up; and in the flickering and flowing moonlight, we remain in each other's arms, naked. Pretty primitive.

Awake and clearheaded now after the drink and the dream, he asks me, blushing, "Should I go and confess?"

"I'm the one who should confess." My face is also red with shame.

As a matter of fact, neither of us confesses. We go to work as usual, posing as people of high morals; we eat and sleep as if nothing ever happened.

My husband and I go to the court for divorce. At the very first hearing the judge gives us a lecture, "According to the Marriage Law, the court can grant a divorce only when emotional attachments on both sides have completely dissolved. Now you are in conflict only because you have no child. That won't do. The Law does not allow a divorce under such circumstances. You should understand and care for each other. Even if you can't have a child of your own, you may as well adopt one."

The judge shoots a glance at me, implying obviously that I am the main cause of our trouble since I do not want to go through with it.

Yet the judge misses the point of our problem. He does not want to pinpoint the reason why our emotional attachments for each other are over. Are we really fighting over the child, or is that a handy excuse to cover up the fact that this marriage is really over? After all, a low divorce ratio is a sure sign of national peace and stability, as the judge firmly believes.

As soon as we get home, my husband declares unequivocally, "Be prepared, I'll file it again in six months."

We do not negotiate our settlement, as both of us have become quite stingy. Each feels he has lost too much, and would hate to lose more by way of compensation. So we fight over every little item, and finally it has to be settled by the court.

Though I had only one chance encounter with Bai Feng, his good work shows up in me two months later. Nausea, stomach cramps, and crazing for sweets. Based on my feminine sensitivity, I know I am pregnant. A wave of exhilaration strikes me dizzy. At long last my sense of values and dignity is vindicated by life itself. "I am a mother, I can be a mother!" A wild outcry from the depth of my heart vibrates through my hands and feet, setting me dancing for joy. After I tell my husband the news, he becomes hilarious first, and then shocked and furious like a hurricane strikes the earth and an erupting of a volcano. "We didn't make love, where did the child come from?"

"It came from heaven." I would rather die than betray the colt that made me pregnant.

My husband would shoot me through my head on the spot if he had a pistol at hand. Unfortunately, traffic police don't. So he slaps my face twice, and moves out to his work place and never returns.

I make an appointment with Bai Feng in the South Lake Park. On the island in the lake I tell him the news of my pregnancy. It is late autumn; the wind blows up layers of green waves on the face of the lake, which are soft and tender like silk brocade and satin.

He sits dull faced on a rock, smoking, then he shoots the butt far into the water. Ever since I told him, his expressions have been as complicated as a magic block: Joy, worry, fear, and shame show in turn.

"Do you want us to get married?" he asks me with his eyes shut.

"No."

"Are you going to hide the truth and cheat on your husband?"

"No."

"Then what are you going to do?"

"I won't get anybody in trouble. But I'm going to give birth to my baby."

He opens his eyes suddenly, and looks in weariness at the sky. It is very clear, only the sun is hanging in its azure vastness. An autumn swallow skims the surface of the lake and soars into the sky with a twitter.

"Do you recognize this molecular formula?" He writes a few letters on the ground with his finger.

I know, it's the formula for alcohol.

"We drank too much that day. A sperm and an eggcell drugged by alcohol won't produce a healthy life. There have been too many deformed lives in this society. We have no right to bring any more into it."

"Stop!" I moan in a low voice, leaning on the pavilion in the middle of the lake. The formula for alcohol flashes back and forth before my eyes like bolts of lightning, piercing my heart and making it bleed.

"A mother without due respect, a child deprived of his social position. Such reproduction is doomed. At least I won't allow it," Bai Feng is still rattling on.

I realize that I did not fall in love with him simply because he is too smart for his own good and has too much worldly wisdom. Except for love making, he knows everything else. He is a good man; he is a good worldly man.

"I need purification!" I shriek through the sky like the autumn swallow.

VIII.

The news of my divorce has been spread through the clinic. Anyone's private affairs are everyone else's morphine. Even before the computer age, the speed of spreading news about someone's private affairs had already surpassed that of the computer. Several of my friends in the clinic come rushing to me after they hear about it. They gather in my department and discuss with me the pros and cons of marriage.

"What kind of education do you have, and what's his? You don't match at all."

ABORTION

"In my opinion, you have to stick to your marriage, like they say, 'You marry a blind man, and you go with him hand in hand.' Divorce is something you mustn't agree so easily."

"Now is the time for the sexual revolution. To hell with all the feudal customs and tradition. Long live the sexual revolution, a long, long life to the sexual revolution!"

I feel so manhandled by these windbags that I can neither cry out nor flare up--I cannot muster the tears or the strength to support myself. Acid wells up in my esophagus, and unable to hold it back, I vomit right in front of them. Women are too familiar with this symptom. At once they look at each other in blank dismay, then they avoid each other's eyes, not knowing what to say.

It doesn't make any sense to try to hide something; that only makes it more scandalous. I have decided to face the new chapter of my life. Bai Feng discusses with me in private the various places to have an abortion. I tell him that as things stand I will not go to anywhere else but will have it done in our own clinic. His whole body shivers at what I say. "Gossip is cruel," he reminds me.

"But it's no more than gossip." I raise my head in contempt.

I visit Wu Dalan in the food store, asking her for some nourishing food like spareribs and eggs.

"You're going to entertain some friend?"

"No, I'm going to eat it myself."

"Aren't you going to have an abortion too?"

I nod yes, not bothering to hide the truth.

"Well, well, equal opportunity. Even obstetricians can't escape the fate. Don't worry, I'll send it to you with satisfaction guaranteed. But, Doctor Xie, I have to ask you a favor."

"What's that?"

"Though we saleswomen here wear white overcoats like you do, ours are not to be compared with yours. The material of your coat is good; it's got the right color, the western-style suit collar, and the opening at the back. It fits your waist and head just right, and it makes you look so nice. Look at mine, no fashion, no style, no nothing, just like a body bag. I look simply terrible in it. Doctor Xie, let's exchange our coats so I can show off too."

"No, I won't."

"Is that so, Doctor Xie? We've connections between us, and we should help each other," Wu Dalan's face alters, and it does so instantaneously.

"I don't want to buy spareribs or eggs." I turn and leave, my lips turning blue with anger.

IX.

I am called to the office once more before my abortion operation. The gentlemen are all sitting up there in their proper seriousness. I touch my hair lightly behind the ear and sit down on the chair they have reserved for me.

Big Joker opens his mouth, "Today we call you here to verify a few things."

I smile faintly, "To say all I know and say it without reserve."

Encouraged, he goes on in a grave voice, "According to reports from the people, you are going to have an abortion."

"That is correct."

"According to these reports, the child you are about to abort is not your husband's."

"Those people were not there snooping when we slept together."

ABORTION

Big Joker is confronted head on, so he circles about, "Isn't it true that you two have been separated for a long time? So how do you explain your pregnancy now?"

"No comment."

"How can you try to cover up your immoral behavior before established facts?" Small Joker grows angry and can not help cutting in.

Big Joker walks around me twice, his hands crossed behind the back. "We know your problems already. Now everything depends on your own attitude."

"Exactly. It depends on your attitude," Bai Feng offers.

His words are but a hint for me: both Jokers know nothing more about it. I move my head a little and say to Big Joker, not without sarcasm, "It would be more dramatic if you told me this with a folder in your hand. You should study more modestly the techniques on how to induce, trap, and trick a person into confession!"

Big Joker is disheartened. He beats his chest and wrings his hands, sighing, "Comrade Xie Ning, you are really doomed!"

Bai Feng shivers all over; he wants to say something but does not.

Lying on the operation table, I wait silently for the moment to come.

Xiao Ru and Doctor Shen will operate on me today, which pleases Doctor Shen no end. Her face is adorned with an animated smile: this has erased her hatred for me. However, she has not found out the man who fathered my child, and she feels she could not die with such an everlasting regret. So she keeps on asking me shamelessly. Xiao Ru is more sympathetic and sincere to me. Holding my hand, she whispers in my ear, "Doctor Xie, we'll start."

I nod my head.

The vacuum is turned on, and the familiar sound fills my ear. The gate of my womb is dilated, exposing my burning acupoint of life. In the instant of their severing and cutting my flesh, I am fantasizing that I am a new born baby wrapped in pieces of afterbirth, bumping and rolling in a huge birthway, but it is so bumpy, so abysmal....

"Doctor Xie, are you hurting?"

Xiao Ru's soft voice reaches me. I nod painfully. This is an abortion of my body and soul all at one time. How could it not hurt? The pain of the abnormal lovemaking with Bai Feng, the despair about my future career, the suffering from the bankruptcy of my marriage--hurt from all directions, and torture upon torture--I have had it all today.

"Doctor Xie, it's over," Xiao Ru's low voice rings in my ear.

I wake up with a violent start and struggle to sit up. Xiao Ru picks up that ball of creamy yellow fine hairs with a pair of tweezers and shows it to me, asking me what to do with it. I tell her to dispose of it in the sewage, as always. She stares at me for a long time, and then lets go of it as directed, murmuring sympathetically, "It's over, another tiny life."

"No. A wart that bears no life in it," I correct her sorrowfully but firmly.

I leave the Department of Gynecology and Obstetrics with the help of Xiao Ru, and find Bai Feng waiting silently outside the door. Upon seeing me, he rushes forward to take Xiao Ru's place. The eyes of my colleagues in the clinic have already weaved a net, waiting for the two of us to come out. A commotion of voice rises from every direction. Bai Feng helps me walk out of the front gate as if there were no one around.

"How do you feel?" he asks.

"Phoenix nirvana."[3]

Outside the gate a red taxi is parked.

---

[3]Detached from reality, as the phoenix rises in fire to the heaven in Buddhist doctrine.

SMART LADY

Liu Yufeng

People on the Plateau can drink, especially in the west. Men drink; so do women, who sometimes even know more about drinking than men. Qiao Niang, the smart lady who lives in this street, is one of them.

Qiao Niang is already forty-two, but is still quite attractive. Her full figure does not look fleshy; on the contrary it seems rather well-proportioned. From her delicate and fine eyes one can see the beautiful girl of twenty years before. It is strange that so much wind and sand in the west have left no traces on her white and smooth face. Even the wild sunshine on the Plateau has failed to do any damage. Her face remains milky and shiny.

In the past, Qiao Niang was a famous star with a voice of gold in the Chaidamu[1] Beijing Opera Troupe, who had for several years been the rage of the time in the vast desert land. She became a household name, as well-known as the sun. Later, during the Cultural Revolution, she was caught with a man by the representatives of the People's Liberation Army,[2] and was paraded for the fun of it with a pair of torn shoes[3] hanging from her neck. From then on, her reputation was ruined. She was demoted to minor roles. Several years flew by, and Qiao Niang no longer had her crisp and golden voice; her youth also slipped away little by little. The man she had been in love with married and had a son and a daughter. But she still remains single. Though she keeps on working in the troupe, what she does is no more than taking care of the costumes. Now she no longer has anything to do with things that would bring fame or scandal. Yet she enjoys her peace of mind. She has less to worry about, and with enough money, she often drinks alone in her house, which helps her kill the time and relieve her sadness. Life for her is not all that bad. As time goes on, she becomes increasingly fond of drinking.

Qiao Niang likes to drink, but she never drinks more than she could take. And with the precaution and sensitivity characteristic of women, she

---

[1]A desert area in northwest China.

[2]These army officers and soldiers were sent to take charge of different civil institutions during the "Cultural Revolution."

[3]"Torn shoe" is a traditional nickname for adulteress.

develops naturally a knowledge of wine and liquor, so her judgment in this regard is usually superior to that of others.

Qiao Niang has been living in this street for quite some time, but she never mixes with any other wine-drinking people there. All her neighbors are just nodding acquaintances. And she has never had a drink with any man.

One bright warm Sunday, Qiao Niang is shakily carrying a gas tank on her bike out of the gate of a gas station. And there she meets her neighbor Zhao Tongyou.

"Oh, it's you, Qiao Niang. Look, your bike is shaking, let me give you a hand."

"That is very kind of you." Qiao Niang is at her wit's end, so she steps aside and hands the bike over, taking advantage of the offer without too many words of courtesy.

And that is how Zhao Tongyou steps into Qiao Niang's house for the very first time. After he enters the door, it takes him just a few minutes to put the tank in place and connect it with the pipe. By then, as if by magic, Qiao Niang has already put four cold dishes and a bottle of wine on the table.

"Master Zhao, sorry to have bothered you." As she says this, she has already opened the bottle, "Nothing really good, just have a few sips."

"Why bother, you don't need to." Zhao Tongyou takes a step back and stammers, "It won't do, it's so embarrassing...."

"Look at what you said." Qiao Niang smiles and invites him to take the seat. "Don't stand on ceremony. We're neighbors, aren't we?"

Zhao Tongyou hesitates for a while, then sits down.

"All right, I'll rip you off this once."

"Please try it. It was sent to me by a friend from Beijing." Qiao Niang hands him a cup full of wine.

"Ah, it's Wuliangye."[4] He gulps it down. "Good stuff, good stuff!"

"Please have as much as you like. There's enough for you." Before he puts the cup down, Qiao Niang fills it to the brim again. At the same time she pours herself a cup, then holds it lightly to her lips in her white and fine hands. With a lift of her chin, the red lips part a little, and the two cheeks tighten to draw down all the liquor in the cup.

"Looks like you drink pretty often too?" With three cups in the stomach, Zhao Tongyou becomes excited and talkative. "How long have you been drinking? Do you have a craving for it?"

Qiao Niang smiles faintly; she waits for a moment and replies, "It's pretty lonely by myself, and when there's something to worry about, I like to have a cup or two. As time goes on, I learn it." She says this in a very natural and relaxed manner, and without the slightest trace of pain or sadness on her serene face. Only two pink clouds rise gradually on her cheeks, pretty and colorful like the buds of peach flowers about to bloom. Zhao Tongyou is so fascinated that he forgets to drink but stares at Qiao Niang with his mouth wide open, which surprises Qiao Niang momentarily and causes her to tip the cup over in confusion. What a pity to waste such fine liquor.

"Please drink, Master Zhao."

"Ah, ah...." Zhao Tongyou regains control and grins awkwardly, "There're so many slips in one's life. I mean, just take it easy and don't think of them all the time. Later on, just let me know if you need help. I'm not afraid of anything and I don't care. If you like, I'll come often and drink a few cups with you. I'm over fifty now, and I've seen so much. Only this is the best thing to do. Come, Qiao Niang, bottoms up!" As he finishes, his drains his cup.

"Is this liquor all right?" Qiao Niang maintains her composure.

"Of course, isn't it a famous brand? But it's not as strong as the Xifeng liquor of our Shanxi province."

Qiao Niang listens quietly; only a smile dances around her mouth. After

---

[4]An expensive and famous brand of liquor.

a while, she sips a little and says, "You're more accustomed to the aromatic types, the strong and heavy stuff, so you'd feel less so when drinking the lighter, leaven type of wines. As a matter of fact, Wuliangye is strong too, but it has a delayed effect. You don't feel it as much at first because it tastes kind of sweet in the mouth and it's smooth for your stomach. But if you drink too much, you'll suffer worse heartburn than if somebody poured molten iron into you." Qiao Niang stops for a little while, then goes on with fervor and assurance.

"The alcoholic content of Xifeng is a bit higher than that of the leaven type, but it has a delicate, attractive smell, tastes strong and highproof, and has an aromatic aftertaste. Men love it. Try some and you'll know."

Qiao Niang's knowledge and appreciation of wine really stuns Zhao Tongyou. He's never thought that the middle-aged lady before him not only is still attractive but also knows so much about wine, which really deserves respect and admiration. So he reverses his role as a guest by filling Qiao Niang's cup and holding it to her with both hands.

"This is really amazing! Qiao Niang, I started drinking at twenty, and have wasted so much money, and after thirty years I still don't know anything about it. Today I've come to realize what wine really is. Qiao Niang, let me drink to your health!"

"Don't say that." Qiao Niang, smiling, hurries to stand up and take over the cup. "How could you compare what I know with your experiences. You make me feel like singing in front of a virtuoso." After she says this, her mouth opens and the liquor glides down; from her throat comes the ringing of lively and hearty laughter.

....

Unable to repress his fascination and excitement, Zhao Tongyou speaks highly of Qiao Niang to his wife as soon as he enters the door of his house. And the more he talks, the more agitated he becomes. And he finally takes off his shoes and socks and continues talking in bed. It is not until his wife pulls a long face and begins to curse him wildly that he stops.

"You've lost the dignity of your forefathers! A man about to die should act so shamelessly. You sneaked into the house of that shameless woman and lost your head after drinking a few drops of cat's piss. Bah!"

SMART LADY

Zhao Tongyou, feeling snubbed, thrusts his wife angrily aside with his eyes, then he turns his back to her, pulls the quilt over his shoulders, and goes to sleep.

The old couple say nothing more to each other that night.

The night is very quiet....

From then on, Qiao Niang's reputation spreads far and wide in the small city, like the spring breeze sweeping through the street.

So because of Zhao Tongyou's blabbering, people visit Qiao Niang with fine wine and liquor in order to compete with and test her.

Since then, Qiao Niang's name has again become the rage of the time over the vast desert land. Everyone knows her in the west. She is the outstanding representative of the western wine connoisseurs. People visit her every few days. And during this period, Zhao Tongyou is also much sought after; he puts on the airs of a Bo Le,[5] looking very proud of himself. At the same time, he has not only tried many wines and liquors that he has never tasted, but also learned a lot more about wine connoisseurship, and suffered no milder tongue-lashings from his wife.

A little later, Zhao Tongyou shows a man into Qiao Niang's house; he comes from the provincial capital and claims to be affiliated with the Xining Restaurant.[6] The man is in his thirties and wears a pair of glasses over his dark and yellow face. He has an easy manner and a fine way of conversation. Once he enters Qiao Niang's house, he acts as if it were his own home. After a few greetings, he begins to wax eloquent about wine. Every few sentences he stops to see how Qiao Niang will respond. Yet Qiao Niang simply sits there and says nothing. She is only listening respectfully and smiling from time to time out of the corner of her mouth. After rambling about wine for quite a while, the wine connoisseur takes from his black leather bag two unlabeled bottles of wine and puts them on the table. He opens one of them and fills a cup, giving it to Qiao Niang.

---

[5]See footnote on p.45.
[6]Probably the best restaurant in the whole province.

"This is our Xining's specialty. I'd like to ask you to try it and see if it's not pure and mellow."

Qiao Niang smiles but says nothing. She lifts it with ease and confidence and takes only a sip. Then her eyebrows smooth out. She places the cup back on the table and remains silent.

"What do you say, Qiao Niang? It's not too bad, is it?" the connoisseur asks with a smile.

"Sure," responds Qiao Niang neither too quickly nor too slowly. "The famous Maotai liquor can't be bad at all."

"What? Maotai?" he sneers. "It's obviously a fine leaven liquor made in Xining, how can it turn Maotai in *your* mouth?"

"Sir, you have probably mixed up the bottles," says Qiao Niang, smiling quietly. "Mellow and rich, it has a unique aroma of its own; its alcoholic content is lower but it never tastes weak. Plus its long sweet aftertaste. What liquor has all this except Maotai? You must have forgotten. If you don't believe me, please try it once more." As she says so, Qiao Niang actually pours one for him.

"No need to try it again, Qiao Niang. Since I didn't remember correctly, please try this one." He opens the other bottle and pours her a cupful.

Qiao Niang's white face reddens a little. She stands up respectfully and takes the cup, but she is not in a hurry to drink the liquor. She places it under her nose and smells it lightly for a moment. Then she puts the cup back on the table without touching the liquor.

"Perhaps it's the Three Flower Liquor from Guangxi Province?"

"How do you know?"

Qiao Niang touches her hair, composes herself and opens her mouth, "First, it has the aroma unique to the rice grown in that area; second, only this kind of rice could make it so fine that it mellows your bones when you smell it. Being aromatic first and pleasantly tasty later..."

Nevertheless, her house grows busier and busier. Drinkers from the street come and go more and more frequently. And the fine white face of Qiao Niang looks brighter. Sometimes you can hear her happy voice betting out Beijing Opera from her house at midnight, ringing through the street like flowing water.

But good things never last long. On a bright, moonlit night, when drinkers are tasting wines and liquors at Qiao Niang's house, Zhao Tongyou's wife barges in. She smashes two bottles of wine right in front of Qiao Niang, points her finger at her and curses ferociously, as if Qiao Niang were a grandchild of hers. "You shameless slut! You think no one knows you? You were dragged out of a man's bed when you were just a girl. Why aren't you singing your opera? Why can't you get on the stage again? For shame, you fox!"[8]

The wine party is ruined. Qiao Niang, unable to breathe, falls flat on the ground. At once everything falls into chaos: the timid escape, the bolder try to restore her breathing in a frantic rush. They find with surprise that from Qiao Niang's tightly closed eyes come two drops of bright red blood.

Since then, Qiao Niang's busy doorway becomes deserted once again. None of the numerous drinkers of the street dare call on her; even Zhao Tongyou disappears without a trace. Qiao Niang seems to be suffering from a serious illness. Her bright face lost its luster and color; she seems thinner and looks ten years older.

Time flies by; with a blink of the eye it is already late autumn.

In gusts of autumn wind, the fallen leaves cover the street, which was green a few days ago but is now all golden yellow and desolate.

At dusk one day, Zhao Tongyou appears from nowhere with two bottles of wine. He sneaks up to Qiao Niang's door like a thief. Then he collects himself and reaches out his hand to knock at it. He knocks for a while, but no one answers. He is puzzled--but then he hears a sneer from across the

---

[8]In many traditional Chinese folklores, a fox becomes a beautiful woman to lure men into disasters.

courtyard fence:

"What are you knocking for? She left the day before, moved back to Beijing. No use to keep knocking, it's an empty house."

Zhao Tongyou, stunned, stands in front of Qiao Niang's house like a fool.

A gust of wind blows over; the withered leaves it blasts up dance in circle before the door, making a "sha, sha, sha" sound. Suddenly Zhao Tongyou feels a fit of dizziness; his hand slips, and the two bottles of wine crash to the ground.

The autumn wind carries with it the sweet smell of the wine and disperses it along the street, which is soon floating in a strong aroma.

Qiao Niang is gone. She never returns.

At first the drinkers of the street do not feel anything, as if Qiao Niang has never existed. But as time goes on, whether they acknowledge it or not, a baffled feeling creeps into their hearts. What is it? No one can explain or define it. It is like the vast and empty gobi behind the street. Even Zhao Tongyou's wife, who has never touched a single drop of wine, stops before Qiao Niang's door one day and blurts out hesitantly:

"This woman...."